MW00567093

COL🚀NISTS

by
Roger Graves

DORRANCE
PUBLISHING CO
EST. 1920
PITTSBURGH, PENNSYLVANIA 15238

Dorrance Publishing Co
585 Alpha Drive
Suite 103
Pittsburgh, PA 15238
Visit our website at *www.dorrancebookstore.com*

ISBN: 978-1-6393-7139-6
eISBN: 978-1-6393-7950-7

CONTENTS

CHAPTER 1

Julia was becoming increasingly frustrated. The committee meeting had lasted nearly all day, and while on their rare good days everyone seemed to pull in the same direction, at other times such as today they were like a bunch of starving dogs snarling at each other. Julia could cheerfully have strangled Lansky several times. She had also tried with all her formidable skills to put Dr. Kuwahara down, but nothing she could say or do seemed to breach his inscrutable superiority. (As it happened, Dr. Kuwahara was terrified of her and used inscrutability as his defense.)

The problem was that, while the committee's mandate was to send a group of human beings to the stars, no one had said how many. Since the politicians were always strapped for cash, it was a case of the cheaper the better. "Of course there is vast public enthusiasm for the expedition at the moment," said the Administration's representative at the meeting that day, "but when the bills start coming in, well, Dr. Lockmeyer, would you really want to have to tell the electorate of all the extra taxes they are going to have to pay over the next few years?"

Pompous little bitch, thought Julia, but with an effort maintained her poker face.

Lansky had enthusiastically adopted the smaller-is-better philosophy. Probably just to get one up on me, thought Julia.

"I'm not in the business of building interstellar cruise liners," he said. "I don't even know if I can get two people there, let alone two dozen." She didn't think it was an opportune moment to remind him that about four dozen was in her opinion the absolute minimum.

"Okay," she said, taking a deep breath and starting again in the manner one uses to explain something very simple to rather dim children, "so we get a bunch of people to another planet in another solar system. What then?"

"I guess someone will set out a program for them to do sciencey things when they get there, but that's not really our concern. Our job is just to get them there."

"Yes, but we've already established that it's going to be a one-way trip. The distances are far too great for a return trip. So rather than them just going there, living out their lives and then dying a long, long way from Earth, which seems a bit futile, we should be thinking in terms of establishing a viable human colony there. This means women having babies there." Julia noticed that Dr. Kuwahara seemed a little shocked at her mentioning such a thing but considered that was his problem, not hers. "And if we're thinking in those terms then we have to think in terms of sending several dozen men and women if you want to establish a viable population, otherwise you would have a horrendous inbreeding problem."

"Well, that's all very nice in theory, but we've only got funding to send three or four people at most. Sending several dozen would

require a huge increase in the life support systems and hence the overall ship size, and we just haven't got the budget for that."

Julia's instinct at this point was to scream, "Screw the goddamn budget, do you want to set up a viable human colony in a new solar system or not, and if so stop giving me your pathetic excuses about money," but realized this would do more harm than good so restrained herself (just).

When she got home, Julia kicked off her shoes and collapsed into an armchair. The day had been one of the worst she could remember. Her head was splitting—why were women so damn prone to headaches? —she wanted a bath, a drink and a meal, and she felt too tired and sick to do anything about it.

She sat slumped in her chair and allowed a few tears of abject misery to roll down her cheeks. Whether this relieved her feelings or whether the self-disgust it engendered spurred her on was a moot point, but she slowly heaved herself out of her chair. A couple of pills and a hot bath later she surveyed herself critically in the mirror. Not much of a waistline any more, boobs were beginning to droop a bit, and don't even think about the face, but still—not bad for fifty-two.

She shrugged on some comfortable old clothes and pottered around with an old-maidish fussiness. So what, she said to herself, I am an old maid. In the past she had had various relationships with both men and women but nothing had lasted. She had at various times considered having a child (it mattered little nowadays if one was in a permanent relationship with the father or not), but the urge had never been strong. Well, perhaps it had been strong when she was in her late thirties and could hear her biological clock ticking, but she was enough of a physician to recognize it for what it was and resist it. What really mattered for Julia was her driving ambition to succeed.

And succeed she had. She was one of the foremost space medicine physicians in her generation. In the closing years of the twenty-first century, when space flight to the Moon and Mars was commonplace and beginning to be commonplace to the Asteroids, it had become apparent a long time ago that humans did not readily adapt to space flight conditions. Prolonged weightlessness, which was the real problem although there were plenty of others, affected practically every organ and system in the human body, and the longer their bodies were in a weightless state, the worse things became. While a great deal could be done with medicines and exercise, every space traveler seemed to need a customized regime of them.

And now they were going to send astronauts on a voyage to another solar system altogether, on a journey lasting not just weeks or months but many years.

Julia had taken on the task of Medical Director for the project as little more than light relief from her more pressing tasks. At first it was a one-day-a-week consultancy, a sort of 'let's see what it would take to get the voyagers there in a more or less functioning state.' For a woman who routinely worked sixty or seventy hours a week, it hardly ate into her other activities; it just meant she worked seventy or eighty hours a week. But it is a truism that nature abhors a vacuum, and since there didn't seem to be anyone on the Steering Committee whose function was to look at the long-term implications of sending people to another solar system, Julia found herself in that role, a role which had claimed more and more of her time until she found herself doing little else.

It had its moments of frustration. She raged inwardly at the political naivety of some of her fellow directors after some particularly clumsy decision on their part, especially Lansky the engineer and Kuwahara the astronomer. You stupid assholes, she wanted to shriek, are you trying to alienate every goddamn vote-grubbing politician between here and the Moon? But being the well-controlled person she was, she recognized the futility of such a course and smiled sweetly at them in the way that only a woman can smile at self-important men. "We could do that of course, but you know, having dealt with that bunch over at the Budget Office before, I think we could save ourselves a lot of grief if we had a quiet word with a few of their top people before we announce our plans publicly. Why don't I give them a call and set it up?"

Little by little they came to rely on her judgment. Yet in spite of a couple of centuries or more of advancement by various women's movements, in spite of legislation by the bucketful which mandated equality between the sexes, men like Lansky still instinctively regarded her as just another uppity broad. Julia knew this, had accepted that he would never change, and just gritted her teeth and resolved to make the best of it. If she couldn't sway him by logic, by clear thinking and experience, she would sway him by flattery. Whatever worked.

Sol Lansky for his part knew nothing of this and wouldn't have cared if he had. His job was to get the ship built, and by God he was going to do it. If the ship had to carry a bunch of goddamn air-breathing, food-eating, shit-producing humans, so be it; it was just another design input to consider. Personally he would much rather have outfitted the ship with some sophisticated robots, but it seemed the wet-brained politicians had decided upon a human payload this time so he was stuck with it.

It was difficult to say whether the ship was being built by government or industry. Privatization of government functions over the last several decades had led to a blurring of the lines between the two. Lansky was a senior vice-president and chief engineer of Astro-Mining Corporation, which had the prime contract for the ship, and a government consultant at the same time. All very incestuous, but it generally worked and led to no more corruption than any other way of doing things. Even less in fact because if there was any failure on Lansky's part, rival corporations would be trumpeting accusations across the entire spectrum of malfeasance. It also had the advantage that the ship was, in effect, being designed by one man rather than a committee.

Lansky was firmly of the opinion (he was that way about most opinions he held) that a committee was the only life form known to science with several heads and no brain. Although he was forced to work with the Steering Committee to get the project off the ground, the ship was his responsibility and don't-you-forget-it. He was undoubtedly a self-opinionated, overbearing, arrogant bastard—but he also held the ship, figuratively speaking, in his stubby, hairy paws and breathed life into it. So might one of the gods of the ancient world have seemed to their colleagues. Perhaps that was why Lansky's ancestors had opted for a single God; the more powerful they are, the less easily they tolerate colleagues.

Another of Julia's colleagues on the Steering Committee was Takahiko Kuwahara, known invariably as Dr. Kuwahara, except perhaps by Lansky who had been known to refer to him as "that stuck-up oriental prick." In what manner Dr. Kuwahara referred to Lansky in the fastness of his own thoughts no one knew, but it probably had something to do with hairy barbarians.

No one on the committee knew very much about what went on in Dr. Kuwahara's mind since he kept his thoughts to himself until they were ripe for deliverance. When he did finally deliver his thoughts, there was no possibility of them being contradicted; Dr. Kuwahara did not so much speak as make pronouncements. As the Astronomy Director, it was his task to determine where in all the vastness of the galaxy the ship should sail. To be sure, Lansky would determine how far the ship could go, more or less, but that still left many possibilities. His was a heavy responsibility since once the ship arrived at its destination there was no possibility of it continuing on elsewhere if conditions turned out to be unsuitable. If he chose wrongly, the ship's human payload might be left in orbit above a planet incapable of sustaining life, slowly starving to death. What made failure unthinkable for Dr. Kuwahara was that the astronauts had the means to report this back to Earth. While he might well be dead by that time, his family and their name would be shamed by him.

Julia now pottered around in her apartment remembering the events of the day, and felt somewhat remorseful. She knew she had been a miserable bitch, but she had to have a commitment to a larger ship, otherwise the success of the whole expedition was in jeopardy.

Whereas Lansky's responsibilities effectively ended when the ship sailed and Dr. Kuwahara's ended a few decades later when it reached its destination, hers went on for generations. Success in the long term was largely dependent on the number of voyagers they sent in the first place. "How do I get through to these turkeys that we have to have several dozen human beings on this ship. Adam and Eve was just a fable, or we'd all be drooling idiots by now through inbreeding."

With her salad and a steak (mainly soybean), a small glass of wine, and the soothing rapture of Mozart's Requiem in the background, Julia reviewed the events of the day. She was blocked, she was frustrated, and she knew she could do nothing about it at present, so she took a book (one of her soppy romances, as she called it) and curled up in bed with it and eventually slept the sleep of exhaustion.

CHAPTER 2

When faced with intractable problems, Julia had recourse to a small number—a surprisingly small number considering her vast range of acquaintances and professional colleagues—of friends with whom she could discuss things uninhibitedly.

Charles Lansdowne (always Charles, never Charlie or Chuck or any other diminutive) was an old friend of Julia's. Years ago they had briefly been lovers, but while they were temperamentally unsuited in that role—Charles was too fastidious to arouse Julia to anything more than mild interest—they had rather surprisingly remained good friends. They had met in medical school, and while Julia had gone on to specialize in space medicine, Charles had early on announced his distaste for, as he put it, the blood-and-pus side of medicine and had taken a side track into pharmacology.

Charles was now a very senior professor, although unlike many of his professorial colleagues at his age (he and Julia were born in the same year) he was still active in research. Whereas many academics when they reach a certain level of seniority seem content to sit back and let their junior colleagues and research students do all the hard work while ensuring that most of their achievements are credited to themselves, Charles actually did some serious research work himself. It was largely this attitude of mind that attracted Julia, herself an active researcher, to him. Having been briefly married, he was now contentedly a bachelor once more, so when Julia called he was happy to entertain her.

"Come on over and I'll cook dinner for us."

Since Julia knew him to be a gourmet cook she accepted gladly and remembered in time not to say "I'll bring the wine"; Charles's cellar was legendary and he liked nothing better than to display and comment upon his choicest wines for his guests.

Charles's apartment was not too distant from Julia's and with its heavy, solid furniture was very much a fastidious middle-aged bachelor's home. His dinner protocol was rigid, and woe betide any guest who broke it. Small talk before and during dinner, and serious conversation only after dessert.

"So what we seem to have here, Julia, is a political problem rather than anything technical. From what you tell me, and I'm a complete layman here, we have the technical capability to send several dozen people to a nearby star, but it would cost a lot more money than most people have envisioned, and more importantly, has been authorized to date."

"That's it in a nutshell. Money. How do we convince people that, oh I don't know, that the world is full to overflowing, that it's in everyone's best interests to seed the human race somewhere else and start over again, no matter how much it costs?"

"Well of course the first problem you have is that there's a significant number of people here in the US who seem to think of the human race as a kind of plague that must be stopped from spreading. You only have to look at some of the drivel being spouted in the media nowadays—I read an article the other day by some academic wishing that a virus would come along and wipe us all out—to see the kind of opposition the starship project is facing."

"I think I read that one too, Charles. I get the impression that there aren't too many people who actually think like that, but such people are a godsend to media outlets trying to get the attention of a jaded public."

"Journalists, goddamn journalists. Mind you, you have to sympathize with them to a certain extent. If you have to produce several hundred words to a deadline every day, I suspect the temptation to slap down any kind of nonsense as long as it's vaguely believable would be difficult to resist at times.

"And of course there's the funding referendum barrier, with which we're both only too familiar. After the great crash of the 2040s when governments found themselves almost choked to death with debt, nobody trusts elected officials to have anything to do with money anymore, so the goddamn thirty-first amendment, which we've both run up against before, means that major projects have to be directly authorized by a popular referendum. It certainly keeps the politicians from running amok with taxpayers' money or borrowing us into bankruptcy just so they can win a few more votes at election time, but it does mean that anyone trying to get a major project funded has to be very, very good at persuading Joe and Jill Taxpayer to part with their money."

"So how do we go about persuading Joe and Jill?"

"I think you're looking at a fairly lengthy public relations campaign to get people's attention. Let's face it, although Earth has a population approaching twelve billion, here in the US where we've kept it down to less than half a billion, life is pretty good all things considered, so overpopulation doesn't seriously affect them. However, in the overcrowded parts of the Third World, life can be a constant struggle for mere existence. And then of course there is the age-old problem that the more there is of anything, the less its value becomes."

"I'm not quite sure what you mean by that, Charles."

"Well, suppose you live in a small town of a few thousand people here in the US and suppose there's a murder. Everyone in the town will know about it, everyone will be interested, and there will be immense pressure on the police to find the murderer. But if the same murder happens in a crowded slum in one of the Third World megacities, there will probably be no more than a file-and-forget response, if that. And the real problem is that the greater this lack of regard for human life becomes, the greater the probability of some really nasty abuses springing up."

"So somehow we need to bring everyone's attention to this—no, more than that, we need to get them concerned about overpopulation at a gut level. Okay, that's problem number one, but how do we link this to the need for colonizing another solar system?"

"Perhaps we need to think of travel to the stars as a kind of lifeboat, in case conditions here on Earth really go sideways? We've already set up colonies on the Moon and Mars, and it's become painfully obvious that these will never become self-sustaining.

Conditions are inimical to life and the only way people can survive is with constant, ongoing supplies and services from Earth. If we want to set up self-sustaining, growing colonies we have to look to some other solar system."

"I agree Charles. I know you're right, but how do we convince Joe and Jill Taxpayer that you're right?"

"There, unfortunately, you have me. The naysayers will undoubtedly say at this point that we shouldn't be wasting our resources trying to go somewhere else while we have such problems at home. Of course, they probably said that when Columbus sailed to the New World in 1492. You just have to have prepared the ground so that when the funding referendum goes out, everyone will automatically say yes."

"So I guess what you're saying is that we need a really good PR campaign to convince the general public that going to the stars is in everyone's best interest?"

"That, plus some fortuitous event that brings home to everyone the necessity, or better still the urgency of doing this. A gigantic earthquake or volcanic eruption that kills millions would be just the thing, loath as I am to say it. And don't forget of course that you will only get one shot at this when the funding referendum goes out. If you get a No vote it will be very difficult to get another referendum."

But in the event the problem solved itself.

CHAPTER 3

The wolf had been chased by riders on all-terrain vehicles. Great noisy monsters with brilliant staring eyes, they had terrified the wolf and caused it to flee blindly. Its flight took it out of Yellowstone Park where it had lived its life and onto a nearby sheep ranch. It was just its bad luck that a rancher spotted it and dropped it with a single shot.

When the rancher rode up on his ATV, he noticed the wolf had a radio collar, which was bad news as far as he was concerned—all that paperwork for a start. Deciding to use the time-honored method of shoot, shovel, and shut up, he quickly dug a hole, rolled the carcass into it and, pausing briefly to blow its radio collar away with his shotgun for good measure, he quickly filled in the hole and rode away.

And thus perished the last wolf outside of captivity in the lower forty-eight States of the US. It was a few months later that a wildlife census of the US brought to light the fact that there had been no sightings of wolves anywhere for a long while, so much so that it was feared, correctly as it happened, that the wolf was extinct in the lower forty-eight.

It had been a slow news week—no politicians inserting their feet into their mouths, no film stars getting married for the umpteenth time, so the network decided, more in desperation than anything else, to run a feature on the disappearance of wolves. It was only intended as a filler but somehow the story caught people's imaginations and grew legs.

"So let's get this straight—there are no more wolves, they've gone the way of the dodo and the passenger pigeon. What happened to them?"

"In a word, increasing land use. Large predators such as wolves need a lot of land in which to hunt and feed, and there just isn't any land left any more. Everywhere in the US is either built-up or is being farmed, ranched, mined or otherwise used by humankind. Even in wilderness parks such as Yellowstone there are so many visitors that there are traffic jams most days, and wolves can't and won't coexist with humankind en masse in this way. We just haven't left any space in which wolves can live."

"What about in the rest of the world? Surely there must be some untouched wilderness somewhere."

"I'm afraid not. If you think the US is in bad shape, the rest of the world is worse. Most of Africa is under intense cultivation to feed their four billion population, and the only lions, tigers, elephants and so on left anywhere in the world are in zoos or hanging as trophies on someone's wall. We seem to have filled our planet to the bursting point. There isn't any room left for any other species except ourselves."

"Can we do anything about it, such as building wildlife sanctuaries?"

"Good luck with trying to persuade people to give up the necessary land, because we're not just talking about a few acres here and there but hundreds, even thousands of square miles."

"So do you see any hope for the future?"

"On Earth? Not much. It's easy to destroy wilderness, but very difficult to re-create it. I think we have to accustom ourselves to increasing urbanization of our planet. The only way we'll ever see wildlife again is to go somewhere else."

This simple exchange, begun out of desperation on a slow news day, somehow struck a chord in people. Soon, bumper stickers appeared saying, "Let's go somewhere else." The manned expedition to the stars, which most people if they thought of it at all regarded as a boondoggle in which a few astronauts would go 'out there' and do more or less incomprehensible things a long way off, began to have more meaning in their minds. It was not long before Julia found herself in a holovision studio. She was an accomplished interviewee, having been interviewed many times in the past after some particularly hair-raising or otherwise newsworthy space voyage.

"... delighted to have with us once again Dr. Julia Lockmeyer, the well-known astronaut and space medicine expert. Dr. Lockmeyer, I gather you're now involved in planning the first manned expedition to the stars. Perhaps you would give our viewers a brief overview of the project."

"Well, as you know, the development of fusion technology and its application to space flight has meant that very lengthy voyages are now possible. Voyages to the limits of our solar system can now be undertaken in a matter of a few months, but voyages to even the nearest stars are something else altogether because of the vast distances involved. A voyage to a typical galactic neighbor of ours would require years, or more likely decades to complete. This means that a spaceship with human passengers undertaking such a trip not only has to provide food and air for the passengers, it has to provide a complete living environment for them. You can't expect people to stay in cramped quarters for years at a time and remain sane and healthy. This means that a ship to send even a few passengers has to be very large indeed.

"Any spaceship that we send to a different star with our present technology will be on a one-way trip, because of the vast distances involved. We have the technology to get people to the stars, but not to bring them back again. That means that whoever goes will be staying there—permanently. We should be thinking in terms, not just of scientists or explorers, but of colonists. Their task will be to seed the human race on a new planet, to give the human race a fresh start with the hope that this time we do it better. We've grown too big for this planet; it's time to move on to the next one."

"So we'll be launching another Mayflower. How many will be aboard her?"

"That's the problem. Right now, we only have funding to send three or four at most. Assuming they all survive the voyage, all two or three decades of it, their chance of successfully starting a new branch of the human race elsewhere is not good. To begin with they would probably have to start having children during the voyage, because they would probably be too old to do so when they reached their destination. But more importantly, there simply won't be enough genetic diversity. Even if they do survive, future generations would have a horrendous inbreeding problem because the gene pool would be so small."

"What exactly does that mean?"

"It means that future generations of colonists would all be having children with their first cousins or even their siblings. After a few generations of this, any latent genetic defects—and we all have them—would rise to the surface and would probably result in a population of village idiots or something of the kind. You must, absolutely must, have genetic diversity for a healthy population in the long term."

"So how many would you like to send?"

"I think for a reasonable chance of success we need to send fifty to a hundred. The more the better obviously, but as many as current technology will permit."

"And how much would this cost?"

"I'm not the expert on this," (although she had taken great care to do her homework before appearing on the show), "but I think we need about ten times the amount of money that has been authorized so far. Question is, are people prepared to pay this much to give the human race, or more specifically our own citizens here in the US, the chance to start afresh on a new world?"

The answer came in the next few days in a social media avalanche. **Yes!** A nation can jog along, contented with its daily life for years, decades, even centuries. But sometimes a single idea infects them, and they act with one purpose. Some of the crusades in the Middle Ages had caused whole towns and villages to drop their daily life and go marching off to distant lands. So now, the USA was infected with the idea of sending colonists to the stars.

The referendum to authorize the money for the Mayflower Project, as it soon became known, received overwhelming approval. The mechanics of it were quite simple. Every voter received an electronic message of the form *Do you agree that funding to a maximum of ... should be gathered by general taxation for the purpose of ...* A simple yes/no response was all that was required. Of course, a lot of people automatically said no whatever the purpose might be, but in this case over seventy percent of responders said yes, which was nothing short of miraculous for a generally jaded, cynical voting population. All that now remained was to get on with it.

CHAPTER 4

Of volunteers for the Mayflower there was no lack. The problem lay in selecting them. The expedition had captured the public imagination, and every aspiring politician, single-agenda pressure group, religious cult, and plain old busybody wanted a say in the selection. The government realized early on that however the choice was made it would leave most people dissatisfied so it quickly distanced itself from the process. It announced that the choice would be left entirely in the hands of the Steering Committee, whose members luckily had already been chosen.

The Mayflower Committee, as it became widely known, had originally been set up to oversee the design and construction of a spaceship, and its members were administrators, scientists, and engineers. They had vaguely assumed that the human payload would be chosen by some other government agency, would arrive as government-furnished equipment as it were, and that would be that. Being placed in the political hot seat, or thrown to the lions as one member observed, was not what they had signed up for at all. As Julia Lockmeyer put it, "Thanks, you bastards." However, anyone who managed to work his or her way up to Steering Committee level in the increasingly raucous and individualistic USA had of necessity more than average resilience and strength. Consequently none of the committee members resigned; they just kept their heads down and got on with the job.

Julia was the obvious person to be placed in charge of candidate selection, or more precisely was the least unlikely person for this role.

"Since we have all these various organizations demanding that their voices be heard, I guess we'll have to give them a hearing, otherwise we'll be accused of disregarding the wishes of the taxpayers. So you lot," she said with a grin, indicating the members of the Mayflower Committee, including Lansky, who was horrified by the idea of having to deal with the general public, "are going to have to listen to their presentations."

In the course of the first month, the committee listened to briefs from twenty-seven different organizations, beginning with the Gaia Liberation Army. The GLA, as it was generally known, had a wide following, particularly in academia, and regarded the human race as an evil virus that had infected Earth, or Gaia as they called her, and their whole purpose in life was to prevent its spread. Their highly professional presentation along with sound effects left the Mayflower Committee with raised eyebrows, and the audience (since these were public hearings) with the impression that launching a starship would probably result in the death of the galaxy.

Most of the following presentations were equally dramatic, based presumably on the assumption that you have to make a lot of noise if you want to be heard. After the first few Lansky had such a look of baffled incomprehension on his face that Julia took pity on him and excused him from further attendance at the hearings. Dr. Kuwahara meanwhile had his usual inscrutable look at the hearings, so much so that Julia suspected he was simply sleeping with his eyes open.

Various other more shadowy groups took a more pragmatic approach and bypassed the formal presentation process in favor of simply trying to intimidate the committee members into resigning in favor of their own nominees.

After a month of this, the members of the committee emerged shaken but wiser. They had of course set up the usual security precautions, which intercepted two letter bombs in one week.

"Okay, ladies and gentlemen," said Julia, "we are going to have to change our thinking on this. If we just announce a slate of candidates we will have almost every one of the organizations we've heard from so far screaming that they have been ignored. I shudder to think what that's going to do to our peace of mind and frankly, considering those letter bombs, our physical safety."

It was Lansky who suggested accepting applications from anybody and everybody. "We'll say we've set up a computer app that will accept anyone as a potential candidate, then we can sort them out later. Okay, it's kicking the can down the road, but it'll give us some breathing space right now."

And so they did. But while they had reckoned on a few thousand applicants, they had failed to take into account the vast enthusiasm for the Mayflower Project that currently existed in the public mind, and the final tally was almost two million. Meanwhile, the committee, under a suitable screen of PR verbiage, attempted to decide among themselves how to choose the colonists.

"Number one priority will be ensuring that we have a fifty/fifty male/female ratio," said Lockmeyer. "Since the gender privacy laws prevent the physical sex of individuals being recorded anywhere, if we ask candidates their sex we'll almost certainly have the media screaming at us. But we'll look damn silly if we get everyone on board the ship and only then find out that they're all male, or all female. We'll just have to infer it from their DNA, and even doing that is of doubtful legality. Luckily we should be able to get access to their DNA since everyone's in the US has been recorded at birth for the last thirty years."

"We'll need a bit more than just the same number of men and women," said Lansky. "There's no point in sending people all that way if they don't have the skills to set up a technological society when they get there."

At that point an unpleasant thought struck Julia. Up to now her role on the Mayflower Committee was to deal with the problems of choosing the colonists, then getting them safely to their destination and ensuring their survival once they got there, insofar as they could plan for this on Earth. But what then? What would they do; how would they be organized? There didn't seem to be anyone on the committee whose task it was to think of such things, so Julia suspected it would probably become her responsibility.

But the question still remained of how to select the colonists. As Julia remarked in one of her by now regular dinners with Charles Lansdowne, "Would we do any better if we just selected a bunch of people at random?"

"I think you can do a lot better than that, Julia, and indeed you must. Not to do so would be dereliction of duty as far as you are concerned. What you're really trying to do is to ensure the breeding success of a small, isolated group of animals who just happen to be human beings."

"Okay, I think you're right. But what's the best way of going about it?"

"I think you have to use genetic selection. You're going to have a limited number of people on that ship, and if you want to maximize the chance of them successfully bringing into being a new branch of the human race, with absolutely no help from the rest of us once they get wherever they're going, then not only will you need as much genetic diversity as possible, but you have to weed out any genetic weaknesses such as a tendency to develop cancer at an early age or anything of that nature. And while you're at it you may as well select the most intelligent, mentally stable, and physically healthy specimens you can find."

"Agreed. The problem is that if the media get the slightest whiff of it they will leap on it like a cat on a mouse. Don't forget, there is a small but highly vocal minority that thinks we shouldn't be planning to go to another planet at all, that regards humanity as a kind of virus that needs to be contained. You can just imagine the headlines— *Mayflower project trying to breed a new super race*—which is likely to start a firestorm that could result in project cancellation. There are so many touchy special interest groups out there who are just looking for an excuse to scream blue murder at us."

"Unfortunately I think you're right. And of course the other problem with genetic selection is that it's based upon the assumption that some people are better than others, at least with regard to siring a new race. In today's world, even hinting that anyone is better than anyone else is likely to raise a firestorm. Anyone who considers themselves to be head and shoulders above the rest is pretty well guaranteed to be torn down and trampled upon in very short order. Being different is one thing; today's inclusive society tolerates everyone's little quirks. But to be better than anyone else—Heaven (or its non-sectarian equivalent) forbid!"

And so was born Operation Joe Average, as Julia described it to her immediate colleagues.

"What we're going to do is to announce that the selected colonists will be totally representative of the US population. We'll use the DNA record of every applicant to create a multi-faceted profile of them. These will then be thrown into a pot and stirred around, so to speak, and the resulting mixture will be used as a template. Anyone selected against this template should be completely average in every way, physical and mental."

This announcement effectively defused what was rapidly becoming a rather tense political situation, with protests and demonstrations almost daily by pressure groups who felt that they, and only they, had the right to represent mankind in its first trip to the stars.

One effect of the announcement was a massive new flood of applicants. While very few of these seriously wanted to go to the stars, they all felt they wanted some part of themselves, some defining characteristic, to be included in the final template. If they did not go themselves in the flesh, some part of them would be imprinted on those who did go, and that was good enough.

Predictably enough, there was also a flood of representations by various religions, cults, and assorted special interest groups pointing out that their particular beliefs, philosophies, prejudices or whatever

should be a fundamental part of the Template of the Average Person. This time, however, the committee was better prepared and deputized a panel of functionaries with the sonorous title of 'The Commission for the Guidance of Humankind's Extraterrestrial Advancement' to listen to the presentations. The members of this panel were invariably of patrician or scholarly appearance and could be trusted to sleep with their eyes open and not snore. The panel members drank a lot of coffee, were given excellent lunches, and were under strict orders not to laugh whatever the provocation.

Meanwhile, as a necessary part of the formation of The Template, as it was soon known in the media, some attention was given to what did *not* constitute the average of all humankind. This of course was a task relegated to a few unimportant technical types who mumbled to each other in technical jargon and generally did things which were incomprehensible, and therefore uninteresting, to the media. This group, under Julia Lockmeyer's tight control, searched throughout the millions of volunteers for the cream of the human race.

INTERLUDE: ZILLA

Zilla brushed a strand of hair out of her face with an impatient gesture. Realizing just too late that she had paint on her fingers, she swore abstractedly then forgot about it. Her whole attention was focused on the half-finished painting in front of her. There was something missing, some essential quality lacking which, if only she could visualize it, she knew would flow from her into the painting. It was like having a word on the tip of her tongue, not quite there yet infuriatingly close.

After staring at the painting for several minutes, she decided she was getting nowhere and gave it up for the day. In any case she had promised to go to a party that evening and knew from experience that it took quite some while to wash the smell of paint off herself. As an artist she was talented, dedicated, and rather messy.

At eighteen, Zilla Starr was a tall slender woman. Her face lacked that perfection of symmetry which has always been considered the hallmark of beauty throughout the ages, but there was a happy vitality about her which more than compensated. When everyone else around her was in their usual state of being weighed down by the cares of the world—lack of jobs, new taxes, gloom and doom in the media—Zilla breezed through it all with a smile on her face and an almost tangible aura of carefree enjoyment. It was positively indecent the way the younger generation carried on nowadays, as her elders remarked.

Having cleaned up, Zilla walked into the living room just in time to hear her stepbrother Stephan's rather petulant cry of "What's for dinner, Mom?"

Stephan was a jobless twenty-year-old with little education and even less inclination to get one, who spent most of his time in front of a holovision set watching anything that came up, but mostly sports, like his father. He was, however, the apple of his mother's eye.

"I'm cooking your favorite tonight, Stephan dear, and we'll eat just as soon as Daddy gets home."

Coming into the living room, Maria caught sight of her adopted daughter and gave an exaggerated sigh. Miniskirts were back in fashion, and Zilla's long elegant legs seemed to go on forever. Maria's legs had never been that shapely, and with middle age approaching they had lost most of their appeal. She felt a twinge of jealousy as she

looked at Zilla, and the thought of her new name made her feel worse. What was wrong with Bronya, anyway? If it was good enough for Maria's mother it ought to be good enough for the little waif that she and Victor had rescued and given a new life, how dare she change it...

When they had brought the little waif home, Victor and Maria (mainly Maria, Victor had very little say in their household) had named her Bronya, after Maria's mother. However, as Bronya grew up, she developed a pronounced dislike for her name, which she considered impossibly old-fashioned and boring, and since very few of her friends could pronounce her last name, Wojnowicz, she changed both names on the day she legally became an adult to Zilla Starr. To make it worse, Bronya, or Zilla as she now was, didn't seem to realize how deeply this had hurt Maria. "It's just a name, Mom. Names don't mean anything nowadays; you just change them to suit your mood."

The fact that this was largely correct was irrelevant as far as Maria was concerned. Although everyone was issued a 16-digit Personal Identity Number at birth, or in Zilla's case when she was brought into the country, which was then your real identity for the rest of your life, it did nothing to assuage Maria's hurt feelings. In any case, what a ridiculous name she had chosen...(As Bronya/Zilla explained, the Starr part was for a classical musician from the previous century who had something to do with all those dreamy songs, while as for Zilla, she just liked the sound of it.)

Maria's objections to the name change hadn't been helped much by Victor either. Although he would never admit it to his wife, he felt a little in awe of his adopted daughter as she changed from skinny child into this tall earthy goddess on the brink of full womanhood, and simultaneously developed an artistic talent that seemed to him miraculous. Not, as he admitted to himself, that he knew anything about art, but he was inordinately proud of the way Bronya, or Zilla as he supposed he should call her now, could daub paint on a canvas and make it come alive.

Victor was also proud that it was he who had encouraged Bronya to start painting. It had all begun when he had joined an art sponsorship group. It was the latest thing in those days; you bought shares in an organization that subsidized artists of one sort or another, and in return got tickets to exhibitions. Not first performances, naturally, they didn't subscribe that much, but they got there ahead of the common herd, assuming that the common herd bothered to attend at all.

Victor tried taking his whole family at first, but Stephan had no interest and Maria always complained about having to stand around in high heels (why she had to wear high heels Victor could never make out), so in the end it was just himself and Bronya. It was fun taking his eleven-year-old daughter; she usually had something to say about what she saw, and often her comments had that devastating accuracy that only the young can achieve. One day they were standing in front of a new work which seemed to be highly regarded by the cognoscenti.

"Er," said Victor, trying to find the appropriate page in the program, "oh, here we are. It's called, er, Dynastic Dream, and one of the critics said it was, er, 'a tour de force of psychokinesthetic symbolism', er, 'encapsulating the essential angst of today's society and the dynamic tension between our inner feelings and outer selves'." The object in question was a double-sided canvas about three feet

square suspended from a light spring so it bobbed in the breeze, painted a harsh, glittery white on one side and a soft peachy orange on the other.

"Looks like he's waiting for the paint to dry so he can get on with it," said Bronya, and they both started giggling. They were glared at by a large lady with a knife-like nose protruding above jowls that wobbled when she swung round to them, which caused Bronya to go red in the face trying to suppress a further set of giggles. In the end they had to leave because neither of them could control themselves any longer.

On the way home Bronya asked, "Dad, what did artists do in the old days?"

Victor had a vague idea that they spent a lot of time painting things that you could see, sort of like photographs, although why anyone would want to spend time putting paint on a piece of canvas when you could just as easily click off a few camera shots, he couldn't say. But he was sufficiently intrigued to forgo his baseball re-runs that evening and switch a holo set to the Net instead.

It took a little while to find what they were seeking. Finally they were looking at a flat, two-dimensional representation of some flowers. *Sunflowers*, it said, by somebody called Van Gogh. At first, it was hardly worth looking at. And yet, and yet, there was something about it that demanded their attention. Victor had the oddest feeling that a bright summer's day was blazing its warmth onto the flowers, even though it was dark outside and the room lighting was subdued. There was a hypnotic quality about the painting which would not let them take their eyes away.

It was late at night before Victor shooed an exhausted Bronya to bed. So many paintings, so many artists. She had a vague idea that there were many, many different styles of painting, and that in each picture the artist somehow put a little bit of themselves into it. How it was done, she didn't know. But she knew what she wanted to do with her life. She wanted to paint pictures like the ones she had seen tonight.

And now, early on a Saturday evening seven years later, the skinny little Bronya that had become the elegantly mini-skirted Zilla was standing in the living room of her home, listening to her mother's exaggerated sigh. She bit her lip to stop her usual disparaging remark about her mother's sigh, knowing all too well how easy it was to get into a flaming row that would ruin her whole evening.

"I suppose you won't have time to eat with us again," said Maria in her hurt voice.

"Of course I will, Mummy." Calling her 'Mummy' usually calmed her down, and in any case she had an appetite like a horse. Painting always made her feel hungry.

At that moment Victor walked in. Short and balding with the beginnings of a paunch, he still retained an air of youthful innocence that endeared him to Zilla. She was somewhat taller than him and by standing on tiptoe could kiss the bald spot on the top of his head, which she proceeded to do. Victor gave her a quick hug while Maria looked rather sour.

After dinner Victor and Stephan parked themselves in front of a holovision set. Victor had recently gained his Registered Football Critic status and considered it his professional duty to watch all the major games, while Stephan just gravitated there in the absence of any other interests. Zilla cleared up, involving as it did little more than stacking everything in the dishwasher, then scooted out of the house, barely hearing her father's plea that she be home at a reasonable hour. Of course I will, she said to herself, so long as I get to say what's reasonable.

Not that she had any reason to worry about being out late. The suburb of Salt Lake City where they lived was well lit and well patrolled, and in any case the party was at a friend's house a quarter of a mile away. Dad always wanted her to call when she was coming home so he could walk over and escort her back, but she felt silly having her own father fetch her. In any case it was much more fun to have one of her numerous admirers escort her back.

Zilla had decided recently that she was definitely heterosexual. Girls were nice as friends, but somehow they just didn't attract her as bed partners. This was not something one would want to be made known publicly. Young people were expected to experiment, and with population pressure mounting (The Problem, as the media usually referred to it), being a het was, well, not exactly frowned upon, but somehow not something you wanted to boast about.

None of this worried Zilla. She just liked being in the company of boys (or men—when did they stop being boys and become men?). When she arrived there was already a crowd drifting around, in that aimless but expectant way that people have before a party spontaneously ignites. She burst in with her usual happy smile and whether by coincidence or whether she was the spark, the party seemed to ignite at that moment.

Jon's house, where the party was held, was larger than most of the others in the neighborhood. His parents were away for the weekend, so they had it to themselves. Down in the basement the noise was deafening and it was just as well that the rec room was soundproofed, else there would have been lawsuits flying the next day. Zilla and her friends could never understand why old people, over thirty or so, got so stuffy about a little bit of noise.

Conversation had been a dying art ever since the invention of television over a century and a half ago. Not that it would have been possible above the noise in the rec room. Hog thrash was this year's music, composed and played electronically. What it lacked in melody, harmony, and counterpoint it more than made up with exuberant rhythmic volume. If, unaccountably, anyone at the party wanted a respite from it, they went outside. It was a warm night so from time to time small groups would lounge around in the backyard, gossiping in the way of partygoers since time began.

"What are you working on now?" said a voice behind her. Zilla turned to recognize the slight, blonde figure of Tony. A few years older than Zilla and determinedly gay, he was one of the few people of her own generation with whom she felt able to discuss art. He had endeared himself to her by cheerfully admitting to playing with dolls as a boy, then discussing the aesthetic merits of various types of doll. Big hairy jocks were all very well, she thought, when you wanted someone big and hairy (although quite a number of those turned out to be gay), but the only people she knew besides herself who appreciated art were either slightly weird females with whom she had nothing else in common, or gays like Tony. Perhaps artists like me are meant to stay single, she thought in her darker moments.

"What am I working on? I don't quite know. I mean, I thought I knew what it was supposed to be, but it's not working out that way at all. It seems to have a life of its own."

"Well, on the assumption that it's a painting we're talking about and not Frankenstein's monster, what was it meant to be in the beginning?"

"A sort of abstract essence of a flower. I know that sounds a bit corny, but I was trying to capture the flowerness of a flower without actually painting a flower. Trouble is, it wants to be something else, but I don't know what. It's hiding there, just inside my head somewhere, but it won't come out. I dream about it. I know exactly what it is I have to paint then, poof, I wake up and it's gone. It's infuriating."

"The only advice I can offer is to keep on dreaming. Celibate dreams, of course. You have to maintain your virgin purity while the Muse is upon you."

"No problem about that. Living at home isn't exactly the best way to expand your sex life, at least with a family like mine. And much as I like you, Tony, you really aren't of much use to me in that direction."

"I know, sweetheart. But at least I'm not a rival. I have the feeling that any man you'd be interested in would have to be one hundred percent hetero. Come to think of it, they do seem to be getting a bit scarce, don't they? When I was down in the party just now, I think there were more boys dancing with boys than with girls."

There was a slight pause. "Why is that, Tony? It wasn't always like this, was it? Where the two sexes seem to be losing interest in each other? You read in the old books how men chased women, and as soon as a woman decided to be caught she just flopped onto her back and starting making babies."

"I guess they did a bit too much of the baby-making bit in the past. Nowadays there are just too many of us. Maybe being gay is Mother Nature's way of solving the problem. At least nobody can accuse me of causing any more babies."

Zilla's thoughts drifted to her own childhood. Maria had had Stephan and declared that enough was enough. Being pregnant was uncomfortable, it ruined her figure, and actually giving birth was something she wasn't going to go through again for anyone's sake, thank you very much. But Victor wanted another child, and Maria had to agree that they would be company for each other, so they set out to adopt one. A girl this time, though—someone for Maria to dress up and fuss with. Boys were all very well in their way, but girls were so much more, well, ladylike than boys.

Adopting was easy enough. With the Third World bursting at the seams, there were agencies practically begging you to take a child. Maria and Victor chose a sweet little one, almost white really, it could just be a slight tan, and Maria proceeded to convert the little waif into a real American child.

Trouble was, Bronya had not grown up in her adoptive mother's image at all. Maria wanted her daughter to be a ladylike credit to her mother who would have the glittering social life that she, Maria, had never quite managed. (Wants me to be another overdressed bubblehead was Bronya's way of putting it.) Instead, she found herself with a tomboyish, scabby-kneed whirlwind who, if dressed in a pretty party dress could almost be guaranteed to come home with it dirty and torn, having got into a fight with some horrid boy. Maria finally gave up in despair, and was consoled only by the fact that Stephan was so much more dependable, so much more caring of his Mama, and so happy to spend time at home with her. (Never gets off his fat butt to do anything, in Bronya's words.)

She often wondered who her real parents were, but had decided she didn't really want to know. She guessed she came from some Third World country—certainly she had dark glossy hair, brown eyes, and somewhat darker skin than her adoptive parents—but Victor and Maria said they didn't know where and she believed them. If she was from the Third World, what she saw of it on holovision made her quite content to be where she was now.

"Come back down to us mortals," she heard Tony saying. "You've gone all glassy-eyed. It must have been the mention of babies that did it. You're getting the nesting instinct, I can tell. Any day now we'll see you knitting baby clothes."

Zilla threatened him with her clenched fist with mock ferocity. Then she grinned. "Someday I'm going to get down to it in earnest and have lots of fat little babies, and the hell with everyone's disapproval of big families, but not for a long while yet. There's too much I want to do first. When I do though, I want you to be their favorite uncle. You can bring them presents and take them to the zoo."

Tony hugged her briefly. "Come on, let's get down to the party again or someone will start spreading nasty rumors that I'm dallying with girls."

There was little else to do in the party room except drink beer, smoke marijuana, and occasionally smooch around the room with one of the few men who were neither intimidated by her nor interested only in their own sex. A couple of times she danced with girls just to show she was not rigidly hetero, but when the last one clutched her in a passionate belly-rubbing embrace, she decided she had had enough and retreated to the backyard again. It was empty this time except for a couple of young men totally absorbed in each other, oblivious to the world around them.

Being alone never bothered Zilla. She was not a hermit by nature, but lacked that insistent need for the company of others which so often passes for sociability. If others were there, all well and good, she could enjoy their company, but if she was on her own then so be it.

Thinking back on her past, it had always been like this. The family had moved to Salt Lake when she was ten. Before that they had lived in one of the satellite towns that had sprung up around Chicago during the great exodus from that city in the middle of the century. She thought it was called Pleasant Creek, or something of the kind, but there were so many new suburbs with similar names that it was easy to be confused. Life had been a lot tougher in Pleasant Creek. They had been uncomfortably near Chicago itself, with its constant threat of raiding parties sent out by the gangs that controlled the city. At least she didn't have to report her movements in advance to the Patrol Centre here when she went out at night. Back in the old days in Pleasant Creek you mostly stayed in at night, so if you wanted to have a friend over they had to sleep over as well. Maria tended to discourage this; she always seemed to find some reason why so-and-so was not really good enough for Bronya, not quite up to our standards, you know.

Like most of their contemporaries, Bronya's parents had a great deal of leisure time. It was only quite recently that the education system had finally accepted that its primary function was to prepare people for what they did most of the time, which was leisure. Maria Wojnowicz had a diploma in holovision appreciation, while Victor was both a Registered Baseball Critic and a Registered Football Critic, which represented quite an achievement. Of course, Victor had to spend several hours a day in an insurance company, but he always felt this was somewhat of an imposition. "Most times I just check what the computer says. Maybe once a day I change something, but for all the difference it makes, I might as well not bother."

But Victor must have been doing something right, because when Bronya was ten he was promoted to a head office job in Salt Lake. When most cities had collapsed into lawlessness earlier in the century, everything worth moving had been moved to heavily guarded suburbs such as Pleasant Creek. Almost everyone now lived and worked in suburbs and exurbs surrounding decaying city cores, like planets orbiting a black hole. Yet there were always some functions which required humans to congregate together instead of talking to each other via holophone, and thus there was a need for a few functioning cities. Salt Lake City was one of the few which had escaped the blight and by the middle of the century had become one of the major commercial centers of North America. A move there for Victor Wojnowicz was a definite step upwards.

Salt Lake was still a Mormon town, no doubt about it. Alcohol was frowned upon, tobacco was illegal, and even marijuana was hard to come by. But at least you could walk out of your house at night without having to report your movements in advance to the Patrol

Centre, and there weren't even any guards on the school buses. Maria never did feel comfortable seeing her children going to school without one or two armed guards in sight. However, the schools were used to mothers like her and faithfully reported the safe arrival of every school bus over the Net. For as long as her children were at school, Maria could never relax until that reassuring message arrived that the school bus had safely reached its destination five blocks down the road.

Bronya's new school in Salt Lake was a progressive establishment which had recently instituted a program to teach all its students to read and write. Of course, anyone taking an advanced university degree was generally expected to learn reading and writing, and certainly Victor would have to improve his skills in this area if he wanted to advance further up the corporate ladder. But learning as young as ten years old was almost unheard of. Maria was doubtful at first.

"I don't know, Victor, I mean, is it going to stunt their development? All this memorizing enormous amounts of things by rote with no chance to do anything creative? After all, I've never learnt that stuff and it hasn't done me any harm."

"Well, children used to learn it at a much younger age a couple of centuries ago."

"Oh, that doesn't count. That was in the dark ages and you simply can't compare what happened then to today's world. I do wish you wouldn't wander off the subject when I'm trying to discuss serious things."

"Well, er..."

"Besides, if you ever need to write anything you just tell a computer to do it for you and it makes those funny little squiggly things, you know, letters or whatever you call them, and if you want

to know anything you just ask the Net and it tells you. Who needs all this reading and writing?"

"I guess there are some things you need to know which aren't available in the Net."

"Nonsense. Anything worth knowing is in the Net somewhere, always has been, always will be."

It was the art book that Victor bought for Bronya a year or two later which finally convinced Maria. It was not so much the reproductions of Impressionist paintings as the creamy sensuousness of the paper which exuded a feeling of voluptuous luxury. If this is what books were like, maybe reading wasn't such a bad thing after all, she thought. She even thought about learning herself but somehow never found time for it.

When Bronya was twelve, Maria finally ceased thinking of her as a little doll, and started to refer to her as a trial and a disappointment. "Look at the mess in your room, your grandmother would have a fit if she saw this, and you've ruined your new blouse." This last with a wail of despair as she saw that her daughter for some incomprehensible reason had liberally rubbed paint into the offending article. (Bronya had been experimenting with a way of spreading background color and had used the frilly blouse her mother had bought her with savage delight.) Where was the delicate little china doll that she had worked so hard to mold in her own image? Maria's thoughts oscillated between maternal misery and feral dislike at such times.

But there was always Stephan to console her. You could always count on Stephan to do the right thing, dress the right way, say the right thing. Manly little fellow too, used to sit with Victor often and watch baseball. None of this running around outside and getting dirty like Bronya.

The final confirmation that Bronya was a Problem Child came one afternoon when she had, as usual, been running around outside. Maria received an indignant phone call from her neighbor.

" ...ought to be ashamed of yourself, letting that disgusting child of yours assault my poor Richard. His eye is so bruised he can hardly see out of it. We're going to sue you for this. If I ever see that child of yours near mine again I'll call the Sector Patrol. How can you live with yourself knowing what a monster you've raised..."

At this point Bronya walked in the house. Maria swiped off her phone with an extravagant gesture.

"What have you done now, you stupid child? Richard's mother says he's going to lose his eye."

"Oh poo, Mother. I just socked him one 'cos he grabbed my ass, and then he ran off screaming to his mummy. He'll be okay in the morning." Since Richard was older and heavier than Bronya, Maria was a little confused. Admittedly, sexual fumblings with pre-pubescent girls were rather frowned upon, but one didn't like to be a prude about these things. Heaven forbid one should get a reputation for prudishness. But to physically assault a person with such little provocation? Besides, what was she doing, playing with boys anyway? Maria determined to have a long talk with Bronya that evening, then dropped the idea with a mental shrug. So many long talks already, and they slid off her daughter like water off a duck's back.

What irked Maria was that Victor in his quiet way could easily talk to his daughter, whereas Maria and Bronya seemed to live on different worlds. Maria knew only too well the glazed-eye expression that would come over her daughter whenever she tried to explain to her how she ought to behave. Victor, on the other hand, could chat with Bronya on easy terms about anything. More and more nowadays the talk would be about art, and Victor was bemused at times to realize that his twelve-year-old daughter knew a lot more about it than he did.

It was only when Maria finally faced the fact that she couldn't talk to her daughter that she swallowed her pride and decided that Bronya needed professional help. It wasn't as if it was anything to be ashamed of, as she explained to Victor that evening. Lots of children needed professional guidance; in fact she was surprised the school hadn't suggested it already, but Bronya was really getting out of hand and there was no knowing what might happen next.

Victor's somewhat feeble protestations having been overridden, Bronya was duly deposited one day in Dr. Ostrofski's office. Dr. Ostrofski described herself as a Juvenile Social Adjustment Consultant, and prided herself on her ability to reach an easy rapport with almost any child or teenager. She smiled warmly as Bronya walked in, noting the child's rather hostile body language which was only to be expected in the circumstances. There was no desk in the room, just a few armchairs and sofas.

"Sit anywhere you want, Bronya, or stand and walk around if you want. I'm here to help you," she said in her most warm, comforting voice. Bronya returned a who-the-hell-are-you look. Dr. Ostrofski realized she was going to have her work cut out with this one.

It is always distressing for a learned adult called upon to provide guidance and counseling to a child to realize that the child in question is more intelligent, and in some ways more learned, than herself. When this sunk in to Dr. Ostrofski during the third session with Bronya

Wojnowicz, she nearly panicked. Children weren't supposed to be cleverer than her; she was the mastermind around here and had a string of degrees to prove it. Unfortunately, none of this impressed Bronya who went on alternately telling her about the Pre-Raphaelites, whom she had just discovered, and remorselessly dissecting her mother's personality.

Later that day, Dr. Ostrofski reported to Maria Wojnowicz that she didn't really think there was a problem with her daughter, that these apparent problems usually sorted themselves out with increasing maturity, and she didn't think much would be gained by her seeing Bronya anymore.

Zilla was woken from her reverie by a group of partygoers coming out to the backyard, presumably like her for some respite from the noise inside.

"Did you guys see that thing on holo last night about the starship project?"

"What, another one of those boring old sci-fi things?"

"No, this one's for real. They're sending a spaceship to another star and they want volunteers to go on it."

"I wouldn't mind doing that as long as I could come back after a year or two."

"No, you don't get it—it's going to be a one-way trip. You're going to spend the rest of your life there."

"You're kidding!"

"They gave a web address, so just for fun I input my PIN. You're now looking at an actual interstellar volunteer."

"So when do we get rid of you?"

The conversation degenerated somewhat at this point, but returned to a more philosophical level later on. In the end Jurgen the volunteer brought up the website on his smartphone and most of the party, fueled by alcohol and peer pressure, input their PINs. They also added the PINs of a hog thrash singer whose number someone just happened to have plus someone else's ninety-year-old great aunt.

And forgot all about it the next day.

Six months later, Zilla received a message: She had been shortlisted for the Mayflower Project.

She was never quite sure why the idea of making an irrevocable break with everything she knew and was familiar with had so much appeal for her. She had the prospect of a promising career as an artist ahead of her and no lack of friends and admirers. Perhaps it was the thought of a world where babies were welcome, and the more the merrier. Perhaps it was simply an inexpressible urge to explore new frontiers, new ideas, new ways of looking at things, in whatever form they might take. At all events she went ahead with the next step.

Her family's reaction was predictable. Maria expressed a formulaic regret that she would be gone but didn't seem unduly upset. Truth to tell, it was a relief for Maria who was feeling increasingly uncomfortable with this cuckoo-child who was maturing into a glamorous and accomplished woman with whom she had little in common. Stephan hardly seemed to care, which was also predictable. Victor, though, was a different matter. He didn't try to stop her, knowing it would only make her more determined to go, but he had a lost puppy air about him that made Zilla want to hug him and tell him that everything would be okay. On the day she left for her initial screening, she did hug him and told him she would be back. This much at least was true. The launch date was still three years ahead.

It was to her friends, perhaps inadvertently, that she expressed her real reason for going. At another party at Jon's house (same people, same music), the backyard conversation, not unexpectedly, centered around Zilla. Reactions ranged from awe—"Wow!" —to cynical amusement—"Gonna have sex with those little green men out there?"—to puzzlement—"But why? Your whole life is ahead of you here." She listened to them for a while, not contributing much but seemingly lost in a dream. In the end, when the discussion had turned to what the rest of them intended or wanted to do with their lives, those of them that had thought about it at any rate, Zilla smiled softly and said, "And I shall be the mother of nations."

CHAPTER 5

Until recently the starship project had been just another of those things at the back of the public consciousness, but it had suddenly been catapulted to the forefront. Someone with diplomatic skills was needed to head it under such conditions. Old Zablinsky who had headed it up to now was a moderately competent civil servant who could be trusted to keep a run of the mill project humming along nicely, but was completely out of his depth in the high profile venture into which the Mayflower Project had developed. It was no surprise to anyone when he took early retirement and scuttled thankfully away.

His replacement parachuted in as Chairman of the Mayflower Committee, Harold J. Merriweather IV, was a Boston Brahmin of impeccable background, but more importantly a diplomat with steely nerves. It certainly took all his diplomatic skills to hold such headstrong individuals as Lansky and Lockmeyer in check, but he did. Miraculously it seemed at times, he even got them to work together.

There finally came a day when they had agreed that there would be fifty colonists on the Mayflower.

"Even with careful genetic selection, I have to have an absolute minimum of forty, twenty men and twenty women, to ensure we don't have inbreeding problems and end up with a bunch of village idiots," said Julia. "And because we must realistically expect some deaths along the way, I want a total of fifty to begin with to allow for a safety margin."

"How are you going to deal with the fact that the Mayflower voyagers we select are going to be anything but average?" asked Merriweather.

"I was rather hoping you would give me some help there," replied Julia. "After all, we brought this Joe Average business into being just to protect our backsides when the selection process started looking rather ugly from a political viewpoint, not to mention the personal safety of some of us on the Steering Committee. But there's no way I'm going to allow a bunch of completely average people to be put on that ship. If I'm responsible for selecting a bunch of people to start a new branch of the human race, I'm going to select the very best individuals I can from a genetic viewpoint. Which does give me some qualms with regard to deceiving the public, but not half the qualms I would have for not selecting the very best."

"I think the expression here is 'between a rock and a hard place.' Hmm, this might call for some delicate handling, which I guess is going to be my job. Tell me, is there any genuine reason we can give out for using genetic selection?"

"Well, apart from selecting for ordinariness, which is just what we don't want to do, we can justifiably select for general health and disease immunity. For example, some people are genetically less likely than others to develop cancer, and obviously we would want to select such people. And before you ask, I know that most forms of cancer can be cured nowadays, but the cure usually demands a massive infrastructure of hospitals, medical equipment, pharmaceuticals and so on, which they simply won't have where they're going."

"So we can reasonably give out that the Mayflower voyagers will be genetically screened for the likelihood that they will retain good health into old age. Very well, it's a start. Are there any other genuine reasons we can give out for further screening? You can see where I'm going with this. We can't tell an outright lie because the selected voyagers will doubtless be interviewed ad nauseam by the media, and it will soon become apparent that they aren't ordinary at all. But if we can tell them a partial truth, that they've been screened for this and that genuine reasons, then the fact that they are all exceptional individuals might be blurred a bit."

"Funnily enough this brings up something I've been working on, and that is the tendency towards physical deterioration on long space voyages, which happens to be my field. There is some evidence that some people are genetically less likely to suffer serious effects from prolonged weightlessness than others. It's not a simple relationship; there isn't a single gene that causes the problem, but there are a series of genes that people less likely to have problems tend to have, or not have as the case may be, and we have actually been screening for that anyway."

"So if we announce to the media that we're screening them for lifetime health and for resistance to weightlessness problems while on board the ship, we could announce it in an 'oh, by the way' manner that the media could not reasonably take exception to?"

"Ye-es, I think so."

"Very well, Julia, if you will draft me some suitable words, I'll see about gently inserting them into the public consciousness. I do know one or two reasonably honest reporters, although there seems to be fewer and fewer of them every year."

It was the requirement for a safety margin in the colonist numbers which finally convinced Lansky. Genetics, inbreeding, and anything else of that nature were outside his field, and therefore unimportant as far as he was concerned. But safety margins were something as an engineer he could understand, so with some discreet prodding from Merriweather he accepted the whole fifty. Not very logical, but then outside of engineering he was not a very logical person.

This was brought home to Julia when a press conference was held to announce the expanded version of the Mayflower Project, followed by a cocktail party, and Sol brought his wife along to, as he said, 'protect him from all those bloody reporters.' Miriam Lansky was a large, placid woman, although Julia had the impression she was quite a formidable person in her own right. At all events she was the one who initiated the conversation.

"Hello, I'm Miriam Lansky. You must be that terrifying Dr. Lockmeyer that Sol tells me about," she said with a grin.

Coming from almost anyone else this would have caused Julia to bridle, but somehow Miriam's cheerful openness disarmed her.

"Do I really come across as terrifying? And by the way, it's Julia."

"Miriam. And I suspect that Sol is really just in awe of your knowledge and achievements."

"I must admit I have much the same regard for him. And while we certainly have our disagreements and have been known to get into

shouting matches, perhaps you would tell him from me that there is nothing personal about it, and I have enormous respect for him."

"Oh, I guessed that. You're two people at the tops of your respective fields, two bulls in a field—oops, that was a rather clumsy way of putting it..."

"I know what you mean, and I've been called a lot worse. But you're right, neither of us is used to being gainsaid, so when our professional roles clash, as they inevitably do from time to time, we do tend to explode in righteous fury. I've gone home many a time knowing I've been a miserable overbearing bitch, but sometimes you just have to be an overbearing bitch if you want to get the job done."

"It's not a whole lot different from being a mother, believe me. When my kids were little they were a rambunctious bunch and you had to lay the law down at times or there would have been chaos."

"How many do you have, if you don't mind my asking?"

"Five, three boys and two girls."

At this point Miriam showed a little hesitancy, as if waiting for the formulaic disapproval of large families that was the usual response in an overpopulated world. To her surprise and relief, Julia beamed her approval.

"How wonderful to find a family that rejoices in their children. I've never had any myself. I guess I was always too busy doing other things, but it somehow makes up for it all knowing that there are people who want and love children. If you and Sol were a few decades younger I'd have loved to have you both as part of the Mayflower's team."

"I guess my career has been my family. I went to university with the explicit intent of getting my MRS (pronounced Mrs. in most circles) and reckoned I'd graduated summa cum laude when I met and married Sol. All I ever really wanted out of life was a loving husband, a large house, and lots of kids, and I haven't been disappointed."

At which point Julia saw Harold Merriweather bearing down on her with a gaggle of reporters in tow.

"Miriam, I have to go, but I'm so glad to have met you. Please tell Sol that I'll try not to be so bitchy, but if I am, it's nothing personal."

INTERLUDE: MAIREED

"So you'll be doing political science at college then? Well, maybe we can arrange for you to have my seat when I retire."

Maireed regarded her father's suggestion with some contempt. She had considerably greater ambitions than merely occupying a seat in the state legislature, but forbore from mentioning it at this time. While she had no particular compunction in belittling his suggestion, she didn't think much was to be gained by doing so at this time.

Maireed Shaughnessy was a young woman of great intelligence, high energy, and boundless ambition. As a child she had always been the leader in whatever they were doing at the time. Perhaps she had to be a leader, because with her domineering personality it was a case of take charge or be lonely. Close friends she never had. Hangers-on and admirers, usually of her own sex, she attracted easily and was generally to be seen sweeping from place to place with her entourage behind her. But confidantes she never seemed to have or need.

Maireed's great grandfather Seamus had emigrated to the U.S. in the twentieth century from the then Northern Ireland. He claimed he was sent by the Irish Republican Army as a permanent fundraiser, although it was rumored he had had a falling out with an IRA boss and had fled for his life. At all events, he remained the rest of his life an ardent IRA supporter, fanatically opposed to the British whom he regarded as several degrees worse than Hitler's SS or Attila the Hun's cohorts. He had the gift of the gab and could talk the hind legs off a donkey, as the saying went. He was a familiar figure in the bars of Boston, holding forth with great eloquence on the tribulations of Ireland and the iniquity of the British.

Seamus Shaughnessy considered he would have failed in his duty had he not inculcated in his children the same intense hatred of the British that smoldered within him. Although he himself never went on active service again, he helped to send millions of dollars back to Ireland, and no doubt much of that was used to create mayhem in Northern Ireland over the years.

It was not surprising therefore that there grew up in the Shaughnessy family a tradition of fighting for the underdog. Any old cause would do, as long as there were recognizable underdogs and more importantly, arrogant colonial usurpers against whom a blow could be struck for freedom. True, colonial powers in the old sense had become rather scarce by the twenty-first century, but that just meant one had to use a little imagination. Shaughnessys fought in various guerrilla actions in South and Central America, and two were killed in China in the 2040s and '50s during that country's long drawn out civil war after the Communist regime finally collapsed.

Members of the Shaughnessy clan often had old Seamus's easy facility with languages and weapons. It was nothing for one of them to join a war in Central America, pick up a working knowledge of Spanish in a few weeks, then go to China and do the same with some backwoods Chinese dialect. Perhaps the facility with weapons came from the family tradition that every one of them practiced with rifles and handguns from an early age. "You never know when some bastard Britisher is going to come into your sights, boy," as Seamus used to say. But Seamus was a traditionalist, or male chauvinist pig, depending on your point of view. Fighting was for the menfolk; staying home and rearing children for the women. This was unfortunate as far as family harmony was concerned, because several of his daughters and granddaughters inherited his fiery disposition.

Maireed's father, Patrick, was one of old Seamus's grandsons. The fire that had burned in Seamus was but a weak spark in Patrick, although he had inherited his gift of the gab. Patrick had no inclination to go trotting around the globe looking for wars to fight, but instead stayed home and studied law. The Shaughnessys had little respect for the law as such—certainly, Patrick never intended to spend his life settling divorces or chasing ambulances—but recognized it as a convenient springboard for politics, which was regarded in their family as almost as honorable as fighting. Like many of his family, he was articulate about anything political to the point of monomania and would argue any cause just for love of arguing. But he lacked the truly successful politician's empathy with people. He made it to the Massachusetts House of Representatives where the party bosses used him from time to time as a one-man filibuster, but never made it any further.

Patrick married a girl of good Boston Irish stock, and between them produced three children. Patrick Jr., the oldest, took after his father: articulate, voluble, yet withal a plodder. He would be a worthy individual in his own way, but he would never set the world on fire. Sean, the next, was different, so much so that his family often wished

they could disown him. Sean was a poet, for the love of Mary, a limp-wristed, verse-spouting pansy, as his father often declared in disgust.

Sean was a throwback to the noble profession of the Irish bard. In centuries gone by he would have travelled the length and breadth of Ireland, and maybe of Europe as well, as a minstrel or a storyteller, or perhaps both. In little country towns he would have walked into the marketplace and waited calmly while his apprentice drummed up business and spread the word. Then, when the sun was low in the sky and the day's business was coming to an end, an audience would have gathered expectantly around him and he would have told tales from the mists of Irish legend, when giants walked the land and faeries wove their spells.

Storytelling in those days combined the roles of theatre and holovision. The storyteller took people out of their ordinary, humdrum lives and opened up a whole new world of fantasy to them. For many of these simple rural people it was not fantasy but fact, and many of them went home afterwards nervously expecting hobgoblins to leap out of the shadows at them. The storyteller had a prodigious memory, a wealth of knowledge, and a poetic flair that could turn the most ordinary of events into something remarkable, but above all he had the power to spellbind people with his voice. The Irish call it the gift of the gab, and many of the Shaughnessys had it to some extent. Sean had it as much as old Seamus had. The difference was that Sean was totally uninterested in politics, and used his gift as his ancient storytelling forbears had done.

It was into this family that Maireed was born in 2078. She was the youngest of the family, being some five years younger than Sean. Patrick Jr. was eight years her senior and was at that time a lumpish creature who regarded girls as generally beneath his contempt. (He didn't change much in later years.) But between Sean and Maireed there was a strange bond. Sean was a gentle, introspective boy, the butt of all the thuggish humor that prevails in schools, who loved to tell Maireed stories almost from the day she was born. Maireed for her part was a fiery, restive little dragon who would allow no one to gainsay her. With her glossy black hair and flashing blue eyes, most people of her age were a little afraid of her. Yet she loved Sean and from an early age had appointed herself his protectress. "Keep your hands off my brother, you bastards," she had screamed at age five to a group of eleven-year-olds who, twice her size, were bullying Sean. And they had backed down. Truly, she was the spiritual heir of old Seamus.

Apart from Sean, Maireed had no close friends. It was difficult to be close to a fire-breathing dragon; one tended to get singed. She was not a gentle child and in this she did not change as she grew older. While most teenagers still had a soft, puppyish look about them, Maireed had from an early age a sharp-edged angularity. It was as if she proclaimed to the world, "I'm for doing, not for looking. You want ass, go look somewhere else." Not that, as a woman, she was sexless. Far from it. But Maireed initiated, Maireed chose her partners, and Maireed discarded her partners, whenever it suited her.

When she felt like it, Maireed would happily take bed partners of either sex. They were invariably rather submissive creatures, particularly the male ones. Maireed had had one experience with a man who wanted to dominate her in bed, and that was enough. She had been bruised, although he was crippled for a week.

As a student Maireed had a quick, rapacious intelligence that could take a new subject, chew it up, digest it, and retain just enough of it for her needs. She was not a deep thinker nor would she have cared to be one. Knowledge for her was a tool to be used, like anything else—sex, force of personality, power of voice—to gain her ends. She wasn't quite sure where she wanted to go, only that she wanted to go to the top.

Maireed won a scholarship to an Ivy League university at age seventeen and opted for political science. She reasoned to herself that this was as good a preparation as any to get her hands on the levers of power, and since it wouldn't require so much hard work as, say, law or finance, she would have more time to get involved in university life. After all, the whole point of going to university was to make useful connections, to run things, and in general to practice what she wanted to do later on. Spending long years of study to get to the top was not part of her plan at all.

A few days before classes began, Maireed arrived to take up residence. A motherly but somewhat harassed woman in the accommodations office smiled mechanically at her as she walked in.

"Gay or straight, dear?"

"What?"

"Well, you'll be sharing a room with another student, and we always like to put people of the same persuasion together. Saves a lot of trouble if you decide to sleep together."

Maireed fixed her with the basilisk stare which had made people around her quail since she was out of diapers. "Let's get one thing clear. I choose who I'm going to sleep with, if at all, and anyone who tells me I have to share a room in this half-assed craphole is going to get their arm broken. Now, you're going to find me a large single room, and you're going to do it now."

The motherly woman on the other side of the desk began to look even more harassed. She opened her mouth to protest that she wasn't used to being spoken to in this way, that single rooms were reserved for senior students only and that she would complain to the authorities, but only an indecisive little squeak came out. She wilted under Maireed's glare, decided discretion was the better part of valor, and hastily allocated her a single room. As Maireed strode out, the motherly woman gaped at her blankly and felt cold sweat gathering under her armpits.

Maireed's University, as she now thought of it, was a thoroughly progressive institution. The School of Social Sciences, by far the largest in the university, had recently been taken over by the Gaia Liberation Army. To be more precise, the GLA had so many of the professors in its ranks that one day it merely announced to the world at large that the School of Social Sciences would henceforth be known as the School of Gaian Sciences and would be run by, for, and on behalf of, the GLA, and that was that. Any of the professors or students who published, said, or otherwise communicated anything not in accordance with Critical Gaia Theory would be cancelled. The university president was informed he could either have his office occupied on a semi-permanent basis by one of the screaming homicidal mobs which the GLA seemed to be able to whistle up at the drop of a hat, or quietly accept the situation. He opted for the latter.

The next day Maireed started signing up for political science courses. Critical Gaia Theory was mandatory, as was EcoGaian Concepts, or CGT and EGC as they were invariably known. She chose a mixed ragbag of other courses on the principle that what she studied didn't matter; it was the fact of being there that counted. She also joined the Gaia Liberation Army as a student member, and looked around for other societies to join, but found there weren't any. "As long as you're a GLA member you won't have time for anything else," said Bronwen, her new GLA Squad Leader, "and frankly, anyone who isn't prepared to give one hundred percent to the GLA shouldn't even be here."

Maireed quietly looked at Bronwen and decided she would have her job before six months were up.

Lectures started a day or two later. The first morning started with an introductory lecture on the principles of Critical Gaia Theory. As the professor said, everything else they would study was simply an extension of CGT, so getting the basics of CGT firmly in their minds was fundamental.

"You and I and everyone in this room are a part of Gaia. All living beings on Earth, all plants and animals, all the rocks and soil, the oceans and the atmosphere, are part of a single living being called Gaia. In this sense Gaia is Earth, but we always refer to her as Gaia in her role as a living being. Earth is simply the physical embodiment of the living being which is Gaia. You'll notice I refer to Gaia as she; this is because Gaia is female in nature, Mother Earth if you will.

"Gaia is a self-organizing being who acts in such a way as to keep her individual components in an equilibrium which is conducive to the continued life of all of her components. We, the human race, are but one component part of Gaia. You can think of the human race as a virus living within Gaia. And as with viruses in our own bodies, some can be benign, while others can be harmful, even deadly. Whether the human race is a benign or a harmful virus is largely up to us.

"And just as our own lives must be in balance—our diet must be balanced or we shall become obese, our physical activity and periods of rest must be in balance or we shall become unhealthy, so Gaia's components must be in balance or she will become sick. It is our duty as part of Gaia to do whatever we can to help Gaia maintain this balance.

"The human race has become out of balance with respect to the other components of Gaia. It has become too large, too demanding on Gaia's resources, and must be pruned back. We must restore the balance, restore the balance. Everybody now—"

And the entire class, prompted by a couple of teaching assistants, chanted, "Restore the balance, restore the balance."

The professor went on, "Evolution unfolds from cell to organism to planet to solar system and ultimately to the whole universe. It is possible that the human race, which you must never forget is a part of Gaia, may ultimately evolve with Gaia into the universe as a whole. However, any attempt at this time for the human race to take matters into its own hands and spread out by itself into other parts of the universe is unacceptable and must be opposed by any means. You will learn more of this later.

"The essence of Gaia is harmony and cooperation. Competition for resources means there are winners and losers, and this in turn leads to excessive demands on resources. It is not in Gaia's nature that there should be any losers, nor should there be excessive demands on resources. Here in the School of Gaian Sciences we explicitly reject the idea of competition. You are not here to compete against one another by taking examinations; you are here to learn about Gaia, to make her the central focus of your lives, to become Gaians in other words.

"Those of you who have elected to study political science and related subjects will learn that, just as Gaia is a living being, so human societies are living beings as well. Our understanding of Gaia can be used to create a better society and design a better political system.

"And finally, Gaians do not simply ask of the world around them 'what is going on,' but rather 'what should we do to restore and maintain the balance.' You will find in your EcoGaian Concepts course that we deal here with practical means of restoring the balance. We expect everyone here to sign up as student members of the Gaia Liberation Army, if you have not already done so, and take part in activities aimed at helping to restore the balance."

Maireed was a little bemused by all of this. Her ambition was to get to the top of whatever she was associated with, and how could she do this if she wasn't allowed to compete? However, she then remembered reading previously while deciding upon a university that since the population reduction ideas of Critical Gaia Theory aligned fairly well with government concerns about population pressure overseas, the GLA, and the School of Gaian Sciences in particular, had grown wealthy on government research grants, so perhaps this was a route to the top. (It didn't hurt either that the GLA had developed a capability to put large, noisy and violent mobs on the streets whenever they felt that government policy needed to be nudged in a direction more in accordance with Gaian principles.)

In accordance with Gaia non-competition theory, all the courses were designed on the basis that no-one should be disadvantaged merely because they were mentally challenged, so Maireed found her attention wandering at times. However, as long as she joined in the chanting choruses associated with most of the courses (*restore the balance, restore the balance* for CGT, *burn, burn, burn* for EGC), not much else was required of her.

After a couple of weeks of this, Maireed was bored senseless. She tried talking to her academic supervisor. Sister Flame had until recently been known as Dr. Constance B. Sproggett, but the School of Gaian Sciences had recently declared all names, all titles to be yet another manifestation of the hated white supremacist anti-Gaian patriarchy, which was responsible for all the hurt and harm to Gaia. Consequently, names and titles were to be discarded without regret, and all professors henceforth known as Sister or Brother (mainly Sister, male professors and students seemed to be very much of a minority in the School of Gaian Sciences). Sister Flame did feel some regret that she could no longer publish papers under her own name in the New England Journal of Gaian Metaphysics, a journal which she had helped found a decade ago, but realized bravely it was her own particular sacrifice for The Cause. She would just have to make Sister Flame as well known in academic Gaian circles as C.B. Sproggett had been.

Sister Flame had not been at all sympathetic when Maireed confessed her boredom. "Your Personal Feelings of Superiority to the other class members are a Disgraceful Manifestation of the kind of Senselessly Aggressive Competitiveness which We in the GLA are Devoting our lives to Overthrowing." (Sister Flame inclined to the upper case when heated.) Maireed endured a few minutes of this, toyed briefly with the idea of answering her in language which would have shocked even old Seamus, then decided it wasn't worth it. As she reasoned to herself, there had to be something else here besides these pompous old farts, else the GLA would never have gotten where it is.

She approached her GLA squad leader. Up till now, Bronwen had done nothing except lead them in various training exercises ("Hold your Molotov cocktail upside-down so the wick doesn't dry out. And don't forget it always counts as a peaceful protest if you're throwing it for Gaia's sake"), preceded and followed as always by the obligatory chanting. At first, she approached the subject obliquely. "Do we get onto anything further, anytime soon? I mean, like advanced discussions of anything, field exercises maybe, something of the kind?"

"You bet your sweet ass we do, Sister Maireed. I shouldn't be telling you this, but in a few days time we're all going on a protest march downtown, and there are plans—big secret, don't tell a soul— to occupy one of the big buildings there for a couple of days, or at least until the media gets there."

"Er—what will we be protesting about?"

"Shit, I don't know. Who cares? Don't you worry yourself about these things, just leave the decisions up to the Group Leaders and make sure you're where they tell you to be when they need you."

Maireed mentally consigned Bronwen to the ranks of the boneheaded and gave up her efforts for the time being. She decided to wait for the promised protest march and see what transpired.

The march occurred as planned. They all got into buses, laid on for the occasion by the School of Gaian Sciences, and assembled at a park about a mile from their destination. They then marched downtown in squads and groups with banners, having been told to chant "Down with Bill T-405," whatever that might be, and "No Limits on Postpartum Abortion," which was somewhat more intelligible if not altogether intellectually satisfying. Finally, they arrived at a large building which proclaimed itself to be an office of the US Government. It was apparently deserted, all its usual occupants having been given the day off when news of the demonstration had been leaked two weeks previously. The marchers swarmed into their pre-arranged places in the building, where they could best be seen by the media, and remained chanting their slogans. Soon, the holovision crews began arriving.

Maireed's squad had been assigned a spot on the tenth floor. She doubted the holovision crews would come anywhere near her, and her rebellious spirit was smoldering by this time. Finally it burst into flame. Grabbing the two people nearest her, Stella and Pauline, she began hustling them towards the stairwell. "Come on, let's show these driveling idiots a thing or two about protests. Grab that banner and follow me." As she moved off, Bronwen squawked, "Where do you think you're going?"

"Shut your mouth, bonehead. We're off to organize a real protest. You stay there and look after the little girls and boys."

They left Bronwen gaping at them, indecision written in every line of her. People didn't act independently in her experience; they waited until they were told to do something then they did it. Well, she couldn't be held to account for it if those women disobeyed orders; it wasn't her job to go chasing all over the place after them, and in any case...

Two flights of steps up and Maireed and her slightly dazed companions were as far as they could go. In front of them was a metal door which looked as if it should lead onto the roof, but it was locked. Maireed kicked at it and it rattled slightly; it seemed to be quite flimsy. On the way up she had noticed a heavy looking fire extinguisher on the floor below. Motioning the other two to wait for her, she ran down, unfastened it from the wall, and staggered back up with it. It was indeed heavy. Pausing for a moment to regain her breath, she lifted it up and ran with it as a battering ram against the door. The door buckled, but held. Once more with all her strength and the door burst open, letting in the clear autumn sunshine and a vista of the flat roof.

Stella and Pauline stood there nervously. Stella looked as if she was about to wet herself, but Pauline seemed to be halfway to enjoying it. "Come on," said Maireed, pulling Stella but merely ushering Pauline. In front of them at the edge of the roof was a flagpole, with a large US flag lazily flapping in the gentle breeze. Bringing their GLA banner with them, Maireed tried to lower the flag, but the mechanism was locked with a heavy padlock. Evidently the usual occupants of the building were used to protesters.

The flagpole was nearly twenty feet in height. It was metal, and the flag rope tapped against it with a ringing sound in the breeze. Maireed looked at her companions, sizing them up. Stella was a heavy-looking woman, while Pauline was lighter, but still quite strong-looking. "I'm going up the flagpole. Stella, stand against the pole, grab hold of it, and brace yourself. Pauline is going to climb on your shoulders, and I'm going to climb on top of her. If either of you let go and I fall, so help me, my ghost is going to come back and tie your bellies into knots forevermore." So saying, she pushed Stella against the pole, helped Pauline climb onto her shoulders, then stuffed the banner inside her windbreaker. Luckily, Maireed was wiry but light and managed to scramble up both of them. On the way up she noticed that Stella by this time really had wet herself.

Standing on Pauline's shoulders, her head was several feet below the top of the flagpole. She was able to undo the lower flag clasp but could not reach the upper one. With a silent prayer she clasped the pole in her hands, pulled her legs off Pauline's shoulders and painfully shinned up the rest of the way. After what seemed like an eternity, she finally threw a hand over the flat boss at the top of the pole. It wasn't the most secure of holds, but it was better than nothing. Trying not to look down, she released the last clasp holding the flag in place and let the wind take it away. It fluttered over the edge of the building and was filmed beautifully as it floated downwards by the holovision crews on the ground. Carefully pulling the GLA banner from her windbreaker she let it fly loose. The wind almost took it out of her hands and threatened to pull her off her perch, but she managed to tie one corner around the flag rope. Now came the trickiest part. Holding on to the lower corner in her teeth, she slowly disengaged her hold from the flagpole boss and allowed herself to slide down two or three feet. Tying the last corner to the flag rope without the boss to support her weight was hardest of all, and Maireed could feel her muscles trembling with the strain. "Only a little while longer, just a few seconds more," she whispered to herself. It took her about thirty seconds altogether before it was secure, and she could let herself slide slowly to the ground; not too fast, the wind was strong enough up here to take her over the edge if she let go too soon.

The other two by this time were on the ground staring up at her. The insides of Stella's thighs were quite wet. Pauline had sufficient presence of mind to stand at the base of the flagpole and let Maireed

use her shoulders as she came down, then hugged her tight the moment her feet touched the ground. As Maireed stood there, feeling slightly sick but thankful enough to have Pauline holding her, she felt something warm trickling down her own legs. Shit, I've done a Stella, she thought, then looked down. It wasn't urine; it was blood. The insides of her legs had been scraped raw.

Maireed was an instant heroine. The holovision cameras had got some quite good telephoto shots of her, her face screwed up in concentration as she tied the banner to the flag rope, and made much of the affair on the evening news. A GLA spokesperson said that Maireed's action had shown the world the relevance and importance of the GLA's mission and everyone else had the sense to shut up for the time being.

A week later, Maireed was in her room wondering what to do next, when the door opened behind her without the customary knock. A slim, hard-looking woman came in and closed the door behind her, then stood looking Maireed up and down. She said nothing and Maireed had the feeling she was outclassed, so said nothing either. Finally, the other spoke.

"So, the instant heroine, leading her pack of girl guides up a flagpole. Do you do that to every phallic symbol you come across?"

Maireed was about to answer with a tirade of injured abuse, but stopped herself. She's trying to needle me—why? came the thought. And she looks like she's a tough one.

"What's your problem, lady?" said Maireed. She wasn't quite sure, but she felt the term 'lady' with its connotations of effete respectability would needle her opponent, particularly the way she had stressed it.

Much to Maireed's surprise, the other chuckled, walked further into the room, and hitched one leg onto Maireed's desk. "Just how much longer do you want to spend here, doing feats of girlish derring-do with the rest of these pathetic little jerks?"

"You mean, I have a choice?"

"That's what I'm here to offer you. The GLA is more than just a bunch of clapped-out academics, and it's always looking for new recruits. Capable recruits, who can be trained to do useful things for the movement."

"Like what?"

"You'll find out if and when we decide to take you on. First, we'll put you on a real training course, not this girl guide shit you're doing here. If you pass that—if—you'll find out more."

"Why all the secrecy?"

"We're fighting a war, sweetheart. Do you think all the white supremacist capitalist pigs on this planet are going to lie down and fade away just because we ask them?"

Maireed thought furiously. Apart from Sean, she had no particular use for any other person on this world, and it looked as if she was being offered a real opportunity to do something, get somewhere, be important...but what about Sean? a small voice in her said. I can look after Sean, I can protect him, haven't I always done that? another voice in her said. Finally ...

"When do I start?"

The hard-looking woman looked at Maireed as if she had passed her first test. "Right now," she said. "In precisely fifteen minutes from the time I leave here, walk to the corner of the block opposite the bookstore and a car will draw up. Get in the back seat. Don't take anything with you. We'll deal with your things later."

The woman turned to leave. As her hand was on the door handle, Maireed blurted out "How do I contact you, Ms. ..."

The woman half-turned, said over her shoulder, "Don't be such a stupid shit," and was gone.

Maireed spent the next year in a training camp. It was a female-only camp, and while she thought there might have been a male-only training camp somewhere else, nobody ever mentioned it. She guessed she was somewhere in North America, but since she had been drugged as soon as she got into the car with a short needle slapped into her thigh, she had no way of knowing. Nor apparently did any of the other trainees, who had all suffered the same fate. She was allowed one message to her parents, after which her phone was taken away and no further communication was allowed. Nonetheless, she counted it as one of the happiest years of her life.

They were being trained as GLA warrior priestesses, or so they were told by the Commandant. The latter was a burly woman in her early forties with man-like physical strength, a strident voice, and a noticeable moustache who ruled trainees and instructors alike with a rod of iron. Maireed guessed she had a military background, and undoubtedly was an expert in various forms of unarmed combat who delighted in joining in training sessions. "Come on, put your backs into it. Don't tell me you're afraid of bruising your pretty little skins. I don't give a damn. Anyone who shirks this session does sixty seconds kick boxing with me afterwards." In spite of her muscular frame, she could rotate her piston-like legs to incredible heights and could lay trainees out cold with one blow.

The physical training was arduous, but they were all young and fit and most survived it well. Unarmed combat was high on the list of activities, and in a short while it became obvious which of them were not going to be of any use. After the first month, the trainees were weeded out. No special announcements, just that some of them quietly disappeared and were not seen again. In Maireed's training squad of eight, only one disappeared.

After the weeding out, they were introduced to weapons training. Maireed had already in her short life fired both pistol and rifle, and was delighted to be doing so again. But this time they spent hours on the range, firing at moving targets, field stripping weapons, and going over assault courses with full combat gear. They also spent considerable time learning about explosives, how to make bombs of all sorts, booby traps, demolition charges and so forth. It was exciting and the young women were given no time to think or reflect. Finish one exercise and on to the next, all day, every day, falling exhausted into their bunks at night.

They spent long hours in the lecture rooms as well. Besides practical instruction, they were heavily indoctrinated with the basic GLA philosophy of population balance, and shown hour upon hour of grisly horror films showing the effects of overpopulation, including starving children and cannibalism, the latter in close-up detail. Maireed wondered sometimes how they made the films, then decided she didn't really want to know.

At the end of her year, Maireed, already a squad leader, was ordained as a Warrior Priestess (Third Class) in the GLA Commandos with the name of Sister Sirocco, and sent to join her first operational unit. She was still required to be drugged before they would let her leave ("What you don't know you can't be made to reveal"), but this time they let her administer the needle herself. She found herself in a suburb of Los Angeles in a commercial building in a rather seedy, run-down district. The Unit Commander, Warrior Priestess (Second Class) Sister Sundancer, greeted her warmly and informed her they were preparing for a mission in a week's time.

"We're going to destroy the Astro-Mining plant here in L.A., which is pivotal to the Mayflower Project. We're going to destroy it because the Mayflower is being built with the express intention of infecting the galaxy with the uncontrolled virus of the human race. The Gaia Liberation Army," (Maireed had noticed she never used the expression GLA, considering it too sacred a name to be abbreviated), "is firmly committed to restoring the balance here on Earth and is unalterably opposed to allowing the present imbalance to be propagated elsewhere." Pompous bitch, thought Maireed with sinking spirits.

Maireed had to admit to herself that, pompous or not, Sister Sundancer was a competent organizer and seemed to have every last detail of the raid in hand. The plan was to place incendiary devices at strategic locations while simultaneously rupturing the water mains with explosives. The entire plant was surrounded by a high fence and was brightly lit, so any attempt to sneak in through the fence would be foolhardy. Instead, they would drive a transport truck through the main gate shortly before the end of the day with the Commandos hidden inside. The truck would be driven to the reception dock, the trailer disconnected and in place for unloading the next day, while the tractor portion would drive out of the main gate again to avert suspicion.

It went as planned. At about 2 a.m., the commandos quietly crept out of the trailer through a concealed hatch and dispersed to their assigned tasks. Maireed had a large incendiary device to lay inside the main engineering building. Because physical security in the building was tight, the plan was to make an opening in the outer wall of the building with an explosive charge then fire the incendiary from a mortar through the hole. She reached her assigned position and began laying out her equipment.

A gun was poked into the back of her neck, and a male voice said with a rather weary drawl, "Okay, lady, knock it off will ya."

They took her to a cell in what she guessed was a police station. On the way she had tried some unarmed combat moves, but the result was a large hand around her throat and the same weary drawl of "Knock it off, lady." In the cell she was told to strip: "You can either strip yourself, or we'll do it for you. It's all the same to us." They took everything away, examined her every orifice, then handed her some clean but well-worn coveralls to put on. After that they left her alone to stew for several hours.

Maireed had no way of telling the time but guessed it was mid-morning when they came for her and took her to an interrogation room. A large wall screen showed an image of her equipment from the previous night—gun, explosives, mortar, incendiary device, all neatly laid out on a table. A rather weary-looking, middle-aged man sat on the opposite side of the table, and that was all. A tray with a mug of coffee and some sandwiches was put in front of her. She thought at first of refusing to eat or drink, but then did so, partly because she was starving, and partly because Dogface, as she decided to call him, did not seem to care whether she ate and drank or not.

Dogface waited until she had finished, then sat looking at her for a while.

"I don't know what gets into kids like you, Maireed, I really don't."

"My name is Sister Sirocco."

"Yeah, and I'm the Angel Gabriel. Get real, Maireed Shaughnessy."

Maireed felt deflated. They hadn't trained her for anything like this. What did she do next? Dogface took the decision out of her hands.

"In case you're wondering how we know who you are, you can thank that bunch of amateurs at the GLA. Imagine, pulling you off to Camp Kinky only a few days after your face was splashed all over the holovision news after you climbed up that flagpole. I remember watching it on holo. Got to hand it to you, it must have taken some guts. Of course you were missed when you disappeared, and since we know exactly how long the GLA commando course takes, we were waiting for you to appear on the streets again. It was a reasonable bet that you'd be posted to Hepsibah's outfit here in town."

"Hepsibah?"

"Hepsibah Liebowitz, otherwise known as Sister Sundancer. She's been trying to blow these plants up for years."

"You're bluffing. If you really knew all this, you'd have arrested her years ago."

"Why would we want to do that? If she gets arrested the GLA lawyers will spring her the next day, and we've shown our hand. Much better to have her bumbling along where we can keep an eye on her. In any case, if we did manage to get rid of her, the GLA might replace her with someone who knows what they're doing. Besides, the GLA have probably got the cops paid off so they wouldn't arrest her anyway."

"What do you mean, the cops? Aren't you the police?"

Dogface looked at her in surprise, then burst out laughing. "Hasn't anyone told you yet? I'll have to kick someone's ass for that. Us, the cops? Not likely. We're SoCal Security. Most of the aerospace plants in Southern California pay us to protect them from people like you. We do a much better job than the cops because if we fail, we're out of a job. Gives us what you might call job security incentive. Which brings us to the question of what we're to do with you.

"We don't have the power to legally arrest you, and handing you over to the cops simply puts you straight back on the streets again. The GLA lawyers would soon see to that. Of course, since you officially disappeared a year ago, we could make that disappearance permanent and nobody would be the wiser, but hell, I've got kids your age, so let's not think about that.

"Now, speaking as a security guard, not to mention a parent, I really don't want to see you back on the street waving guns and bombs. We'd only have to spend time and money tracking you, which of course would get billed to our clients, and sooner or later one of them is going to suggest that you really do disappear permanently. Believe me, our clients can be mighty persuasive, especially when it comes to contract renewal time. So I'll tell you what we're going to do. We took a few photos of you in your cell when you were stripped off last night. I know, I know, it wasn't polite of us, but there, this isn't a polite business. Those photos and your voiceprints are now in a computer studio not too far from here, and with the aid of some clever techniques we'll shortly have a neat little holovideo showing you having a real nice orgy with a couple of horny studs. Same studio, incidentally, that makes the stuff they showed you up at Camp Kinky, and yeah, I've seen 'em. We're going to keep that holovideo in our safe here, but if you ever get mixed up again in this business," here Dogface waved his hand at the image of Maireed's arsenal of the night before, "it goes out on general release with a special preview copy to GLA headquarters. Fair enough?"

Maireed ground her teeth but was a realist enough to know when she was beaten. The GLA senior command would recoil from her in horror if they saw the video. Although they would probably guess it was a fake, they demanded dignity and rectitude of their warrior priestesses (apart from blowing things up and burning them down) as a mark of respect to Gaia. The blow to their prestige and self-image was simply too great to allow themselves to associate with her if such a video was released.

"So what do I do now?"

"You can just walk out of here as far as I'm concerned. But since having you hanging around could be embarrassing, we're going to give you a ticket to New York, a change of clothing and some money. Take off, kid, get lost, don't come back, good luck, oh, and no hard feelings?"

Dogface ushered Maireed to the door, left her in charge of a couple of competent-looking women, and walked off. As he walked into his office down the corridor, a technician poked his head in the door.

"I've got the skin pics and voice prints from that skinny broad we took in last night, Chief. Shall I send them down to the porn shop?"

"Nah, waste of money. Just keep 'em on file in case we ever need them, but ten to one we never will. The kid's had her fling, struck her blow for freedom and all that shit. She'll probably just go off and marry some poor jerk and devote her life to making him miserable."

They took her to an obscure airport on the outskirts of Los Angeles. Like most major cities in the world, Los Angeles was ringed with a circle of airports. Air travel had become progressively less expensive during the last fifty years until it had all but eclipsed road and rail for anything longer than fifty miles or so. Of course, that meant the skies were practically black with aircraft near major cities, but no matter. The profession of airline pilot had faded into history as airliners became fully automated by mid-century, and aircraft movements were now as rigidly controlled as trains on their tracks. Airliners made their way in and out of the city airspace within a few hundred feet of each other as a matter of everyday routine. Accidents were a thing of the past.

Dogface's crew had a choice of at least a dozen airports to spirit Maireed away. It was possible that Sister Sundancer or one of her team would be watching for Maireed and would attempt a rescue, although Dogface didn't think it likely; they had dealt too hard a blow to Sister Sundancer's organization last night. Nevertheless they took Maireed to a busy little commuter airport and put her on a plane to Bakersfield, from whence she would change for San Francisco, and thence to New York. Of course, once she landed at Bakersfield there was nothing to stop her coming straight back again, but Dogface reckoned he had got her, psychologically speaking, where he wanted her, at least for the next day or two, and that was enough. He was right. Maireed sat slumped in her seat on the flight in a state of abject misery. It had all come to pieces so fast, after that wonderful year spent training. She felt belittled, crushed. She had come out fighting and the world had slapped her aside as if she had been nothing more than a buzzing fly.

After what seemed like an eternity of hanging around crowded airports and being jammed into crowded aircraft, Maireed landed

at one of the New Jersey airports that served the sprawling urban blight that was New York. The no-go areas were spreading like cancer and were already lapping at the airport boundaries. Maireed, having little experience outside her well-protected New England suburban life, took the subway (fully automated, like the aircraft) downtown with a vague idea of finding somewhere to go to earth like a wounded animal.

Chico was feeling good. He'd knifed a rival pimp last night and left him dead. Now Chico had undisputed possession of his strip of turf plus the other's string of girls. He could hardly believe his eyes when he saw this broad walking on her own, no escort in sight, looking around her as if she was a complete stranger. Which she obviously was. Chico had never seen her before and it was his business to know every broad in town. Thinking it was his lucky day, Chico closed rapidly on her then blocked her path.

"Goin' somewhere, kid?"

Maireed barely glanced at him. "Get lost."

Chico grinned to himself. This broad had spirit; it would be fun breaking her in. Grabbing her arm and pulling her round to face him, he was about to tell her some of the preliminary facts of life when a sharp blow to his solar plexus and a kick to his crotch left him gasping for breath on the ground. But Chico was tough, fit, and wearing protection where it mattered. He bounced back to his feet, no longer pleased with the day but deadly angry. No one, but no one did that to Chico. Besides, if anyone had seen him knocked down, and by a mere broad at that, it would be all over town before nightfall. Chico would have a rough time persuading his rivals he wasn't slipping if he didn't kill her.

Chico's knife appeared in his hand like magic. Chico had grown up with a knife in his hand. He was pretty good with guns too, but to get on in the gangs you had to show you weren't afraid of blood, and that meant knives. This stupid broad was going to get sliced up like salami.

Maireed had no weapon. Everything of that nature had been taken from her back in Los Angeles. She slipped into the unarmed combat stance she had practiced so often in the last year and warily eyed her opponent, looking for an opening. Chico noticed her posture, and realized he had something more than the eye-scratching, bottle-throwing hellcat he sometimes had to tame in his business. No problem though. He was a match for any ten broads.

Maireed realized she was in trouble. Her opponent had a deadly intensity about him, an assured manner she had never met in her year of training. This opponent had spent his entire life fighting like this, and winning. Losers didn't live in fights like this. They circled around each other, Maireed looking for an opening, Chico enjoying his sense of superiority and the growing unease he could feel in his opponent.

Chico moved in, deciding the time was ripe to mark his opponent. Not to kill her, just to make her bleed a lot for his own enjoyment and to show off his skills for the sake of the bystanders he was vaguely aware of behind him. He would finish her off later in a spectacular and very messy fashion, he decided.

Without warning, a heavy wooden stave was swung at him. It took him on his knife arm, shattering the bone and tossing him into a heap on the ground away from Maireed. His scream was cut off as a large boot descended on his neck and pinned him in place.

Maireed abruptly became aware of her surroundings. Facing her was a large bearded man in grubby overalls with a heavy stave, now held in his clasped hands in front of him in an almost biblical fashion. Several others were nearby, in a circle around both her and Chico. Most were armed with shotguns or other heavy-looking weapons.

"Fifth Avenue Vigilante Patrol, ma'am. We've been looking for an excuse to hang Chico for a long time, and I think we've just found one. Now would you like to tell us why we shouldn't hang you alongside of him?"

For a moment Maireed's voice wouldn't work. She opened and shut her mouth several times but nothing came out. "Take your time, ma'am," said the large bearded one. "We ain't goin' nowhere till you've told us all about yourself. You're a stranger here, and we tend to get upset when strangers come in and start making trouble."

Maireed found her voice. "I'm looking for refuge. I, I was part of a far-out religious cult in L.A., but I couldn't stomach some of the things they were doing, so I ran away."

"What sort of things, ma'am?"

"Blowing up buildings, shooting people on the streets, that sort of thing."

"And they taught you to knock people like Chico over, did they? Must have been a real rough bunch. I think your story stinks, but I'm interested enough to hear the rest of it. You come with us now. Maybe we'll hang you later, maybe we won't. But just you be sure of one thing. You try running away and Manuel here will blow you away."

Manuel turned out to be a gap-toothed older man with a shotgun in one hand. He grinned at Maireed. "Like the man says, behave yourself. This'll make a real mess of you if you don't."

79

They took Maireed to a building several blocks away. Along the way she noticed many of the buildings were once imposing but now were deserted and looked as if they had been looted several times. The building they entered was grubby and unkempt but it had a definite air of purpose about it. They sat Maireed down at a table with the bearded elder on the other side and two other men standing near the door. She thought fleetingly that there seemed to be a pattern forming, that sooner or later in a new city she would always find herself sitting in an interrogation room opposite an unknown man.

"Okay," said her interrogator, "I'm going to start by telling you who we are. Then you're going to tell us all about yourself. Then, if we think fit, we're going to hang you. Your friend out there who you were dancing with is dancing on the end of a rope right now.

"We're the Vigilante Patrol. In case that doesn't mean anything to you, it means that we are the law around here. We make the law, we enforce it; we're judge, jury, and executioner all rolled into one. If you want a lawyer, go find one and we'll hang him alongside you."

Maireed by this time was beginning to recover her wits. "Where I come from, there are policemen, and the judges don't hang people."

Her interrogator snorted with a mixture of exasperation and amused contempt. "Where you come from, ma'am, appears to be about a million miles from here. Now, are you going to tell us about yourself, or shall we just get on with it and hang you? And before you make up any more lies, I might as well tell you that lying is a hanging offence around here."

There was something in his manner, something so matter-of-fact about the way he spoke, that Maireed's normally feisty spirit quailed. Deciding she had nothing to lose, she launched into a description of

her year at the training camp, the few days in Los Angeles, and her ignominious expulsion.

When she had finished, her interrogator looked at her for a few moments. "Well, I guess you told us the truth this time, especially the bit about being stopped by the security boys. Those guys are professionals, as we well know."

"They took me so easily; it was as if they were just waiting for me."

"They probably were. It's their job to be way ahead of you. If you'd had about twenty years experience and street smarts to match you might have avoided them, but for a kid like you, fresh out of college—not a chance. But now you're here. What did you expect to do here?"

"I don't know. I guess I wasn't much good at the terrorist game, and in any case, now I think about it, it does seem a bit silly doesn't it? I mean, it was fun while we were training, but you never had time to think, and I guess I don't really want their kind of a world. Besides, while most men are either arrogant bastards or useless idiots, my brother Sean is one of the sweetest people alive, and, and..."

Had Maireed been a weaker woman, the thought of Sean would have made her burst into tears at that moment. Instead, she broke off and bit her lower lip for a moment, then continued.

"I came here because I couldn't think of anything else to do. I've never been here before in my life, but I don't want to go back to the GLA or to university, and I'm certainly not going to crawl back to my parents with my tail between my legs. I want to do something worthwhile, but right now I haven't a clue what that something might be."

Her interrogator regarded her solemnly for a few moments. "If I read you right, you might find something worthwhile here," he said.

"Listen now. I'll give you a choice. We'll either escort you to the subway, and you leave here and don't come back. Or you can stay and work here. But before you make up your mind, let me fill you in on a few things.

"This here is New York City, and it's been without the rule of law for nearly thirty years now. Way back when, the good citizens had become fed up with their police in years gone by and had kept on reducing the funding for them. The less police you have, the more petty crime you get, so people and businesses started moving out of the city—after all, who wants to live in a war zone if you don't have to. The more people moved out, the less tax revenue there was to pay for the remaining police and all the other services, until one day the whole thing just collapsed. Since then New York has been ruled by the street gangs. At first it was fun; I should know, I was a gang leader at the time. But there was a lot of people just couldn't afford to leave. Besides, many of them were like me; this is my city, it's my home, and I ain't leaving for nobody's sake. But after a few years things were getting pretty desperate.

"If everything is ruled by the knife and the gun, young men don't live long. Businesses, such as there are, get robbed so often they soon close down. Delivery trucks won't come into the city from outside unless they have armed guards, which puts the price of everything way up. It's difficult to get out of here now because the folks who live on the outside have hired more armed guards to keep us in. Can't say I blame them; only reason many of us ever went outside the city was to rob somebody or something. We only manage to keep the subway open by agreeing to strip searches when we leave, as you'll find out. But it wasn't so long ago that a lot of us were facing real starvation.

"So, 'bout ten years ago, we decided we had to do something. A lot of us older folk got together and decided we had to have law and order, and, things being what they were, we had to provide it ourselves. Nothing fancy, mind. Just don't rob or kill, that's about all. If you do, we don't have any of those fancy trials they have in the world outside. No ma'am. If we catch you, we hang you on the spot. Like Chico.

"Which brings us back to you, ma'am. We're beginning to bring law and order back to the city. But our kids are running wild. Very few of them have fathers. Like I said, life expectancy for a young man isn't great around here, and there's little incentive to settle down and be a good father anyway. Even fewer of our kids have any education. Before the last policeman left, thirty years ago, the schools had all closed down. So we're setting up our own schools. Discipline is no problem; the vigilante patrols will hang anyone who makes trouble, no matter what age they are, but we're desperately short of teachers. We don't need anything fancy, just people who can teach them elementary reading, writing, and arithmetic. The conditions are lousy and the pay's worse, but it's a worthwhile job. What do you say to staying here and being one of them?"

Maireed sat and thought for a while. She wanted to do something with her life, and whatever it was she wanted to get to the top. She wasn't interested in long years of study and the GLA no longer appealed to her. But New York looked as if it might be growing into great things again someday. Certainly, there was no lack of resolution that she could detect in the people around her. Maybe this was an opportunity to get in on the ground floor.

"Okay," she said. "I'll give it a shot."

They boarded Maireed with a family struggling to maintain a vestige of middle-class living in the wasteland around them. Not only was it close to the school where she would be working, it afforded greater safety. "We can let you have your own apartment, no problem," said Wally Mendez, the mayor, "but we can't guarantee your safety in it. Besides, if you board with the Santinis you don't have to cook for yourself." The logic of this appealed to Maireed so she accepted.

Wally Mendez, as overall leader of the vigilante patrols and ex-officio mayor of New York City, had let it be known on the streets that teachers were sacrosanct. This kept Maireed reasonably safe provided she didn't do anything stupid like walk around alone at night. Not that she had much wish to do so; her teaching left her so drained at the end of each day that at first all she wanted to do was eat and then fall into bed.

Maireed taught in what had been a school many years previously, but had been deserted and vandalized until little of it was usable. However, the population of the no-go areas of New York, which is to say the areas in which the rule of law no longer held, was down to about quarter of a million from its peak of about five million fifty years ago. There were fewer children in the city, and of those only a small part were willing to come to school. For a start, some would have to travel through another gang's territory to get to school, which was a risk many of them were not prepared to take. But for the most part, mothers who had never had any schooling themselves (fathers, being mostly absent or non-existent, didn't count) could not see the value in sending their own children to school. Far better, in their eyes, to have them out on the streets begging, stealing, or working in one of the sweatshops that had begun to spring up again than wasting their time

in school. Even so, there were more students eager to learn than the few available teachers could handle.

The principal of Maireed's school was pragmatic. "I don't care if you're not trained as a teacher. Neither am I. Besides, what they'd teach you in college wouldn't be of much use here. We got no Net connections, no videos, not many books, and paper's expensive. Just do your best to get them to read and write to begin with. If you can teach them to add and subtract as well, that's a bonus. I'm going to give you twenty students to begin with. Better to teach a few well than a lot poorly. You work with them all day, every day. If they give you any trouble you can't handle, let me know, fast. The vigilantes always have someone nearby, and these kids know enough to respect them by now."

What the principal did not mention was that a few years previously, when the schools had started after being closed for a generation, there had been almost daily gang fights in the schools, with an average of one or two deaths each week. Finally, the vigilantes had pounced and had hung three students in Maireed's school yard, amongst others. The fighting stopped after that, at least within the school grounds. It was not the deaths that shocked the students; that was a fact of everyday life. It was the concept, hammered home in an unmistakable fashion, that authority could exist outside of their own gang structures.

Maireed had no trouble keeping order in her class. She had a voice that could crack like a whip and powers of invective that earned her the respect, even the awe of her students. They called her The Witch, and some believed she had the evil eye. But she also had a little of her brother Sean's storytelling ability and would enthrall them by the hour with tales and legends from the past. Some were from books, but these were hard to come by, so she invented many of her stories. She was surprised to find she was quite good at it.

The stories were used as the basis of her teaching. The children of the blighted areas of New York had grown up in an almost illiterate society. There were few if any print newspapers or magazines, and with the lack of maintenance and eventual decay of the city cable and cell-phone systems the only generally available contact with the outside world was radio. There were one or two privately-owned cable connections which could access both holovision and the Net, but for most people these were off-limits and they lived in effective isolation from the rest of the world. Maireed struggled on for the first few months, learning on the job and gradually coming to understand the needs of these children.

Teaching occupied Maireed fully for a year, but then her restless ambition began to surface again. At first, it manifested itself as an urge to take over other areas of the school. With her class now up to thirty students and humming along nicely, Maireed started organizing a library in her spare time. Since this involved working in the school after hours and walking home after dark, the vigilante patrol assigned one of their members to escort her home. Maireed soon had him working with her in the converted storeroom that was to become her library.

At first it was a case of "Ben, do this," and "Ben, lift that." Ben was a still-handsome man in his thirties (forty was considered old on the streets), and they spent a great deal of time together with no one else around. Maireed by this time had been celibate for nearly a year, and before that at the training camp it had been females only. Late one afternoon as the light was fading outside, she brushed against him accidentally and found herself trembling, feeling that old familiar warmth between her legs. Coyness had never been part of Maireed's makeup. She stood for a moment with one hand on Ben's arm, and sensed his own eagerness. To Ben, teachers were sacrosanct, a race apart. One didn't make advances to them; it was almost sacrilege—but there was no reason to push the lady away if she started it. Maireed swung her arm around his neck. "Kiss me, Ben."

They walked back to Maireed's lodgings, satiated and somewhat sticky. She sensed that Ben didn't want to break off the contact between them at this point, wanted to stay around for a while, but Maireed just wanted to be alone. Rather curtly she said, "Goodnight, Ben," and went inside.

She avoided Mrs. Santini, who had a nose for gossip that a bloodhound would have envied, and went straight into the shower. She felt unclean. It wasn't that sex disgusted her, nor that Ben's breath could have been sweeter, to say nothing of his underwear. Rather, she felt for the first time the squalid meanness which was the essence of the city. She wanted theatres, restaurants, spacious homes (her parent's home outside Boston seemed a sybaritic paradise by comparison with her present quarters), and all the comparative wealth and freedom of her childhood. Wearily she went down to Mrs. Santini's spaghetti dinner.

"Look at the poor child, she's working herself to a shadow. Sit down, Maireed, eat, eat." Mrs. Santini's motherly cluckings were so much a part of the scenery that Maireed barely registered them anymore. She absentmindedly made small talk while forking up spaghetti and dimly became aware of Mr. Santini discussing the holovision program he had been watching just before dinner.

"...so now they want to send people to the stars. The stars, I ask you. What do they want to go there for? Haven't we got problems enough as it is here on earth? Spending who knows how much money just because some people ain't content with what they've got here..."

"Going to the stars, Mr. Santini?" asked Maireed. (It was an old-fashioned household whose head was apparently entitled to the prefix Mr. at all times. Maireed sometimes wondered if Mrs. Santini addressed him as Mr. in bed.)

"Something about a project called Mayflower. They were saying they want to colonize another planet around another star. Another star! And calling for volunteers to go, as well. Probably be eaten by green slimy things as soon as they get there, if they get there at all. Hah!"

And with Mr. Santini's universal huff of dismissal, the conversation changed to other topics. But that night in her bed Maireed thought about it again. New worlds. Limitless open spaces. Whoever was the boss there would be king of a whole world—or queen. The latter thought made her sit bolt upright in bed.

The next day, Maireed looked up Mayflower on the newly installed library Net link. Screening out the historical references, she soon located what she was looking for. There it was, Project Mayflower, to be launched in three years. Applications were invited for colonists, none to be over twenty-one years of age. Maireed was a few weeks short of her twentieth birthday. Input your Personal Identity Number to the Mayflower website. She applied without a second thought.

Nothing happened for six months. Maireed toiled on with her students, albeit with less enthusiasm than before. Still, her library was growing, as was the school, conditions were becoming a little better every month, but somehow the spark had gone out of her. Her eyes were fixed on other horizons.

Then one day the message came. You have been accepted as a possible candidate. Report for initial screening. She left New York without a backward glance, supremely confident that she would be one of the chosen ones.

CHAPTER 6

It was the great orbiting telescopes that had originally drawn Takahiko Kuwahara to the US after completing his astronomy PhD in Japan. Telescopes on the ground suffer from the fact that they have to look up through a distorting blanket of atmosphere, and however clever the means used to compensate for this, the fact remains that telescopes can see much better if the atmosphere isn't in the way.

The first space telescopes such as the twentieth century's Hubble were early essays in the craft of space-based astronomy, but it wasn't until the latter half of the twenty-first century that the electronically linked arrays of giant telescopes orbiting the Sun a million miles from Earth gave astronomers the opportunity to peer closely at planets circling nearby stars.

Dr. Kuwahara with his newly minted doctorate had jumped at the chance of working with the new telescopes. Scientifically he was a perfect match for the new possibilities they opened up, but it meant working in the US where culturally he was not quite such a good match. American women scared him with their free and easy attitude of equality with men in all things, indeed of superiority to men in many things. Growing up as an only child in a rather traditional upper-class Japanese family had not provided him with much confidence in a society where casual sex was taken for granted.

After a few attempts to socialize with what he instinctively regarded as barbaric but erotically enticing women, he retired into a shell from which he never really emerged again. American women frightened him, and highly accomplished American women such as Julia Lockmeyer terrified him. As a defense he developed what would become his famous inscrutability. To his colleagues he was a detached remote genius who never showed any emotion and never indulged in personal conversation. Since he undoubtedly was a genius in his field, the fact that he was apparently a one-dimensional individual who lived for his work and nothing else was accepted by most people. "Dr. Kuwahara is a genius," they would say, as if that explained everything.

While Takahiko Kuwahara was a lonely burdened man with almost no social life, he was also a driven man, driven by the need to succeed, to show the world that he could achieve miracles. It was almost entirely his doing that it became possible to provide images of planets circling suns up to fifty light-years from Earth. Not just blobs in space, but outlines of continents, inland seas and rivers, details of the atmosphere. It was his great achievement that these images could be teased out of the torrents of data that the great telescope arrays provided.

The closest Kuwahara ever came to unburdening his thoughts occurred one day after a lengthy planning meeting, and only Kuwahara and Harold Merriweather remained in the room, when Merriweather said, rather gently,

"You seem to be rather troubled today, Dr. Kuwahara. Is there anything I can do to help?"

Kuwahara sat silently for a few moments as if weighing up his words.

"Troubled? Yes, I am troubled, and I have reason to be. I am the only person who can cause the brave young men and women we will be sending to the stars to die a useless, lingering death. Which is what will happen to them if I send them to a planet incapable of sustaining life, and all they can do is orbit the planet until their supplies run out and they starve to death.

"We should wait until the robotic probes we have sent out have sent their data back before we send people, but that won't happen for forty or fifty years or more. The human race it seems doesn't want to wait that long. So be it. But that means the sole responsibility for ensuring that the voyagers can survive at the end of their journey is mine, and mine alone.

"I will not hide from you that this responsibility frightens me. I am no longer a young man and I will probably be dead before news of their arrival reaches us, but my family and my name will be shamed if I fail in this."

"Is there anything I can do, Dr. Kuwahara, to lessen your burden?"

"I thank you for asking, but no. Other than constructing much larger orbiting telescopes, we have all the raw data that we can use, and all we can do is to find ways to unlock the information we need from that data. I do not think I am being boastful when I say that my team is the best there is. We are doing all we can. I will not recommend a destination for the Mayflower until I am at least ninety-nine percent certain that life can be sustained when they arrive—but I can never be one hundred percent certain. There will always be uncertainty, and I must live with that until we have knowledge of their arrival, which will probably not be in my lifetime."

To which Harold Merriweather had no response.

After much agonizing, Kuwahara had made his decision on the destination planet. Although he himself would probably be dead, or at best a very old man when news came of the colonists' arrival, it was unthinkable that they would find the new world hostile to human life. He had to be right.

While Dr. Kuwahara avoided personal conversations like the plague, he was quite happy to give lectures on his work. When the final choice of destination had been made for the Mayflower, he was the natural person to give a press briefing, in his typical lecture mode.

"There are many potentially habitable planets within the radius of fifty light-years that represent the limits of what can be achieved with current technology. Each one was subjected to the most minute and thorough examination that our technology permits.

"The planet we have chosen orbits a star about twenty-eight light-years from Earth, and is as close to Earth-like as we can find. Its sun is just a little brighter and hotter than ours, and the planet orbits it a little further from it than our planet is from our sun, so its surface temperatures are very similar to ours. It has a 26-hour rotation period, so that its day would be just two hours longer than ours. It has much the same gravity as Earth, and its axial tilt of fifteen degrees means that there will be seasons, although summer and winter will not be quite so dramatically different as on Earth.

"The planet has an Earth-like atmosphere, and we have detected a chlorophyll-like substance which is a good indication that there is

plant life there. All in all, we feel confident that this is a planet which could support human life."

"Dr. Kuwahara, if this is such an ideal planet," asked a reporter, "how do we know that there isn't some intelligent life already on it who might not welcome us? After all, if a spaceship from another solar system suddenly landed on Earth, announcing that it was going to colonize our planet, it would meet with a rather chilly reception, would it not?"

"That is a good question, which deserves a good answer. To begin with, astronomers have been searching for some indication of intelligent life in the galaxy for well over a hundred years, with no success. Narrowing the focus to our chosen destination, we have not detected any radio broadcasts of any description in any part of the electromagnetic spectrum from this planet, and indeed from any of the planets we have examined in our galactic neighborhood. In addition, no lights have been detected on the dark side of the planet.

"From this we can infer one of three things. First, and by far the most likely explanation, is that there is no intelligent life on the planet. Second, there is intelligent life, but it has not yet developed a technological civilization..."

At this point Merriweather, figuratively speaking, buried his face in his hands and groaned (actually, being a good diplomat, he maintained a poker face, but if he had had telepathic powers, Kuwahara would suddenly have been struck dumb). Shut up, shut up you damn fool, don't you realize what the media will do with this? But Kuwahara just kept going:

"For example, had you examined our own planet five hundred years ago, you would not have detected any radio broadcasts, and any dark-side lighting would probably not be visible from space. Third, there may be a very advanced technological civilization which has developed some means of communication which is beyond our comprehension, and which we are unable to detect. However, in this latter case we would expect to see at least some dark-side lighting, which as I mentioned has not been detected.

"We have no way of knowing which of these three is true, except by going there. If either of the last two possibilities is true, this will be a risk that we will have to take, but in my opinion, and it can only be an opinion, not a scientific statement, the risk is very low."

Unlike Merriweather, Kuwahara was not a politician. If he had been he would not have mentioned the last two possibilities. Some of the more hostile media outlets immediately put out imaginative stories based on the possibility (which they naturally made look as if it was a near certainty) that the Mayflower voyagers were going to meet and subsequently massacre an idyllic civilization, in the manner of Pizarro and the Incas. Other journalists, acting like the herd animals they usually were, chipped in with their own stories until the general public came to believe that yes, there probably was an idyllic alien civilization on the destination planet, in fact there were probably thriving civilizations on every habitable planet.

A day or two later, Merriweather drew Julia Lockmeyer aside for a quiet word.

"We do seem to have stepped into a quagmire here, Julia. I have to admit, it was all my fault for allowing Dr. Kuwahara to make the presentation in the first place. I should have realized that he has no political sense whatsoever. Now we have to think of a way out. No use

asking Kuwahara for help, and Sol's bull-in-a-china-shop approach is the last thing we need right now. Do you have any suggestions?"

"Well, what this situation has brought into the open is that there has always been a strong ideological group that believes the human race is a virus that must be contained, and that letting it loose on the rest of the universe is grossly irresponsible. Think back to the Gaia Liberation Army presentation a few weeks ago and you'll see what I mean. I don't think this attitude is anything new; in fact I think you can trace its roots back to the concept of original sin in the Middle Ages and earlier."

"True enough."

"But I think there is a much larger group that believes that the human race was meant to expand out into the universe, that Planet Earth is just a nursery and that our destiny lies out there somewhere. I guess if I look into my own soul, that's what I believe, otherwise I wouldn't be here. However, the breast-beating virus believers, while fewer in number, are much more vocal and make their presence felt more than the rest of us. We just have to find a way of convincing the general public that Mayflower represents the future and the sooner we get on with it, the better. Let me bounce some ideas off one or two trusted friends and see what comes up."

Julia's first stop was at her old standby, Charles Lansdowne. After dinner Julia was able to steer the conversation to her current problem.

"... so we are now up against the idea, skillfully inserted by the stay-at-home crowd, that the planet we shall be going to is already inhabited by an intelligent life form and we shall be unwelcome gatecrashers, so to speak. What do we do now?"

"The first thing that comes to my mind, Julia, is the statistical absurdity of such a proposition. The earliest known examples of Homo sapiens—us, in other words—date back no more than 200,000 years, and the earliest civilizations are 10,000 years old at most. If you want to postulate that a life form more or less equivalent to ours and at about the same stage of development exists on the other planet, then you have to assume our respective developments are synchronized to within a few thousand years. Since Earth is four-and-a-half billion years old and we must assume the other planet is about the same, this is, statistically speaking, highly unlikely."

"Okay, I can appreciate that, but I don't think you're going to get very far if you try to explain that to the general public. Once they have something in their minds, nothing short of a prime-time holovision interview with aliens explaining that our selected planet has been vacated by them in preparation for our arrival will change their minds.

"And in any case, the stay-at-homers will probably invoke the precautionary principle. Even if we are a hundred million years away from the development of intelligent life on the other planet, the mere fact of our going there might inhibit its development, so we ought notto go."

"Hmm, a wicked thought just came into my mind, Julia, the Sermon on the Mount, Matthew 5:5—'Blessed are the meek, for they shall inherit the Earth.' What if we were to say to the stay-at-homers that you are welcome to cower here in your misery, and when the rest of us have left for new worlds out there you will indeed have inherited the Earth."

"I'd love to say that, but you know as well as I do the kind of hysterical backlash that would result. But it's a nice idea if we could somehow imply it without actually saying it."

Julia still needed to bounce her ideas off someone with abundant common sense who would represent the general public, and of course would be sympathetic to the Mayflower Project. On a whim she called Miriam Lansky, rationalizing to herself that if Miriam didn't represent fundamental common sense then no one did.

"Hi, Miriam, this is Julia Lockmeyer. We talked at the Mayflower cocktail party a few weeks ago..."

"I remember you well, Julia; you're not a very forgettable person. What can I do for you?"

"Miriam, I need to bounce some ideas off someone with a lot of common sense and I thought of you. Can I buy you lunch sometime? I promise this has nothing to do with Sol."

"You've got me interested. When and where?"

And a couple of days later...

"We've landed in deep shit, Miriam. The hostile section of the media, which nowadays means a large part of it, have managed to convince the public that the Mayflower will most likely be going to an already inhabited planet, and that we will be going as hostile colonizers. Although the possibility of this is minute, the resultant uproar is threatening to derail the entire project. What do we do now?"

"Well, even though you say the possibility of there being intelligent life on the destination planet is negligible, and I'll take your word that it is, the one thing you mustn't do is try to convince the public that that it is negligible. The more you try, the more people will think you're trying to hide something. What you need to do is somehow turn this to your advantage."

"Okay, but how?"

Miriam took a sip of her wine. She gave Julia a rueful grin. "Unlike you, my dear, who seems to have an eternally slim figure, I have to watch my weight. I guess it's one of the problems that mothers like me face in later years..."

Miriam thought for a moment or two, then, "You know, when you think about it, while individual members of the public can be mature thinking adults, the public as a whole seems to have the thought processes of a four-year-old. And when four-year-olds get something into their heads you can't argue it out of them. The only thing to do is to distract them with something else—let's bake some cookies or go to the park and feed the ducks."

"Interesting thought. So what, figuratively speaking, might those cookies or ducks look like?"

"It would have to be something that makes the public see the Mayflower Project in an entirely new light. Umm—how about 'we come in peace to greet you as our galactic neighbors and to learn from you'."

"Yes, I like it—'and we bring you gifts,' although what the hell you could bring as gifts to an unknown life form is beyond me."

"That's okay; you can toss that problem straight back to Joe Public. Just announce that the Mayflower will be carrying gifts, then set up a very public competition to decide what those gifts should be. You'll have them eating out of your hand."

And so it proved.

INTERLUDE: CHUCK

Chuck Woodburn idly scratched his behind. He was bored out of his mind and would have welcomed a bit of action, anything at all, rather than babysitting a bunch of slug-soft city kids on a school bus every day. But the Commander said he was to do this because their unit needed the money, and it didn't seem to make any difference that the Commander was his father. One day he was going to challenge him, call him out regular, and leave him dead. Then he would be the Commander. But not yet awhile. He was enough of a realist to know that his father and several others in his unit could best him. But one day...

Shifting his equipment belt to a more comfortable position on his hips he checked off the children as they climbed onto the bus. When they were all on, he growled a command into his wrist microphone and the bus lumbered off out of the school premises. As its computer guided it along its pre-set route, stopping at each address to let a child off, Chuck wished that he had been assigned a bus with some older kids on it. A couple of these sixth-grader girls looked as if they had something worth feeling up under their clothes, but most of them weren't worth a second glance. He had suggested as much to the Commander, who had just laughed at him.

"I know what you want, boy, which is why the buses with the big broads get run by the married men. If I gave you one you wouldn't have your mind on the job no how, and then maybe we'd end up with a busload of corpses one day. You keep your pecker strapped down till you're off duty."

Chuck had to admit that the Commander had a point there. They were uncomfortably close to Washington here in Alexandria, and

Washington was a bubbling stew of gangs making raids on everyone and everything around them. The Feds in their downtown citadel tried to pretend that it was business as usual, but they still needed several full-strength militia units just to ferry them in and out of the place every day. Chuck's unit used to have a contract, but an armored bus under their control had been hijacked, and by the time the dust had settled there had been precious few survivors. Needless to say they lost their contract to a rival militia, which was why Chuck was now chaperoning school kids in Alexandria. At least he would be on street patrol next month, which would give him a better chance for some action, particularly if one of the Washington gangs decided to go raiding.

Some of the hotheads in the unit had suggested faking another hijacking so the other militia unit would lose their contract in turn, but the Commander had come down hard on that one. "Get it into your thick skulls once and for all, you lame-brained hopheads, that militia units don't fight militia units. No matter how funny some of them talk, they're militiamen just like us. We run things around here because we stick together and respect each other. But if we ever start fighting each other, there's plenty of gangs in the Washington Wastelands would eat us alive. Any man in my unit who tries a sneak attack on another unit will answer to me personally."

And indeed, Commander Woodburn of the Bull Run Militia was not a man to be trifled with. A little past the prime of life, he was still a formidable fighter. Of course, the Bull Runs could not claim to be an aristocratic unit like some of the senior Montana Militias. Nevertheless they were an honest hardworking unit, warriors for the working day, with a generally good reputation. Having had a bus hijacked in Washington was only a minor blot on their record; it had happened to most of the other units in the area, but the Feds had this reflex action of what they called 'competitive procurement.' Commander Woodburn had an idea that the Feds were split into a number of warring factions, and the slightest slip by a contractor of one faction meant an opportunity for another faction to grab power. Realistically, he knew that they would get another contract in a year or two, so in the meantime they turned their hands to whatever they could.

Commander Woodburn had been pondering whether it might not be a good time to get out of the Washington trade altogether. It was becoming obvious that the Feds had less and less money to spend every year. Ten, fifteen years ago, the armored buses were always well maintained inside and out. Nowadays it was a different story and breakdowns were quite common, which was why they'd been attacked in the first place. Of course, had the militiamen on board been alert there wouldn't have been a problem. (Just as well they'd both died in the attack, or the Commander would have made their lives a living hell afterwards.) There was talk that the next round of contracts were going to demand that the militias provide their own armored transports. Commander Woodburn did not fancy that at all; riding herd on buses was one thing, running them was something else altogether. They were a Militia Unit for chrissake, not a bus company.

He stretched his heavy limbs in his office chair in his small, cluttered office. It would be good to get out of these everlasting cities, out into the open country, or what was left of it, and live as God had meant militiamen to live. It hadn't always been this way, he reminisced idly to himself. Militia units were the last bastion of freedom in America, as everyone knew, and belonged in the open where a man could see his enemies without having to wonder if a sniper was concealed behind every goddam window. Trouble was, you needed money to live and buy weapons and ammunition, and just about the only place a man could get that nowadays was in the cities. He'd heard tell that the land used to be divided up into tiny farms of a few hundred acres apiece, each owned by a different family, but he couldn't vouch for it. All he knew was that any land capable of being farmed was owned in county-sized blocks by some shadowy agribusiness somewhere, and had a well-entrenched militia company to protect it. It would be nice to have a contract like that, but those militias passed the business down from father to son.

Looking up at the wall screen, he saw a bunch of his men walking into the compound, evidently just coming off duty. His eldest son was among them. They looked goddam sloppy he thought with disgust. Well, he would soon put that right. Buckling on his equipment belt, he strode out of his office into the yard and began bellowing orders.

As a full militiaman, Chuck lived in the barracks with the other unmarried men. He had moved in a few months ago, on his eighteenth birthday, and had had to endure a lot of ragging from the other men, particularly as he was the Commander's son. His father had warned him he would, and he was right.

"When you move out of this house, forget about being my son. I'll treat you as I would any other man, and I'd be doing you no favor if I didn't. Someday you may be Commander in my place, but if so it'll be on your own merits, not because you're my son. The Bull Runs are going to be led by the best man they've got, and if you're going to lead them you have to be better than any of them. So get out there and learn what it takes to be the best."

When he first walked into the barracks and dropped his kit on an empty bunk, he was greeted with silence until Joe Summers, a lanky individual with a freckled face and a reputation for moving like a cobra, spoke up. "Well, look who's just walked in. Guess Papa's decided his little boy is too big to run around the house anymore."

Chuck looked him in the eye for a long moment. Sure, he could fight him for that. Might not win, but he'd give a good account of himself. On the other hand, starting a fight the moment he walked in seemed a bit stupid, as if he was just another muscle-bound numbskull who had only one way to settle anything. He decided to wait it out for a while.

"My name is Chuck Woodburn. If it's the same name as the Commander's, that's neither here nor there. I'm Chuck Woodburn, and anyone who doesn't like it answers to me, and to nobody else."

"Suit yourself, son," said Joe, and turned away.

Chuck leapt over the intervening bunk and grabbed Joe's arm, forcing him around. "You deaf? I said my name was Chuck."

It was a glorious fight. Joe was faster and more experienced, but Chuck was no novice and was heavier. They fought to a draw while the others cheered them on. After a long while, when they were both still more or less upright but bruised, bleeding, and exhausted, Joe grinned, held out a hand and said through a split lip, "Welcome to the barracks, Chuck."

After that, the other squad members in his barracks cleaned him up and got him ready to start his basic training. Big Bill Kretsky, his squad leader, made sure he knew all he needed to know about drill, small arms, and unarmed combat. The latter was particularly important, since militia units didn't have any formal police powers, but provided security in the absence of actual police who had largely withered away when governments were unable or unwilling to pay for them. Lacking powers of arrest, militia units kept order, for those who could afford to pay for them, largely by their fearsome ability to beat the crap out of any wrongdoer.

Part of Chuck's unarmed combat training required him to fight every member of his squad. It was rough and brutal, and one of its objects was to weed out any new recruit who wasn't tough enough to take the beatings he undoubtedly would sustain when fighting more experienced men. However, Chuck surprised them by unexpectedly winning one or two fights and achieved a reputation as a useful buddy to have in a tight spot.

By the time Chuck had gone through basic training, he was an accepted member of the Unit, in the same squad as Joe Summers whom he counted as one of his buddies. They drank together and womanized together, and went looking for fights where they could. Trouble was, fights were hard to come by unless you were bent on getting killed. Of course, there was no problem in ducking into Washington and picking a fight in the nearest bar, but the chance of coming out alive unless you went there in force was just about nil. Those brothers seemed to shoot each other as a way of saying good morning. They even had meat wagons which went on regular routes past the bars every morning. Why there were any of them left was a mystery to him; he supposed they just bred fast.

Nor was it advisable to start a fight with a member of another Militia. These things had a way of escalating into all-out war as each side attempted to protect its honor. Sure, there were plenty of organized contests, heavy with protocol, but anyone who picked a casual fight with another Militia was liable to incur his Commander's displeasure. And Commander Woodburn's displeasure was not to be taken lightly.

As for the suburban slugs, forget it. For a start, few of them ever went into bars, and even the ones that did would wet themselves if you so much as glanced at them. It always seemed strange to Chuck that these slugs they were paid to protect were the ones who owned everything. He had often wondered why they didn't just take over everything and run it themselves. He had asked old Dan about it once.

"Heard a couple of units tried that once, out West somewhere. Things went fine for a while, until they found that acting as a government ain't as simple as it seems. They got tied up in lawsuits and fleeced by just about every slicker that came along. After that, militia units tended to stick to what they're good at, which is being militias."

Old Dan Fogarty had lived in the barracks since before Chuck was born. He'd never shown any interest in getting married or promoted, but he knew every trick in the book and quite a few that probably weren't. He wasn't too interested in women and rarely came along with the others when they went looking for action. Of course, had there been the slightest suspicion he was queer he would have been out of the Unit in a flash, probably face down in a ditch somewhere, but old Dan's interests lay elsewhere. He spent most of his off-duty time reading, for chrissake, not with holodiscs but actual books printed on paper. The only time Chuck had ever seen Dan angry was when Pete Schwarz had ripped up one of his books. Old Dan was regarded with new respect by the younger militiamen after that, especially by Pete who spent a couple of days in hospital. But for all that he was easy to talk to and liked showing off his knowledge.

"Got to learn to read and write if you want to get on, Chuck."

Chuck forbore to mention that Dan's evident skills in that area had not seemed to boost his career very far. "How come it's all that important, Dan?"

"Why, a militia unit is a business, just like a bar or a factory. We provide services that people want; they pay us. If you're involved in running the Unit, you have to deal with contracts and the like, and that means reading and writing. Course, it wasn't always like that. Used to be, militias formed to protect their freedoms and rights from big governments. But then the big governments choked themselves to death with debt, and the militias stepped in to do some of the things governments used to do, but couldn't any more. We protect people as long as they have the cash to pay us."

"What happens if they don't pay us?"

"Why, we go somewhere else. As to what happens to the people we used to protect, that's their problem. Judging by what I can see in Washington, it won't be too long before the Feds run out of money to pay us, then they'll have to shut the place down. Won't be too soon for me, I could do with a change of scenery."

Dan's wish came true shortly thereafter. The Commander called the Unit together one Sunday after Church to vote on their next contract.

"No need to tell you men that policing streets and school buses ain't the greatest job in the world. Sure, it pays well, but if we do much more of this we'll be losing the fine edge that makes us a good militia. So I've negotiated a five-year contract for the Bull Run Militia to be a

Border Security Unit. The good news is we spend our time in Maine, patrolling the coast. The bad news is we have to take orders from the Border Security Agency."

There were a lot of questions, most of them pertaining to how the Unit would be employed and whether they would be split up. The Commander was emphatic on the last point.

"The contract says we work as a full militia unit at all times. No splitting up, we have our territory to patrol and protect and we stay on it. But within that territory we go where the BSA says we go and do what they say we do."

It was left to Dan Fogarty to ask the obvious question. "Seems to me we're going to have to leave here anyway 'cause the Feds are running out of money. So if they can't afford to keep Washington going, how can they afford to keep the Border Security Agency going?"

"That's a good question, Militiaman." Rightly so, since Dan and the Commander had quietly discussed this very point a week ago, and agreed that Dan should bring it up. "But just remember this. The Feds get to run whatever the voters—that's you and me and everyone else— say they get to run. And it looks like the voters have said they can do without most of Washington, but not without a Border Security Agency. Without them, this country would be swarming with illegal immigrants, and we've got enough problems dealing with all the people we have here already without adding a whole bunch more."

The discussion rolled back and forth well into the afternoon. On major decisions like this, the Bull Run Militia was a democratic institution and everyone had the right to voice his opinion. But they all knew that once a formal vote had been taken, they were bound by the will of the majority, from the Commander to the youngest militiaman. However, Commander Woodburn was well aware that if he wanted to keep his job he had better ensure that the final vote was heavily in favor of whatever he proposed.

In the end, it was. He knew his men and knew the prospect of getting out of the big city was irresistible. So it came about that a few weeks later a convoy of trucks with their heavy equipment took to the Interstate and growled their way to Maine. Half of the men and all the women and children had gone ahead by air, leaving the others to guard the trucks en route.

The northern coast of Maine is for the most part a lonely, inhospitable, rocky place. In other words the ideal place to land a boatload of desperate migrants in the middle of the night, for whom the prospect of drowning while disembarking was considerably better than the thought of returning whence they had come.

The naval arm of the Border Security Agency was supposed to intercept the big ships, stuffed with several thousand migrants, but nowadays they disembarked well out to sea and sent their cargo ashore in high-speed inflatable boats. Just about impossible to pick them up on radar, grumbled Chuck to himself for the umpteenth time, standing on a cliff top in the rain in the middle of the night. "Why can't these goddam bogeys come ashore at a civilized time, say ten o'clock in the morning. Working nights all the time doesn't do my sex life any good."

"At least we're less likely to be drilled in the back by a sniper here," said Joe Summers beside him.

Chuck was about to reply when he caught a movement in his night sight. He thumbed his microphone. "Red zero six to

Foxhound. Looks like we've got visitors. Two, no three, maybe four boats approaching."

The unit went into a well-rehearsed routine. Chuck remained on the cliff top reporting on the situation while Joe maneuvered their truck as close as it could get, then prepared the star-shell mortar in the back. It was a crude, primitive device but had the great advantage that its projectiles were self-powered, would illuminate a wide area, and were almost impossible to shoot down. Sometimes the old methods work best. They waited for reinforcements while the first boat reached the shore. Its pilot pulled in as close as he was prepared to go, which wasn't very close at all, then urged his passengers to jump out.

Looking out at them, Chuck heard a pistol shot during a brief lull in the roar of the surf. Apparently some of the passengers considered that the pilot could move in closer, but the latter had done this run before and was in a hurry to be away. He evidently had a healthy respect for the Militia and persuaded his passengers that jumping out was in their best interests by the simple expedient of shooting one of them. They landed in six feet of water in heavy surf on a rocky shore, and few of them appeared to be good swimmers. Perhaps half of them reached the shore, and lay huddled on the rocks at the foot of the cliff. As the last of them left, Chuck fired a couple of shots at where he thought the engine of the boat lay, but without apparent result. He certainly alerted the pilot, who gunned his engine and left like a scalded cat.

Meanwhile, reinforcements had arrived. Joe fired a star shell, bathing the whole shoreline in a harsh light which cast sharp black shadows. The second boat was in the act of landing its passengers, most of whom froze like rabbits caught in a car's headlamps. Its pilot also persuaded them to continue disembarkation with a few pistol shots, but he was unlucky. One of the militiamen on the cliff top shot him, and he fell backwards into the surf. The other two boats veered round before they reached the shore and headed off, one up the coast, the other down. Chuck reported their movements, then signed off.

Big Bill Kretsky arrived at that moment. "Nice work, Chuck."

"What are we going to do about the bogeys down there?" asked Chuck.

"Well, if you like, you can climb down and offer them coffee and donuts, but me, I think I'll just leave them there till morning. They ain't going nowhere. With a bit of luck, the way the wind's getting up and the tide's coming in, there won't be any left by morning."

And indeed, out of two boatloads numbering perhaps a hundred or so, there were only thirteen left alive by morning. Chuck's squad rounded them up and handed them over to another militia unit who had the contract for illegal alien detention. Where they went after that, Chuck neither knew nor cared.

Chuck's squad fell into a routine after a few weeks. They could generally count on some action every couple of weeks or so, and were getting used to the continuous night patrols. They had tried sleeping on patrol at first, but a series of surprise inspections by the Commander persuaded them that remaining awake was a wiser alternative. In the end they accepted that evenings off duty came only once or twice a week.

Some of the unmarried men (and one or two of the married men) formed liaisons with local girls, but girls were in short supply, and in any case the local inhabitants were a clannish lot, suspicious of these drawling southerners. (The Deep South began at Connecticut as far as

they were concerned.) For want of anything better to do, Chuck, with Dan Fogarty's help, started to improve his reading skills.

Dan kept a collection of books in his locker. "Borrow them, read them, but respect them" were Dan's instructions, and his reputation was sufficient for Chuck to note his words well.

"Who's this guy Shakespeare?"

"Oh, he lived about five hundred years ago. Wrote plays mostly, but it's all poetry of a sort. He was the kind of guy that couldn't put pen to paper without writing something memorable."

"Sounds like hogwash to me." Chuck opened the book at random and with some difficulty read a few lines aloud:

"Disdaining fortune, with his brandished steel,

Which smoked with bloody execution,

Like valour's minion carved out his passage till he faced the slave;

Which ne'er shook hands, nor bade farewell to him,

Till he unseamed him from the nave to the chaps

And fixed his head upon our battlements."

Chuck thought for a while. "Looks like somebody got wiped out. What's a brandished steel?"

"Probably a sword. If it's who I think it is, the blade would have been about three feet long and maybe three inches wide at the hilt. You could carve somebody up nicely with one of those. And that's just what the guy did."

"Shit, this sounds interesting." Chuck turned a few pages:

"... I have given suck, and know

How tender 'tis to love the babe that milks me:

I would, while it was smiling in my face,

Have plucked my nipple from his boneless gums

And dashed the brains out, had I so sworn as you
Have done to this."

"Holy shit, I'm glad she wasn't my Ma. Quite a dame, whoever
she was."

"That was Lady Macbeth, the wife of the guy with the sword.
They neither of them lived to collect their pensions, but between them
they wiped out quite a few people before they were done."

Chuck was hooked. Over the next few days he read the rest of
Macbeth. True, it was hard going, the language was archaic,
convoluted, and in many places just plain long-winded. But the raw,
elemental passions and furies of the characters came through
regardless. He was particularly fascinated by the witches, those senile,
cackling embodiments of malicious deceit. He pictured them in his
mind, toothless, warty, hairy-faced old woman dressed in dirty rags,
breath like a rotting corpse, with wet, red-rimmed eyes that gleamed
with an unholy light. He put the book aside with an inward shudder
as he got ready to go on patrol that night.

That night another boatload of bogeys came ashore. Routine stuff,
except that this time there were young children with them, trapped
at the foot of a cliff at night in a storm. Their terrified screams grated
on Chuck's nerves and made him think of Lady Macbeth:

Have plucked my nipple from his boneless gums / And dashed the
brains out …

And for the first time made him feel guilty.

Chuck was not an unfeeling brute, but growing up in a militia
unit was not the best way to develop finer feelings. Suddenly, for the
first time, he began to think about what he was doing and why.

"Why do we have to do this, Dan? Letting kids drown."

"You mean, keeping the bogeys out? Well, there was a time, oh, before I was born, when they tried letting them all in. Trouble was, it meant the big cities started to become more and more like the places these guys were fleeing from. People were living on the streets and it took more and more money to provide for them and keep order, just when governments were collapsing with all their debt. In the end the voters decided that, yeah, letting them all in was nice, but it just cost too much money and made too much trouble, so gradually the voters said the hell with it, keep 'em out."

"Yeah, but do the voters know what it's like, hearing kids drown?"

"Course not. That's what they pay us for, to do the dirty work for them so their sweet dreams ain't disturbed. And yeah, from time to time a bunch of them get upset and say we should start letting them in again—open borders or something of the kind, but most of these people can't do simple arithmetic. If they could, they'd realize that with open borders you could easily get tens of thousands a day coming in, and with the rate at which most of them breed it wouldn't take too long before we were just as crammed as any Third World country. There's no shortage of people in the Third World wanting to come here.

"Luckily for the rest of us, whenever the idea of open borders pops up it gets put to a referendum vote and loses every time. When there's a collision between noble ideas and hard cash, the noble ideas get sideswiped every time. Get used to it, Chuck; we'll be doing this job for a long time yet."

But something had awoken in Chuck, some newborn, whining, whimpering conscience that nagged at him every time he had to stop a boatload of bogeys. As time went on, rather than becoming inured to the job, it got worse. He felt sometimes as if he were one of the witches in Macbeth, casting dark spells to lure sailors to their death. Then one day, the holovision news described the Mayflower Project and its call for volunteers. Chuck applied, and six months later was informed he was on the shortlist.

The call came at the point where Chuck's conscience was making him think the unthinkable—leaving the Militia Unit. Going to a new world where there would be no population pressures sounded almost too good to be true. He accepted with relief.

CHAPTER 7

At the next planning meeting, Julia regarded Sol Lansky with less professional exasperation than before, having got to know his wife. Somehow, knowing a little about Sol beyond the face at the conference table made him more human and easier to deal with.

Solomon Lansky (Sol to just about everyone except his elderly mother who still called him Solly) had been born in Britain in 2045. While Britain had been spared the worst excesses of the Great Intifada which had resulted in much of the European Union becoming the Caliphate of Europe, there was enough backlash to make life uncomfortable for the few remaining Jewish families still in Britain, so Sol's family had emigrated to the US in 2057.

Sol's family believed in education. They knew all too well how fickle the protection of princes and presidents could be and were determined that their children should have the means to earn enough to make them, if not bullet proof, at least capable of moving away in a hurry from any hotspots. Medicine, law, and banking were the preferred options, but engineering came a respectable second.

Sol took to engineering as a duck takes to water. He was interested in things, not people. For those engineers lucky enough to begin their careers at the start of a new wave of technology, the rewards can be great, and Sol Lansky was lucky enough to start his career when fusion became a viable technology for spaceship propulsion. No longer were deep space vessels limited to chemical fuels. With their new fusion engines the sky wasn't even the limit; it was merely the starting point.

But not only do successful engineers need to be able to harness new technologies, there needs to be sound economic reasons for those technologies being used in the first place. After joining Astro-Mining Corporation as a young engineering graduate, Sol cut his teeth on asteroid mining projects that were beginning to provide raw materials for an Earth whose own mineral resources were rapidly declining. By the time he was in his thirties, Sol ran a design team that built space miners and freighters and was generally recognized as the go-to man for anything out of the ordinary in space. And since Astro-Mining became very wealthy supplying rare-earth minerals to industries that needed them back on Earth, his employers made sure he shared in that wealth. They were determined to keep Lansky and his capabilities for themselves.

As far as Sol was concerned, there were two types of people in the world: engineers who did useful things, and everyone else. Moreover, the only ones amongst the engineers who really counted were those who worked with him, and more and more in recent years, for him, on building spacecraft. Sol was naturally a person who gravitated to the top so he could make his own decisions. In spite of his vast technical knowledge, he was at heart a feudal lord who would have felt quite at home in the Middle Ages.

Sol's social skills were not so much lacking as unpracticed; he didn't see much point in being polite to people unless there was a good reason for it, and in Sol's world there rarely was. Straightforward, yes, but anything beyond that wasn't usually necessary as far as Sol was concerned. Luckily he had a wife who loved and respected him and was proud of his achievements and also, being fully cognizant of his limitations, would cover for him in most social settings, in which arena she tended to treat him as an overgrown child. Which was just fine by Lansky. For two intensely practical people it was a marriage made in Heaven.

Julia was brought out of her reverie by Harold Merriweather as he brought the meeting to order.

"So we know how many we are sending and, thanks to Dr. Kuwahara, where we are sending them," said Merriweather. "What else do you need to know, Sol, before you can get to work on the ship?"

"Only one other thing is significant, and that's how much supplies they'll want to land with them on the planet."

"Forgive me, Sol. I am not an expert in these matters, as you know, and if I seem to be asking obvious questions, please bear with me. But why should their supplies be so significant?"

"What's significant is the total payload mass, the total cargo we have to send. We know the number of people on board, and we know how long the journey will take so Julia's people can give me all the data I need on life support systems on the ship..."

"Life support?"

"While they're on the ship they'll need air to breathe, food to eat, and somewhere to shit afterwards. Fifty people doing that for nearly fifteen years or so will need a lot of consumables and a lot of plumbing—that's life support."

Merriweather wished, not for the first time and very probably not the last time, that Lansky could express himself a little more delicately, but said nothing. Knowing when to say nothing was one of the secrets of diplomacy.

"Wait a minute," said Julia, "if it's a twenty-eight light-year trip, surely the minimum time it can take is twenty-eight years—nothing can go faster than the speed of light is what I've always been led to believe."

"You're quite right, except that for the people on board the ship a little thing called time dilation comes into play, as Einstein announced almost two centuries ago. The faster you go, the more time slows down for you. At the speed the ship will be travelling—about ninety percent of the speed of light—time dilation will be more than a factor of two, so allowing just under a year for the ship to get up to that speed and the same time to slow down at the other end, then as far as the passengers on the ship are concerned a bit less than fifteen years will have elapsed."

"So the only thing we don't know is how much cargo we take along for the colonists when they land. Once we know that, I can work out the total payload. The reason payload mass is so important is that for every pound of payload I have to have several thousand pounds of fuel."

"Ah, now we come to the crux of the matter, Sol. Why so much fuel?"

"This ship is just going to be a big rocket. Like any rocket it carries its own fuel which it squirts out of its ass at a great rate of knots. If you do that, the ship is pushed forward, as anyone knows who's lit off a few fireworks. Problem is, we have to get this baby up to somewhere near the speed of light. If you don't do that, with the distance we have to go, twenty-eight light-years or about a hundred and sixty-four trillion miles, everyone on board will have died from old age before we get there.

"To get to the planned cruising speed of ninety percent of the speed of light you have to accelerate at one gravity for about ten and a half months. When you get near your destination, you have to slow down again, which you do by turning the ship around so it's facing backwards," Sol demonstrated by waving his arms in the air, "and fire your jets for another ten and a half months. Twenty-one months worth of fuel altogether. With the most efficient plasma jets we can make, that adds up to an awful lot of fuel. The more mass you have to accelerate and decelerate the more fuel you need, so every pound of additional payload means more fuel. The problem compounds itself because until you actually burn that fuel it's just dead weight, extra cargo if you will, which has to be accelerated with the rest of the ship.

"As well as the passengers and their cargo, we have to send along landing craft to get them to the planet's surface. The ship itself will be a deep space craft. There's no way it could survive a landing on any planet; it would just break up as soon as it hits the atmosphere. So we have to pack some landers as well as the rest of their gear."

"What about radiation protection for the passengers?" said Julia. "I thought there was a problem with that when you travel at those speeds."

"You're right, radiation is a problem. When you start moving at close to the speed of light, a collision with even a single hydrogen atom will cause a burst of radiation which, if repeated often enough, will sterilize you or even kill you. But we'll arrange the fuel tanks so that no matter which way the ship is facing there will be a wall of fuel between them and the direction in which the ship is moving, so they should be protected no matter what."

"Won't the radiation affect the fuel in some way, like causing a premature reaction in the fuel tanks?"

"Not a problem, because it isn't really fuel in the chemical sense; it's just reaction mass. In fact the tanks will be full of water."

"Water?!"

"Yep, just water. Any rocket works by propelling mass out of its rear end at a great rate of knots. You can do this with a chemical reaction, such as putting hydrogen and oxygen together and igniting them, but to get the thrust we need we'll be using plasma jets. The main engines will essentially be fusion reactors. Water vapor goes in one end, gets heated to a million degrees or more, and goes out the other end in a massive flare of hard radiation. You can't use plasma jets on Earth because the radiation from them is so severe, but in deep space it's not a problem. You can use anything you like as reaction mass, old sweatpants if you insist, but water is convenient."

"And what if the ship should meet something substantially larger than a hydrogen atom, say a small meteorite?" said Merriweather.

"In that case, game over, goodbye, kaput. At the speeds at which they'll be travelling, collision with anything substantial would result in a catastrophic explosion. It's a risk they'll have to take. But the chances of it happening are very small, as far as we know."

"Let me put the question to you in a different way then. Assuming the cost of the ship is kept within the limits we have been set—no point in doing it at all if the costs are going to be so enormous that it gets cancelled halfway through—how much cargo can we send along with the colonists?"

"With fifty of them? About two hundred pounds each."

"But that's impossible," flared Julia. "When they land they'll be totally without resources. We have to provide them with at least two years' supply of food, plus seeds, farming implements and everything else."

"No way. Can't be done."

Merriweather quickly intervened before the usual Lansky/Lockmeyer shouting match occurred. "Julia, what is the absolute minimum weight of supplies we will need?"

"About a ton per colonist, perhaps a little more. We're still working on it, and obviously are trying to get the weight of everything down. But I doubt very much that we can do with substantially less."

"So we seem to have a shortfall of about two thousand pounds per colonist, or a hundred thousand pounds in all. Sol, is there any way we can cut that much out of some other part of the ship?"

"No way. Everything is pared down to a minimum. Only thing we haven't really looked at is the life support systems. If we could seriously reduce the number of passengers or get them to stop eating for fifteen years, that might do it, but not otherwise."

"Back to you then, Julia. Have you any suggestions?"

"Well, one thing we did look at some time ago was the possibility of sending frozen human embryos—actually just fertilized ova—and have the ship grow those embryos into human babies and birth them at the journey's end. The problem is that they then have to spend the next eighteen years or so growing up on the ship, which by then would presumably be in orbit around the destination planet. This means you would need much the same life support systems as if you sent adults on the voyage, and while you would be using the systems at the journey's end rather than on the journey itself, you still have to have them on board the ship. We could of course send the embryos down to the planet's surface and raise them there, but then we would have to have quite a few adult humans with them in that case to take care of them and deal with any problems we might encounter on the surface, which we simply can't foresee at this point. Using robots to do this isn't a viable solution because for all their capabilities, robots aren't much use at dealing with unpredictable situations. And of course if we have a number of adults on the surface we may as well produce the fertilized ova the old-fashioned way. Either way, you wouldn't reduce the need for life support systems very much, if at all.

"The other problem we have to deal with is that we don't have the payload capacity to send along the typical machinery of a technological society, such as farm tractors and fuel synthesis equipment—"

"Plus all the maintenance equipment and spares," interjected Lansky.

"That too, so when they land they're going to have to do pretty well everything by muscle power. And if you do that, you need men. Big strong, sweaty men. This is one of the reasons why we're sending equal numbers of men and women. From a purely genetic viewpoint we could get by with a lot of women and just a few men, but leaving aside the societal problems this would probably cause we need the men for their muscle power."

Julia thought for a moment before she spoke again. "There is possibly a way to reduce the life support burden on the ship, but not one I've wanted to consider before all other alternatives are exhausted. Putting people into deep freeze doesn't work; mammals simply can't survive long-term freezing no matter how you do it, but there has been developed a class of drugs that have the effect of putting people into a coma. Their requirements in terms of food and air are very much reduced, and we don't have to worry too much about recreational facilities for them. One of the major factors in designing life support is that we have to provide things for the voyagers to do while they're on board ship. If you don't, they'll go crazy with boredom and probably start killing each other.

"The problem is, coma-inducing drugs were developed for long-term therapy such as for severe burn victims, but have never been used for more than a few months at a time. We would have to use them for years at a time. There is simply no data on how humans would react to long-term use of this nature."

"Can we find out?" said Merriweather .

"That's what I intend to do."

INTERLUDE: JESSICA

Jessica Thorskill was a big girl. Not fat, just built to a larger scale than most other girls. Nearly six feet tall and well-muscled, with blonde hair and blue eyes from her Scandinavian ancestry, in days gone by she would have been called a strapping wench. A cheerful girl, she tended to play on the boys' teams in sports since she was reckoned to be too physically powerful to play on girls' teams.

Jessica's family had a tradition of service. Whatever you did in life, it had to benefit other people in some way. There were lawyers and judges, doctors, nurses, and social workers in her family. As she reached the end of her high school days, it was natural for Jessica to think in terms of a career along those lines. Becoming an investment banker, or heaven forbid, an actress, was unthinkable.

Since medicine seemed to be her chosen area, Jessica's father, the judge, suggested she have a talk with one of his golfing buddies. "Jim Reinhold's one of the best cardiac surgeons in the business. He can tell you what it's really like, rather than reading about what it's supposed to be like."

A few days later found Jessica in Dr. Reinhold's office.

"If this were forty or fifty years ago I'd probably be too busy to see you, but most of my work is done by robosurgeon nowadays, and to be honest I don't have enough to do. That's the reality you have to face in medicine today—humans are gradually being made redundant.

"All those holofilms you've seen of surgeons in scrubs and face mask—forget 'em. I don't often go into operating theatres today. Sure, I'm responsible for a lot of operations, but what I really do is monitor a very complex robot as it does the work. There are still the odd occasions when something unexpected crops up and I have to take over, but it's almost always done by placing the robosurgeon under local control. I haven't had my hands inside a live human body for years.

"To be quite honest with you, I don't know how much longer I'm going to be required to do even what I do today. Robotic surgeons are getting better and smarter every year, and it won't be long before they can do everything I can do, only better.

"And of course this brings up another problem. The less you use your surgical skills, the rustier you become until you're more of a liability than an asset."

"Don't you practice on simulators? I read somewhere that surgical simulators are really lifelike."

"Oh yes, and I spend several hours every week on them. The problem is, I suppose, that you know at the back of your mind that a human life isn't at stake, so it's difficult to maintain that fine edge of skill and concentration necessary to be a really good surgeon."

"So I guess what you're telling me is that surgery is rather an iffy career choice. What about other branches of medicine?"

"If you think surgery is being taken over by machinery, diagnostics are completely taken over. A medical diagnostic autosystem can measure just about everything it's possible to measure in a human body, compare it against an enormous database of possible medical conditions, and come up with a diagnosis that's correct well over 99 percent of the time. Humans simply can't match that kind of performance, so we don't even try to any more. Every doctor relies on automated diagnosis nowadays."

Jessica was a little crestfallen by this stage. "Is there any branch of medicine that still needs people?"

"Strangely enough, the one branch that people thought was going to disappear first turns out to need human beings more than ever. I'm referring to nursing, of course. People seem to need human contact for the healing process. Experiments have been tried with completely roboticized hospital wards, where the patients get superb physical care, but we get poorer outcomes and the patients take longer to heal than in wards with human staff. It seems we humans just can't get by without other people."

"But don't jump in before you know whether you really want to do it. Something you might want to think about is spending some time with one of these charity clinics that have been springing up lately in Africa and other Third World places. They're always looking for volunteers, and you're likely to see medicine in the raw, so to speak, without all the hi-tech that we have here. Then you can decide whether you want to make a career out of it."

A few minutes searching on the Net turned up the World Social Justice Foundation, which did indeed operate clinics in Africa and Asia, and yes, they were constantly looking for volunteers. A couple of weeks later found Jessica at their Global HQ, which consisted of a rather drab office building in an industrial suburb of Salt Lake City.

"As you can see, we don't go in for fancy accommodation here at Wissjiff because all our funding goes to our clinics and other overseas facilities."

Jessica's interviewer was a rather intense but smart-looking, grey-haired woman. At first Jessica was somewhat taken aback by the term 'Wissjiff,' which she correctly assumed to be a pronunciation of WSJF, because it sounded too much like 'mischief,' but she put that thought behind her as unworthy.

Glenda Lamarr, as the sign on her desk indicated (sounds a bit like one of those old-fashioned film stars, thought Jessica), went on "for the same reason we can't pay you a salary when you're out there because we really do operate on a shoestring budget, but if you decide to become one of our volunteers you will find it to be a life-changing

COL**NISTS

experience. There are people in the less fortunate parts of the world" (by which she meant anywhere outside North America) "who will rely on you for their very existence."

Put like that, Jessica signed up without hesitation.

As Jessica walked out of the building almost floating on air, Robb Lovell, WSJF's chief executive, poked his head into Glenda's office.

"Another lamb for the slaughter, Glenda baby. Make your quota this year and there'll be a nice fat bonus for you."

"No problem, Robb. Now piss off because I've got someone else coming in a few moments."

The World Social Justice Foundation had started as a group of dedicated, compassionate people a few decades ago who had seen a need for medical services overseas and had found a way of fulfilling that need. As they became known for their good works, contributions from like-minded donors had begun flooding in until they were quite a wealthy foundation.

And there the trouble began. Large amounts of money sloshing around with almost no oversight (they were a charitable foundation after all, it says so right here on the label) attracted unscrupulous operators whose interest began and ended with money. As the original directors of the Foundation retired they were gradually replaced by people of a more mercenary frame of mind until WSJF was primarily a vehicle for making a handful of cynical people very rich. Robb Lovell had been hired, at an enticingly large salary, purely for his proven capabilities as a fundraiser.

All of which did not detract from the fact that WSJF did indeed still run a number of overseas medical clinics in particularly poor parts of the world, and these did indeed provide a genuinely necessary service. They just weren't the focus of WSJF's activities any more and received only a fraction of its budget. The rest went to advertising (very slick professional advertising under Robb Lovell's personal direction) and gold-plated compensation packages for directors and senior staff.

The clinic was in rural Zimbabwe, in an area of low scrubby hills seemingly populated by endless herds of goats. Jessica seemed to remember reading somewhere that Zimbabwe had once been known as Rhodesia and had been called the breadbasket of Africa, but that had been in the dreadful days of European colonialism. Funny to think that the Caliphate of Europe would once have been capable of colonizing anything, since it seemed nowadays to be locked in a downward spiral of ever increasing poverty. She wondered briefly if this semi-arid land had ever been productive, then dismissed the thought as irrelevant. Her job was to deal with the here and now, never mind the past.

The clinic was a collection of rather dingy-looking, single-story buildings that acted as the health center and hospital for a wide area. Run by WSJF but largely staffed by a Catholic order of nuns and low-paid local employees, it would have been known in the past as a mission, but such references to anything religious were more or less taboo nowadays so they just called it a clinic. Sister Mary, the nun who seemed to be in charge (there had been a medical director in charge until last year when funding ran out and she left, so Sister Mary just picked up the reins and carried on) was a small, wiry-looking woman of indeterminate age. She never seemed to stop moving, which was just as well since she was doing two or three people's work.

"One thing you need to bear in mind, Jessica, is that being short of supplies is the normal state of affairs here. We just carry on and do the best we can. Our motto can be summed up in three words: we cope, somehow.

"Never forget, in many cases we are often the first and last line of defense for these people. They come to us with their pregnancies, with their children, with all the effects of malnourishment and disease, and somehow we cope. We never turn them away and say there is nothing we can do, even if sometimes the only thing we can do is to hold their hands and comfort them as they die. We can always, always do something for them."

Jessica heard the words she wanted to hear—something about comforting the afflicted—and immediately imagined herself as a kind of junior ministering angel surrounded by adoring patients who worshipped the ground she walked on. She was therefore somewhat disappointed to find herself in the laundry washing sheets, but being of a practical disposition she reasoned to herself that clean sheets were a necessary part of comforting the afflicted, so she got on with the job.

She joined the two girls working in the laundry, Mandida and Chido. Both were dark-skinned Shonas, with Mandida plump and giggly and Chido rather slimmer and more serious in demeanor. As she walked in, Chido glared at her.

"Huh, white girl thinks she come to boss us around and tell us how to run the laundry."

Jessica said nothing, but smiled gently. This was an occasion for doing, not talking. There were a couple of baskets of what looked like wet clean sheets, and she had noticed the long washing lines outside. She picked up a basket. It was heavy, but she was a strong girl.

"This lot ready for drying then?"

Chido stuck her hands on her hips and looked rather belligerent, but Mandida grinned at her and tossed a bag of clothes pegs onto the basket. Jessica walked outside and started hanging up the sheets. She noticed the two black girls carrying out the other basket between them. As she worked, she tried talking to them.

"Hi, I'm Jessica, and I'm new here. Sister Mary told me to work in the laundry. What's next after this?"

After that, Mandida was friendly enough, although it took Chido a day or two to accept Jessica. In the end she did because Jessica was invariably cheerful and willing to work. Since Mandida was not a hard worker, Chido found her workload a lot lighter with Jessica there, and it was difficult to keep on being surly with someone who worked just as hard as she did.

Most of the sheets they washed were old and worn, and required constant patching. When they finally fell to pieces, they were cut up to make bandages. Even the more lightly used bandages were thoroughly boiled and then re-used. As Sister Mary had said, being short of supplies was the normal state of affairs.

Sister Mary always put new volunteers in the laundry or somewhere equally uninteresting for the first month, which enabled her to sort out the truly dedicated from the not-so-dedicated, the down-to-earth from the fantasists. Those who came with the fixed idea that they would instantly become a healing saint, beloved of all with patients worshipping the very ground they walked on, usually left before their first month was up.

Jessica survived her month in the laundry and even seemed to thrive on it, so she was now given the chance to help on the medical side of things. While she still helped in the laundry when required, at other times she was allowed to follow Sister Mary around the wards, learning medicine the hard way and seeing the miracle of birth at first hand. It was here she learned that she seemed to have a natural talent as a midwife. At all events, pregnant mothers seemed to be at ease with her.

The clinic had its own robosurgeon called Charlie. (The Central Health Laboratories prominently displayed CHL logo was presumably responsible for that.) It was a third-hand cast-off from a hospital in Bulawayo, which in turn had been donated from a Boston hospital, but at least you could do simple things such as appendectomies with it. A couple of times Jessica stood by in fascination as it removed an appendix, and found to her relief that she didn't faint at the sight of blood. Anesthetics were a bit hit and miss; as Sister Mary cheerfully said, they were more likely to kill patients with the anesthetic than with the actual operation, but the alternative in the case of appendicitis was a horrible death so you read the instructions and hoped for the best.

The real problem was not so much the lack of medical supplies but the sheer numbers of people who needed their help. With a population of nearly four billion, many of them existing at subsistence level (on a good day), malnourishment in Africa was just an everyday fact of life. And where there is pressure on resources, sooner or later there will be armed conflict.

Jessica had been there for almost six months when civil war erupted in South Africa and rapidly spilled over into Zimbabwe. It happened very fast. One week there was apparent calm; the next week bloody uprisings.

The band of armed men suddenly appeared one morning. Perhaps they had been soldiers who had lost a battle, perhaps they were guerrilla rebels, perhaps they were just a collection of displaced civilians who had obtained weapons and ammunition (not too difficult in Africa) and had decided to strike out on their own. At all events, they burst into the clinic in mid-morning demanding money, food, and medical supplies.

Jessica was in the laundry that morning, lifting sheets out of the boiler with a long laundry pole rather like an overgrown baseball bat. It was noisy in there, and at first she heard nothing until Mandida's screams rent the air. She instinctively rushed towards the sound, still holding her laundry pole, and found Mandida on the ground outside the laundry about to be raped by three men, two holding her down, one with his pants around his ankles. Without conscious thought Jessica swung the pole at the man crouching over Mandida. Jessica was a powerfully-built woman and the pole was long and heavy. There was an ugly meaty sound and a spray of blood as he toppled to one side with his skull crushed. The other two men saw a blonde Valkyrie snarling at them with a bloody weapon raised in her hands, and ran for their lives.

At that moment a burst of gunfire rang out from the direction of the main building and, still running on instinct, Jessica raced towards the sound.

Sister Mary had evidently been remonstrating with the men, and being remonstrated at by Sister Mary was not something one quickly forgot. One of the men had cut the occasion short with his AK-47, that ancient but still popular weapon for untrained militias and gunmen, and now Sister Mary was lying motionless in a pool of blood. Some long-buried Viking ancestor seemed to awaken in Jessica and she hurled herself at the men, screaming an incoherent battle cry and

wildly swinging her laundry pole, a shield maiden out of legend come to life. A part of her mind noted with grim satisfaction the sound and feel of someone's arm being broken.

Cowing nuns and clinic workers when you are armed and they are not is one thing. Facing down a berserker warrior apparently careless of her life or death, even if she is only armed with a piece of wood, is something else altogether. The men scattered and took off as if faced by an angry hippo on the Zambezi.

Jessica stood leaning on her laundry pole, trembling and feeling she was about to vomit. Then she noticed Sister Mary's hand feebly stirring. She knelt down and gently turned her over. The front of Sister Mary's smock was red with blood. Jessica was simultaneously horrified by the sight and felt paralyzed with helplessness. Suddenly she seemed to hear Sister Mary's voice from her first day at the clinic: "We never say there is nothing we can do, even if sometimes the only thing we can do is to hold their hands and comfort them as they die."

Jessica cradled Sister Mary's head on her breast and held her hands, heedless of the blood soaking into her own smock as she watched the life drain out of her.

She stayed holding her lifeless body with tears streaming down her face for what seemed an eternity, until she realized that life must go on. Carefully standing, she lifted Sister Mary in her arms—she was so light! —and saw that most of the clinic staff had gathered around her. Turning to two of the porters—elderly men, but still strong—she said, "Dig me a grave. We will bury her by the chapel." To two of the nurses: "Make her ready for burial. You know what to do."

To her everlasting surprise, the elder of the two nurses bobbed her head down and said, "Yes, Sister Jessica."

Jessica was stunned by the sudden realization that these people were looking to her for guidance. The Sister-in-charge is dead, long live the Sister-in-charge. But I'm not even a nun and I've only just turned nineteen. Oh Lord, what shall I do?

You do the job that is in front of you, a voice inside her seemed to say. You do the best you can. You cope, somehow.

First things first. "Is anyone else hurt?"

"There's one of them by the laundry with his head bashed in," someone said.

Oh, thought Jessica, that must have been me. Am I really capable of killing someone? I guess I am. Then why don't I feel something about it, like shock or horror or guilt? I suppose I will later, but right now I don't so let's just get on with things.

"Just dig a hole and bury him. Rapists don't deserve anything else."

What happened to Christian charity? she thought to herself. Well, wherever it's gone I'm not bothered by it right now.

"Did they take anything?" she asked.

"They took the truck, but that seems to be all. It was standing near the main door and they just drove away with it."

"Well, I guess we'll have to manage without one for a while."

And almost reverently she walked with Sister Mary's body into the clinic's main building, followed by the two nurses. Placing her body in the clinic's operating theatre for want of any better place, she suddenly started shaking as the delayed reaction hit her. The two nurses had followed her in and were looking at her with concern on their faces. One of them said, "You wait here Sister, I'll bring you a clean smock."

Looking down at herself she noticed for the first time that she was covered in Sister Mary's blood, and the shaking became worse.

Then the same voice in her head said, You can't go to pieces now, not in front of the others. It was almost as if there were two people inside her head, one quivering on the brink of hysteria, the other calm and matter-of-fact. So far the calm one seemed to be in charge, but she felt it wouldn't take much for the balance to change. We can't let that happen. These people rely on us now. You can have hysterics some other time.

Promise?

Promise. With an effort she stopped herself shaking.

That evening, just before sunset, they buried Sister Mary. Jessica read the words of the burial service from her prayer book ("earth to earth, ashes to ashes, dust to dust"), feeling uncomfortable doing so because it should have been an ordained priest, but there wasn't one and she didn't know how to fetch one, nor apparently did anyone else. She wasn't even sure if Catholics used those words, but there was only herself to read them, and it was unthinkable that it should have been anyone else at the mission. For Jessica had decided that the death of Sister Mary had somehow sanctified the place, and now it was no longer a mere clinic; it was what it always should have been, a mission.

In the days and weeks that followed, Jessica had no time to think. Of course, she had sent messages off to WSJF in the US, together with a report of the incident ("incident indeed! goddamned catastrophe, more like!") to the capital, Harare, but she didn't know whether any of them got through. The country by this time was fully engulfed in civil war, and all that protected them was that they were in a remote area with no strategic value. Just lots of hungry people to feed and a constant trickle of wounded.

The labor agent had done his homework. He knew the clinic was trying desperately to feed refugees with very little resources, and the refugees included a large number of young people of just the right age.

A couple of trucks arrived about midday with supplies. Jessica was not expecting them, and at first it was a godsend. Two whole trucks full of medical supplies and food which would keep the mission running for at least a month.

The agent stepped out of the lead truck and asked for the clinic director. He was somewhat taken aback when the blonde young woman announced that she was the director, but soon realized it would make his job a lot easier. The previous director, Sister Mary, had been a suspicious old bitch, and had sent him packing when he had called the previous year. So Sister Mary was dead? That was too bad. And Sister Jessica was now in charge?

"We're part of Social Justice Africa, and our mission in life is to help young people get better jobs and lift themselves out of poverty."

It all seemed so plausible to Jessica, even if she had taken a dislike to the man at first sight. Something about the way he held himself, something wolfish about him, grated on Jessica. "I wouldn't like to be alone with him" was the way she put it to herself. But maybe he can't help it, she tried to rationalize to herself, and I can't afford to let my feelings get in the way right now.

"We reckoned you might be having difficulties with all the refugees in this area, so we put together some supplies for you." In fact, they were part of an earlier aid shipment that had been hijacked by one gang, who were promptly slaughtered by a rival gang who did business from time to time with the labor agent, but there was no need for this impressive looking blonde piece to know that.

The labor agent went into a well-rehearsed patter. "SJA and its international sponsors provide education for careers in the hi-tech industry. Young people with a largely agricultural background need to start early and get a good education if they're to have a chance in today's competitive world, so we've established training schools where they can begin apprenticeships, before becoming fully qualified technicians at age eighteen. Our schools like them to begin their education as young as possible, so the intake this year will be for the 10-12 age group."

"You can get more details from our website, but that's the gist of it." (And yes, there was a website saying all the right things, but websites were easy to set up.)

"We're swinging past a couple of the new refugee camps in this part of the country, so if you feel everything is fine here and these people just want to continue with their traditional lives, that's fine too. We'll be on our way."

Jessica could sense the man was a little more tense than his casual words seemed to imply, but then everyone's tense nowadays, she said to herself. She was a little nervous about the deal, but letting two or three dozen pre-teens go would relieve a lot of pressure, and there were certainly a lot of orphans of the right age. In the end, it was the reference to 'traditional lives' that persuaded her. Tradition of starving on inadequate rations, more like, she thought to herself.

They had no difficulty persuading most of the orphans to go, of which there were many. The fact that one of the men with the trucks was handing out T-shirts and ball-caps emblazoned with the SJA logo was irresistible for most of them. Quite a few of the ones with families also went. Parting with children was a wrench, but it was better than seeing them hungry wasn't it?

In the end, the two trucks drove away with thirty-seven volunteers on board. Jessica noticed that the trucks were completely covered with heavy doors at the back, but as the agent said, with all the guerrillas and everything you couldn't be too careful.

That night Jessica wrote her regular report to WSJF, mentioning in it the SJA visit.

Jessica's reports to WSJF's head office were briefly scanned and filed without much attention being paid to them. As long as the clinic was there, doing what it was meant to be doing, nobody at head office cared too much. It was just unfortunate (or perhaps a deliberate leak by someone in the organization) that Jessica's latest report found its way into the hands of one of their major donors. An uncomfortable phone conversation for Chief Executive Robb Lovell ensued.

"What the hell are you guys doing in Zimbabwe supporting those goddamned labor cartels? Don't you know there have been serious allegations about them supplying slave labor for Asian factories?"

Robb Lovell could hardly admit he hadn't seen the report and was only vaguely aware that they had a clinic in Zimbabwe, wherever that might be. However, he hadn't reached his exalted position without being able to think on his feet and calm irritated major donors (minor donors were handled lower down the food chain).

"I fully share your concerns, and we are monitoring the situation closely. It seems that someone over there overstepped their authority and they are being recalled as we speak. We're as anxious as you are to ensure that this kind of thing doesn't happen again. It's in direct contravention of our social justice mandate." And so on for several more mellifluous phrases, at the end of which the donor seemed to be satisfied and Lovell had cold sweat trickling in his armpits from the thought of losing all those millions.

When the donor had disconnected, Lovell yelled for his subordinate. "What's all this crap going on with the clinic in this Zamboni place, or whatever the hell it's called?"

"Er, actually it's Zimbabwe, and yeah, that's one of the places where we laid off the medical director last year when we had a funding problem. It's largely run by nuns and other volunteers who don't take salaries, so it keeps our costs down."

"Well, whoever's running it now has just screwed up big time. Apparently they're giving away underage child laborers to some shady outfit called Social Justice Africa. Hey, they're not associated with us, are they?"

"They used to be, years ago, but they were spun off into an independent outfit for political reasons."

"Okay, but who's running this clinic thingy right now?"

"It used to be a nun called Sister Mary, but she got shot by some terrorists a few months ago. Let me pull up the file on it... I see all our recent reports have been written by someone called Jessica Thorskill, doesn't seem to be a nun... oops, she's only nineteen. Wonder how that slipped through?"

"Only nineteen, you stupid jerk! Get her out of there before she does any more damage. Recall her right now and send in someone else."

And shortly thereafter Jessica received an unequivocal, strongly worded recall order.

Jessica had been at the mission for less than a year when she was unceremoniously thrown out, or so it seemed to her. Huddled in her seat on the flight back, awash in a mixture of emotions—shame, guilt, anger, confusion—she tuned into a news broadcast on the aircraft and learnt of the call for volunteers for the Mayflower Project. Her life seemed to be over, so why not make a new start far, far away. She called up the Mayflower website and entered her personal identification number.

Six months later she learned that she was on the short list. Still emotionally raw from what she saw as her failure, she made her decision and reported for initial screening.

CHAPTER 8

Julia Lockmeyer had a problem. She needed to find out if it was possible to put humans into drug-induced comas, then wake them up years later with no lasting ill effects. Given a callous State with plenty of unwanted prisoners for experimentation and several years to try things out, it would have been simple. But the USA, for all its faults was not that callous, and anyway Julia needed the answer in a few months if the schedule was not to be thrown into a tailspin.

Back to Charles Lansdowne again. This time she would be asking about drugs, which was Charles's area of expertise. In any case Charles would almost certainly ask her to dinner again, which was an invitation that Julia was always glad to accept.

When the meal had been cleared away and Charles had served coffee and liqueurs, Julia was finally able to broach the subject of coma drugs.

"We certainly have drugs that will put you into a prolonged coma, no problem there, but whether you can be successfully revitalized after several years is an open question."

"Testing on humans is out of the question," said Julia, "but what about animal testing?"

"There, I'm afraid, you are up against one of the most vicious and bloody-minded creatures the world has ever seen—the rights activist. Anyone conducting animal testing nowadays is likely to be shot or blown up by any one of a variety of groups describing themselves as animal rights activists. It's another example of the innate contrariness of the human race, that some of the most single-minded killers the race has ever produced describe themselves as rights activists of one stripe or another whose avowed intent is to make the world a kinder, gentler place. It's as if some people need a religion which sanctions bloodshed and violence, and if they can't find a suitable one, by God they go out and invent one."

Julia realized with some dismay that Charles was in his lecturing mode again—he was a professor after all—so she settled back and prepared herself for the inevitable flow of words. But Charles was a good speaker, and it had been a very good dinner...

"Of course, not too many centuries ago, the Christian Church had provided all the bloodshed and violence that anyone could want. Crusades, heretic burnings, religious wars; no end of opportunities for a young man to indulge a healthy taste for blood and violence, and all in the name of God and eternal salvation too. But then a few wimps had begun to say, 'Wait a minute now—didn't this Jesus fellow say something about brotherly love?' and pretty soon it became difficult to get a really good war going in the name of God. Of course, that didn't prevent the priests blessing you when you did get a war going, but the advent of television put a stop to that as well. It was a bit difficult to maintain the fiction that God was on your side when you could see the priests blessing the soldiers on the other side. It began to lead to turf wars between the priests ('lay off will ya—he's my God, not yours'), and that spoiled the whole illusion."

Julia felt she should enter into the spirit of the thing.

"When you think about it, another favorite pastime for those who liked violence was empire building. Back in the good old days when Genghis Khan was alive it was an accepted part of a young man's education to go out into the world and lop off a few heads here and there, or possibly get his own lopped off."

"Yes, but by the beginning of the twenty-first century there had been just a little too much of this kind of thing and it was going out of fashion, at least on a worldwide scale. I suppose most people were quite happy to have it so, but there's always a hard core of individuals for whom bloodshed and violence is necessary, whatever they are doing. These are not common thugs, you understand, for whom violence is merely a means to an end, but dedicated people earnestly striving to put the world to rights.

"Under the sacred banner of Rights Activism, anyone can indulge in shooting, bombing, throwing Molotov cocktails, or whatever, provided you are Doing It For A Cause. The important point is that, unlike common criminals, you aren't doing these things for yourself. Dear me, no. You are, in a spirit of noble self-sacrifice, doing these things for the protection of animals, unborn fetuses, social justice, racial equality, political freedom (please fill in the name of your Cause in the space provided), or the latest revelation of eternal truth from on high. Whatever. All those blown-up or burnt-down buildings give you a sincere feeling of achievement, and the smell of blood is often a real turn-on.

"All of which means, of course, that we had to develop some other means of trying out new drugs."

At this point in Charles' monologue, Julia pricked up her ears and said, "Tell me more."

"There's only one way open to us, and that's computer simulation. Computers, as you know, first evolved to a recognizable form around the middle of the last century, and by the end of that century were beginning to be capable of useful work. The idea of simulation, of building a model of the real world in software inside a computer, was almost as old as computers themselves. You could for example build a software model of a bridge and torture it to see just how much stress it would take before it fell down. Then you built the real bridge, using the lessons learnt from the model. All this was commonplace by the end of the century. But modeling the human body was altogether on a higher scale of complexity.

"By early in this century, computers with sufficient power to take on the enormous task of simulating the human body began to be available. The science of biosimulation, of actually modeling the behavior of living organisms, developed much more slowly. First they had to model the intricate dance of a single protein molecule working its way through a cell to find and mate with just the right partner. Then gradually was developed the ability to model a complete cell, then individual organs within the human body. Finally, two or three decades ago the first halting, clumsy computer models of the whole body were put together. For the first time it was possible to ask a computer, 'If I administer this new drug, what will the effects be? Not just the effect it was designed to produce, but all the side effects as well?' No more thalidomides it was announced, ever.

"The first models were clumsy, and didn't work as well as they were supposed to. One of the first drugs to be developed without animal testing, a new diabetes treatment, worked just as the computers said it would, until the recipients started developing inoperable brain tumors a year or two later. I'm sure you read about it." Julia had. "The media naturally bayed for blood and demanded that honest citizens be protected from irresponsible callous scientists who allowed such criminally flawed products to be placed on the market. They conveniently forgot that it was their agitation a few years previously that had contributed in large part to the demise of animal testing.

"For several years after the diabetes drug fiasco, nobody developed any new drugs. Animal testing was, if not exactly forbidden, far too dangerous for the scientists concerned, and computer testing was distrusted. Eventually the pharmaceutical companies were feeling the pinch and the media as usual was baying about their criminal irresponsibility in not producing any new drugs.

"All this time the biosimulation people had been quietly working on better and better software, in which I've played a humble part, and we think we finally have solved the problem; we have biosimulation software which actually works. It's been checked out many, many times with existing drugs whose effects we know well, and so far it's always given us the answers we expected. However, it's sufficiently new that it has never been used to develop a new drug which has subsequently been put on the market and mass-tested, so to speak."

"So what you're saying then, Charles, is that if we use this software to develop a means of putting people into what amounts to hibernation for several years at a time, it will probably work, but ..."

"Exactly. Caveat emptor—buyer beware."

Julia was silent for a while. I guess this is as good an offer as I'm likely to get, she thought.

"When can I get hold of this software?"

"How about tomorrow?"

There were several coma-inducing drugs available. She and her team, with Charles Lansdowne's active support, asked their computers, "If we give a healthy subject a dose of this particular drug, put them on life support, what condition are they likely to be in at the end of a fifteen year voyage?"

The answer came back, "Probably dead." (Actually, what the computer said was that the probability of survival under those conditions was 5.37 percent, which translated well enough to 'probably dead'.)

So they experimented with different drugs, changed the drug doses, added others along the way, played around with this and that, all on computer, and by trial and error found a way to keep humans in a coma for four to five years at a time. More than five years was found to be dangerous, so they would wake them up every four years and then keep them awake for three months to allow their bodies to recover before putting them into a coma again. (Not only would their organs need time to recover, but their muscles would need exercise to regain their strength if the voyagers were not to reach their destination so enfeebled they could barely stand up.) The computers said they could expect about a ten percent mortality rate over the course of a fifteen-year voyage, provided all were young, fit and healthy to begin with. The chance of survival went down steeply for anyone over twenty-five at the beginning of the voyage, so that would be the upper age limit of the voyagers. Women had a better survival

rate than men. "That's okay," said Julia. "Men are expendable. Women aren't. They're the ones that have babies."

The computers also told them of an unexpected bonus. Keeping humans in this condition slowed down the aging process. If a twenty-year-old woman went on a fifteen-year voyage and spent most of her time in a drug-induced coma, she would be the biological equivalent of a twenty-seven or -eight years old at the end of it, with perhaps ten to fifteen good child-bearing years left. It would, after all, be futile to send colonists to a new world if they were too old to have children when they got there.

INTERLUDE - ZACK

Zachary Gonzales was a large, untidy young man. Although muscular, his shape leant more towards the potato sack than the Greek god, and his shirttail was always seeking its freedom. While capable of moving surprisingly fast on his large feet when the necessity arose, he was normally slow moving to the point of lethargy. Zack was one of those individuals who simply lacked the internal need for action when there was no call for it. If circumstances demanded he run, then run he would, with surprising speed and stamina, but otherwise he was content to amble along slowly.

Zachary's mother was a Kansas Baptist who, to the dismay of her family and friends, had married a Catholic, and a Mexican at that. Sarah's family proclaimed their Christian forgiveness of her for this unnatural act, even to the extent of inviting Philippe into their home after the marriage. But forgiveness or not, the social temperature was always hovering around the freezing mark, and Sarah and Philippe eventually just drifted away.

Sarah did not miss her family much because she and her mother were two strong characters who fought incessantly when they were together. This was fortunate because Philippe's work took him all over the world for years at a time. Sarah soon became accustomed to uprooting herself and her children and setting up house in some strange corner of the globe. Had their mother not been a solid rock around which the household rotated, Zachary and his younger sister Martha would have grown up in chaos. Instead, they grew up in an environment in which there was always a central core of normality, no matter where they were. It seemed that after Sarah's one act of rebellion—marrying Philippe—she had henceforth decided to conform to her own family's norms and create a Kansas Baptist community in miniature wherever she went. Luckily, Philippe had no interest in religion whatsoever so his Catholic background did not get in the way.

Philippe Gonzales was descended from a long line of Mexican peasants. Had he bred true to his strain, he might have spent his life scratching a living on some hardscrabble plot in Mexico, or perhaps slaving in a sweatshop making machine parts. But by some quirk of genes and the luck to be in the right place at the right time, he won a scholarship to a university in California and graduated in the newly emerging technology of hydroponics.

With earth's population pushing twelve billion, there were more and more mouths to feed every year and less and less farmland with which to do it. Philippe's job was to design and build vast factories that, given sunlight, water, and a handful or two of chemicals, could grow crops. Most of the time for obvious reasons these were built in deserts where sunlight was plentiful and the land was of little use for anything else. Had Philippe been an astute businessman he could have become

a very rich man, for he was as essential to his age as the computer technocrats of the previous century or the steam engineers of the century before that. But since he was no more than a competent engineer, he merely enjoyed a comfortable life, albeit one that required him to travel around the world. His family invariably went with him when he was posted abroad for any extended period.

None of the Gonzales family were graceful in build. Philippe was a heavyset peasant, while Sarah had developed into a broad-hipped matron with muscular forearms and a gravelly voice. If she had lived in India two hundred years previously she might have been a much-feared Memsahib, ruling a household of several dozen retainers with a rod of iron. As it was, she had a knack of commanding instant respect from all around her wherever she set up her household. This was fortunate for her and her family. Philippe's work took them into parts of the world where tension between ethnic or religious groups was a fact of life, and bombings and shootings were regarded as little more than Saturday night fun by the locals.

The Gonzales spent a year or two in the Middle East, then moved on to northern China on the edges of the Gobi desert. Although the Chinese civil war in the 2040s and '50s had resulted in 200 million deaths, mainly from starvation and disease, China's population had more than recovered and was approaching two billion. With much of their farmland devastated by industrial and military pollution, hydroponic factories were vital if further civil wars were to be avoided, and Phillipe's skills were much in demand.

They stayed several years in China, and Zack, as he was universally known, grew up speaking Chinese as well as English with an accent composed of equal parts of Mexico, Kansas, and northern China. Two years of schooling after this in California, where Philippe at that time was running a head office design team, left Zack wondering just who he was. At age eleven he didn't seem to be quite an American, certainly not Mexican, yet equally certainly not Chinese.

"Who am I, Mom?" he wanted to ask after a day at school in which he never quite seemed to fit in. Yet Sarah, for all her strengths, was not the kind of person of whom you could easily ask soul-searching questions. She was an intensely practical tower of strength who would defend her children like a lioness if she thought they were threatened. But so sure was she of her own identity that she could not conceive of others being unsure.

Zack's education was continued in Mexico where Philippe managed a large production plant. Here for the first time Zack felt he had some roots. There were real live aunts and uncles and innumerable cousins to visit. Even here though, Zack felt a stranger. He initially had difficulty understanding their street Spanish, and in any case they lived too far away to be part of his everyday experience. By his early teens, Zack had retreated into himself, a shy child lacking the resources, or perhaps too thin-skinned, to bull his way into any new group and become part of it.

By sixteen, Zack was an accomplished linguist, fluently at ease in Spanish and English, and competent in half a dozen other languages. Lacking any real social life he threw himself into schoolwork, achieving academic distinctions that he would never have obtained otherwise. But by his seventeenth birthday Zack had had enough. "I'm leaving school, Mom. There's nothing in it for me anymore."

Sarah, who was the undisputed head of their household when it came to such matters, was not perturbed. Time for Zack to spread his wings a little, she thought. He can always continue his schooling later.

"Okay, Zack, it's your choice. What do you want to do?"

"I don't know. Travel, I guess, but on my own this time."

Three months later, Zack was sitting in a café in Tangier. He had wandered around Europe for a few weeks, done the obligatory sightseeing, and discovered that mere sights quickly bored him. His money was beginning to run low and he needed to find work, but found that the prospects for even the meanest of jobs were worse than in America. A casual acquaintance mentioned that it was easier in North Africa, and since he was in Spain at the time it was easy enough to take the train through the Gibraltar tunnel.

With his American clothing he was every inch a student tourist, yet his calm demeanor and willingness to listen quietly allowed him to fade into the background. He had checked in to a cheap hotel as soon as he reached town—there was usually some kind of accommodation aimed at wandering students in every large town—and now was gradually feeling his way around the place.

He sat with a coffee in front of him, absorbing the atmosphere. The café was a small shabby affair a little removed from the tourist center of the city, which Zack instinctively avoided. The babble around him gradually began to sort itself out into individual voices. Some were French, heavily accented to Zack's ears, while others were in an unknown language. He began listening to the French at the table next to him. There were four of them, heavily built men in their thirties and forties, looked as if they might be off-duty police or security guards perhaps. They all had that arrogant, authoritative air of the minor official who has bulled his way up the ranks, an I'm-in-charge-here-and-don't-you-forget-it look that brooked no interruptions or interference. Zack wanted to strike up a conversation with someone, to ask about the city, but decided very quickly that these were not the right people at all. Instead he sat quietly, idly listening to their conversation.

" ...so the boss gets a new batch, doesn't check that they've been processed properly, picks a pretty boy out and starts screwing him, and a couple of the others just walk out the door. Twenty minutes later, when that lump of dung realizes what's happened, he hits the panic button and expects us to run our asses off to cover his mistake. He can go rot for all I care. May his balls drop off—and they probably will one of these days, the way he lights into everything with an asshole."

"You're right, Jorge, it's a hot day. So what are we looking for, anyway?"

"Oh, the usual. About ten or eleven years old, male, skin color a bit lighter than the locals. Just look for anyone looking a bit dazed or lost and haul 'em in. Alive if possible, but don't pick up one of the locals or we're in trouble. We search this sector; the others will take care of theirs."

They stood up and clumped heavily out. Zack stayed for a while, puzzling over their talk, then got up and walked out himself. He decided to wander around the place, to familiarize himself and see what was to be seen. He was reasonably confident that his sense of direction would enable him to find his way back again.

Perhaps it was the unfamiliar pattern of little winding alleys, or perhaps Zack was too interested in absorbing the unfamiliar sights and smells around him, but half an hour later he had to admit to himself he was lost. He was not unduly perturbed, but continued walking at random deeper into a maze of narrow alleys between tall buildings, confident that sooner or later he would find his way out. He rounded a sharp corner and was nearly bowled over by a small figure that ran into him at full tilt. He instinctively clutched at the child as he fought to retain his balance.

"You there, hold him right there. He's ours," shouted a loud voice about fifty yards off.

The child—Zack could see it was a young boy—was nearly exhausted, and seemed unable to run any further. He clutched at Zack, getting between Zack and the owner of the loud voice, who was approaching fast. "Don't let them take me," he said.

It took Zack a couple of seconds to realize he was speaking Mandarin Chinese, a language he hadn't heard for several years. The illogicality of it struck him: what was this child, obviously speaking his birth tongue, doing half a world away in a North African slum? By this time, Loud Voice had reached Zack, and pushed him aside to reach the child.

That was a mistake. Zack did not like being pushed and was too large to be pushed with impunity. He turned sideways, swinging the child away from his assailant as he did so, and returned the push with a shoulder check, catching Loud Voice in the chest as he reached forward. More by accident than design, it was a well-timed maneuver. Loud Voice gave a surprised grunt and sat down heavily. Zack thought he recognized him as one of the men in the café.

A heavy hand fell on Zack's shoulder and pulled him roughly around. Zack found himself looking at another of the men from the café, holding a nightstick that had evidently seen considerable usage judging by the dents and scratches on it. The child tried to run, but the man holding Zack casually put his foot out and tripped him. He fell heavily, and didn't move. Loud Voice had got to his feet by this time and picked the child up as if it were a bundle of firewood.

"Just keep out of our way, m'sieur," said the one with the nightstick. "This one is our property, we've paid for him, and to interfere with him would be theft. You wouldn't want us to make a complaint to the magistrate, would you? The jails here are not good places for well brought-up young men to find themselves."

Zack wasn't quite sure what he had got himself into, only that whatever it was he felt sorry for the child and quite helpless, since Loud Voice was now about to disappear around a corner with him. He opened his mouth and spluttered the beginning of a protest, but the other simply patted his shoulder, saying, "You meant well, m'sieur, but you are in the wrong here. Enjoy your stay in Tangier." With that he walked swiftly off to join his companion, leaving Zack standing in the street with his mouth hanging open.

Discontented and inwardly seething—although about what he could not say—Zack found his way back to his hotel. Not one to spill his heart out to strangers, he was nonetheless sufficiently moved to tell the desk clerk about his experience. The answer was unexpected. The clerk looked at him as if he had walked in with dog shit on his shoes, and remarked icily that decent people didn't bother themselves about such things.

Taken aback, Zack slouched off to his room, but was unable to forget the incident. He hung around the tourist areas of the city for a few days, but the joy of discovery had gone out of him. Finally he decided to go find the American consul in the hope of acquiring a sympathetic and knowledgeable ear.

Two days later, Zack was ushered into a moderately imposing office in which sat a moderately imposing man next to a very imposing American flag. By his speech he was evidently a local resident, and he didn't look particularly sympathetic, but Zack plunged on regardless. As Zack told his story, the consul's expression changed from boredom to interest to a wholly undecipherable look.

"Well, at least you haven't come to me with the usual hard-luck story I get from students. That's a relief at any rate. But why tell me about this? What do you expect me to do about it?"

"I'm not sure. I just felt an injustice was being done, and I felt sorry for that poor kid. What was he doing here anyway? He was born in northern China, I'm certain of that. I want to do something to help him, but I don't know what to do until I know what it was all about."

The consul looked at Zack for a moment. "I don't think you know much about how the world operates, do you, Mr. Gonzales. Perhaps I should tell you a few of the facts of life.

"That's a nice jacket you have. Buy it in the US, did you? Could I have a look at it for a moment?"

Somewhat perplexed, Zack took off his jacket and handed it over. The consul looked at it for a moment, then examined a label sewn on the inside of one of the inner pockets. Handing it back he said, "As I thought, your jacket was made right here in the big plant on the other side of town.

"Where do you think all these nice cheap things you buy in your shops come from? They certainly aren't made in the States. I can guarantee that. Your labor laws and trade unions have priced your own workers right out of the market. You think you're too good to make all these things, yet you still demand them in your shops. Well, for your information, these things are mostly made in megaplants like the one right here, by ten-year-olds like the one you saw the other day."

"But, but, I thought there were laws against that sort of thing," spluttered Zack, in the beginnings of outrage.

"There probably are in the US, but in the Tangier Free Trade Zone and a few dozen other places like it around the world, there aren't. The rest of the world doesn't care or isn't willing to give up its luxuries so it looks the other way, but it's places like this that supply the shopping malls of the world. The kid you saw was probably bought a few days ago in China and shipped here in a batch of a hundred or so. He'll work for ten years or so at the plant, until he's of no more use to them."

"But doesn't anybody care about these things?" cried Zack. "We were always taught about the dignity and the sanctity of life in our schools."

"Son," said the consul gently, "when you have twelve billion people in the world and rising, there isn't much room for dignity and sanctity. In most parts of the world, life is cheap. It's like any other commodity. When there's too much of it, the price goes down. Didn't they ever teach you that in school? You just happen to be a very privileged young man, born in a privileged society, where you haven't had to come face to face with the realities of life. Welcome to the real world."

Zack sat speechless for a few moments, his thoughts whirling incoherently. Finally, the memory of the helpless child who had come

to him and whom Zack, it now seemed to him, had refused to help, came back. "What will happen to those kids when they become, like you said, of no more use?"

The consul for the first time would not look Zack in the face. "I don't know," he said "and if I were you I wouldn't ask. Just get one thing into your head. The plant out there is making enormous amounts of money, a lot of which flows into this city. Anyone who does anything to interrupt that flow is liable to get squashed very flat, very fast. And now if you'll excuse me, I have a lot of other things to attend to."

Zack walked out of the consul's office confused and unhappy. He could neither believe nor fully understand what he had just heard, but the face of the terrified child kept intruding on his thoughts. As he walked, not caring where he was going, confusion gave way to anger, a deep inchoate anger. Zack wanted to lash out, to rend, to kill, yet there was nothing around him which seemed to deserve his anger. Just a sense of frustrated failure and the face of a terrified child.

He found himself back at the hotel, not quite knowing how he had got there. The same desk clerk was on duty that had rebuffed him earlier. He walked up to the desk and asked, "How do I get to the plant where the foreign children work?" Something in his manner caused the clerk to forget his disdain, and he gave Zack directions.

The plant was vast. Over two square miles of buildings, storage yards, rail lines, shipping terminals and warehouses. It was surrounded by a high, heavy chain link fence that seemed to be designed to keep people in rather than out. Zack started walking around it. It was easy to do so, because there was a perimeter road running outside the fence, with a neatly graveled swath about ten yards wide between the road and the fence. The gravel was spotless, and seemed to be freshly raked. Inside the fence was another ten-yard stretch of gravel, and, Zack noticed, a second fence beyond that.

The sun was hot as he walked the perimeter road. It did not seem to lead anywhere, just around the plant. After about ten minutes, a light truck approached him from the opposite direction and skidded to a halt in front of him. A heavy looking man, reminiscent of the group in the café a few days previously, leaned out of the cab.

"What the hell are you doing here? This is private property."

"There's no fence around it," said Zack, reasonably but rather tensely.

"Don't give me that shit. Get the hell out of here if you know what's good for you, or I'll have you thrown out."

The truck accelerated past Zack, missing him by no more than a couple of inches. Deciding that discretion was temporarily the better part of valor, Zack moved off the road away from the fence into the scrub, and continued on his way. The going was harder, but there were no fences or signs nearby so Zack assumed he was safe.

He crossed a double railway line, which entered the perimeter fence through massive gates. The gates were shut and it was evidently well lit at night, judging by the number of overhead lights. Zack continued on. The sun was even hotter now, and he wished he had brought some water. A few sounds came from the factory, but otherwise there was silence, broken only by the sound of insects in the scrub.

About halfway round, with the plant on his right and unbroken wasteland on his left, a truck came hurtling down the road towards him. It stopped several yards away, and three men wearing some kind of uniform got out and walked towards him. At the same time another truck came up behind him, and disgorged another two men, similarly attired. Feeling that he was in trouble, Zack turned briefly to run, then thought better of it. Apart from several hundred miles of desert there was nowhere to run. He stood his ground and waited.

The five men spread out so as to encircle him, then closed in. Zack waited, outwardly calm but with a fluttering of apprehension in his belly. When they reached him, there were no preliminaries. Two of them grabbed his arms and hustled him to one of the trucks, while the other three followed as escort. Zack was half pushed, half thrown into the back seat, with a guard—he assumed that was their function—on either side. Not a word was spoken while the truck drove inside the main gate and stopped at the back of a building a hundred yards or so further on.

Zack found himself, not altogether of his own volition, in front of a desk behind which sat a large, coarse-featured man looking coldly at Zack. Standing beside him Zack recognized the heavy with the nightstick who had spoken to him a few days previously. As if to confirm this, Nightstick nodded and said, "That's the one, boss. Attacked Jorge when we were retrieving the absconder the other day."

The boss, whatever he was boss of, looked at Zack for a few seconds more. Finally, "You're in big trouble, m'sieur. First, you attack one of my men when he's doing his job. Then, you come snooping around where you've no business to be. So, before we hand you over to the police, who are going to throw you out of the country, you're going to tell us why you're doing this. And just in case you were wondering, the police here won't worry at all if you're, shall we say, a little bit the worse for wear when we hand you over."

Zack was fighting hard not to panic. He had never been in such a situation before. Suddenly, with a flash of inspiration born of desperation, he knew what to do. He had come here to find out what was happening to those children. Very well, now he was here he had to find a way to stay here, and to stay with sufficient freedom to move around at will.

He forced himself to relax, and flashed what he hoped was a confident smile at the boss. "I came here for a job, boss. I knew if I wandered around outside your guys would pick me up, and what better way to meet my future employer. As for that business with, what was his name, Jorge? It was just an accident. The kid ran into me, Jorge pushed me to get at the kid, and the rest was just instinct. Hey, I'm sorry if I hurt his feelings, but next time I see him I'll buy him a drink."

Zack's speech had got the boss's attention. He stared at Zack for a few seconds more then, guardedly, "What sort of a job were you thinking of, m'sieur?"

"Why, a security guard, of course. Plant like this must need a lot of guys who can pull their weight, and I need the work. Reckon I'd be good at it, too."

"What experience do you have, m'sieur?"

Zack cheered up immensely at this. The boss appeared to be showing some interest. However, he had enough sense not to fabricate anything. Like almost everyone else in the world, his life history was available on a computer somewhere. "At this trade, not much, boss. But I'm fit and strong, and I speak several languages, including the one that kid spoke. It's Chinese, and he comes from northern China, if you're interested."

This definitely got the boss's attention. "Where did you learn all these languages, m'sieur?" Zack gave him a thumbnail sketch of his life. The boss turned his head towards Nightstick and cocked an inquiring eye at him. "Well, Pedro?"

Pedro grunted. "Could be useful. Let me do some background checking first. Might be a plant."

The boss turned back to Zack. "We might have a use for you, m'sieur. But we have some checking to do first. My men will take care of you till then."

The next morning found Zack with a new uniform, a nightstick, and a few other implements of the trade, and a Spartan room in what was evidently the guards' barracks. He had tried phoning home to let his family know where he was, but his smartphone didn't seem to work—there appeared to be some kind of interference whenever he tried to use it or to access social media. He made a mental note to look into it later, but dismissed it as a minor problem to be sorted out later. However, the food was good and the other guards were not unfriendly.

"Hey, I hear you're the one that knocked Jorge down. About time someone did that to him."

"Good thing you're not on his squad, though. Reckon he'll bear a grudge for a long time."

Zack presented himself as a bumbling, cheerful dimwit, and it seemed to go down well. Apparently nothing much else was required or desired of him. Abdul, his squad leader, was a dour individual who took him to his assigned station and told him what was expected of him.

"You do what you're told, when you're told and how you're told. I got no use for guards who try to think for themselves. You do what I say and we get along. You screw up and I give you shit. Okay?"

Since Abdul was a mean-looking individual, larger than Zack with a scarred face and aggressively bad breath, Zack was inclined to believe him. He mumbled, "Yessir," which seemed to satisfy Abdul, and meekly followed along behind him.

The plant contained a bewildering array of buildings of all shapes and sizes. They entered one of the larger ones, went up a flight of stairs, and came to a doorway. Abdul placed the palm of his hand against a translucent screen, there was a brief buzz, the door opened, and they went in.

The room seemed to recede into infinity. Lines of apparently identical machines were tended by a number of small, slow-moving figures, dressed identically in drab coveralls. A low murmur of machinery filled the air, but apart from an occasional clatter of sharper sound there was an almost dreamlike, underwater quality about the place. Abdul marched into the room with Zack trailing behind. The door shut automatically behind them with an audible click.

Abdul marched halfway down the room, looking neither to left nor right. He stopped at a station where another security guard stood, idly swinging his nightstick and looking intently around him. "All in order, Franz?"

"Okay, boss."

"This is Zack. He'll be on your shift beginning today."

"Okay, boss." Evidently, small talk was not required on Abdul's squad.

Abdul beckoned to Zack. "Come."

They approached an area where a couple of the workers, who looked to be of Chinese origin and no more than ten or twelve years old, stood as if waiting for something to happen. Zack was struck by their air of dumb dejection. They appeared as if they were barely aware of their surroundings, knowing only that they did not want to be there, but had neither hope nor expectation that things would be better elsewhere. Abdul caught one of them by the shoulder and spun him round in a firm grip. The child staggered slightly, but otherwise made no resistance.

"Most times they're docile, like this, but occasionally they get out of hand. When that happens, you do this." Abdul raised his nightstick and dealt the child a sharp blow to the base of the skull. The little form collapsed unconscious without a murmur. "Now let me see you do it on that one there."

Zack felt sick. His instinct was to throw up, then run out of this hideous place, never looking back until he was across the ocean. But he had come here to help these people, so he told himself, and running wasn't going to help anyone. If he had to hurt some of them to help the rest, so be it. He sensed Abdul watching him intently.

"What's up, kid? Squeamish?"

Feeling that words would be useless, he reached out and grasped the second child. He was struck by how frail it seemed. He spun the child round as gently as he could; it—she, he realized—stood docilely enough. He raised his nightstick in a trembling hand.

"Nah, not like that. You'll do permanent damage like that, and then the Production Manager will complain to the Big Chief. Aim for that spot there, enough force to jolt them, but not enough to send them flying."

Concentrating on the indicated spot on the back of the child's neck, and shutting his mind to everything else, Zack let fly. It wasn't hard enough. The child gave a feeble scream and dropped to the floor, clutching the back of her head in both hands.

"What the hell's going on here?" A tough looking woman in her thirties strode up to them. "How the hell do you expect me to meet my production quota if you go messing around with my operators? Go play your stupid games somewhere else, you fly-blown lump of camel shit."

Abdul grinned at her with easy familiarity. "No problem, just breaking in a new guard."

The woman ran her eye up and down Zack appraisingly. Zack was embarrassed by her frankly carnal look and felt himself blushing. "Hey, he's cute, isn't he," she said.

Abdul chuckled. "You keep your hands off him, you old bag, at least until his shift's over. What are you staring at," he said to Zack. "Take these two," indicating with a nudge of his foot the two children lying on the floor, one unconscious, the other moaning gently, "through the blue door over there. They'll deal with them inside."

Zack picked them up, one under each arm, one limp, the other barely moving. They were quite light. Going through the indicated door, he found himself in an area which had the appearance of a hospital. There was a wheeled stretcher nearby onto which he placed them, as gently as he could. Another woman, whom Zack took to be some kind of medic, was sitting in a small office, dictating something into a computer. She looked up as Zack came in, wiggled a couple of fingers at him, then went on with what she was doing. Not knowing what else to do, Zack stood waiting.

After a couple of minutes the medic came out of her office. "Alright, there's no need to stay. I'll look after everything." Seeing Zack's irresolution, she added, "You're new here, aren't you?"

"Yes, ma'am. Uh, I was, uh, wondering if this sort of thing happens often?"

"You are new, aren't you. Sure it does, happens all the time, that's why we're here."

Seeing Zack's puzzled look, she added, "Look, when we get a new batch of operators they undergo treatment to make them docile. It's called personality suppression if you want to be technical, but most people call it brain-burning. Anyway, there's a delicate balance between too much and too little. If there's too little, they're difficult to handle, particularly when they get older, and if there's too much they become useless. So we have to accept that every now and then one or two of them get out of hand. That's where you come in. Your job is to deal with them with as little harm as you can, then bring 'em to us. We patch them up, like these two, who'll probably be back on shift tomorrow, none the worse for wear.

"Let me see, you must be on Abdul's squad, right? He uses a billy club. He's quite an artist with it. Some of the other squad leaders use gas. That's okay too, but if there's a crowd of them, it means you wheel in a dozen at a time, and the shift managers don't like that. You work at becoming as good as Abdul and you'll be okay. Now be off with you, I've got work to do."

Zack left, deep in thought. Abdul had evidently finished chatting to the supervisor and was checking something on a computer screen at the guard station. As Zack approached, he turned around.

"So what took you so long? I said take them to the body shop, not get yourself laid, not while you're on duty. Next time I give you an order, you do it then get back on station on the double. Understand?"

"Yes, boss."

For the next hour, Abdul toured him around the factory floor. The machines appeared to be making some kind of shirts, each one doing a different operation, and the human operators fed them with raw materials and carted the finished products away. He guessed there were perhaps a hundred children on the floor with, as far as he could tell, three or four adult supervisors, including Abdul's friend. Each supervisor had a cattle prod which he or she used whenever necessary, and a panic button in case things got out of control. Zack was given a receiver, which he wore on his wrist to indicate the area where he was needed. His job was to sprint over there and sort things out, which meant in practice using his nightstick. The children were of no danger to the adults, but unless stamped out promptly a kind of low-level hysteria could spread among them, which interrupted production.

By the end of the day Zack had clubbed a couple more and taken them to the body shop (it was technically the Operator Care Centre, but everyone called it the body shop). He felt sick at heart. He felt he should have thrown his club away and left the plant, never to return again. But something kept him going, a feeling that eventually he could help these creatures—it was becoming difficult for him to think of them as fellow humans—if only he could stick it out for a little while.

The next few days went by in a blur. Zack settled into a routine. The plant operated twenty-four hours a day, with two twelve-hour shifts. At the end of the shift, two of the guards escorted the children back to what he guessed were their living quarters. At the beginning of the next shift, they were escorted back again. For some reason, there was rarely any trouble on these trips; they usually just plodded dully along, two by two, holding hands as they went.

Zack was fortunate enough to have started on the day shift, but next month he would be on nights. At the end of each day he was content to eat, watch holovision for a while, then sleep. He sometimes wondered what the operators—he soon began to call them that, rather than children—did when they were not working. He asked a few people, but nobody seemed to know or care. Apparently they were looked after by a department called Operator Housekeeping, whose employees were considered to be at the bottom of the social scale in the plant.

At the end of his first week he had a day off and decided to go into town. Wearing his civilian clothes, he approached the main gate. As usual it was shut, but there was an identipanel against which he held his ID badge, expecting the gate to open for him. Nothing happened. Zack wandered over to the gatehouse.

"Hey, how do I get out of here?"

"Like anyone else, just hold your badge against the panel and the gate'll open."

"Well, I tried it, and it didn't."

"Let's see your badge then."

Zack passed his badge to the guard, who held it in front of his computer panel.

"Jesus Mary, don't those jerks in security management tell you anything? You've been here a week, right? You don't have pass out privileges until next year."

"What?"

"Listen, son. You signed some papers when they gave you that badge and everything else, right? Well, if you'd read the fine print you'd have found that you agreed to stay on site during your probationary period, which is a year for guys like you. Now piss off and don't let me see you again for a year."

Back at the barracks Zack mooched around for a while. The night shift was sleeping, the day shift was working; nobody was about except for some of the child workers who did menial tasks around their living quarters. Zack hardly thought of them as human by this time, indeed he barely noticed them. He still couldn't get his smart phone to work; there was just a hissing noise whenever he tried to use it. Finally, out of boredom he made his way down to the staff commissary.

Wandering through the aisles of what was in effect a supermarket, Zack began to realize the scale of the plant. There was enough merchandise here for a town of several thousand people. Somehow he doubted that the child workers would ever be allowed here. Indeed, when they were lined up and marched them off to their barracks at the end of a twelve-hour shift, stumbling with tiredness, he doubted that they did much at all until the next day.

He was examining some electronics on display when he felt a finger dragged lightly down his spine. He jumped and turned fast. Facing him with a grin on her face was the tough-looking supervisor he had met on his first morning. Her name was Shana or something like that, he thought. Although he had seen her every day since then, he had not spoken to her.

"Bit jumpy aren't we, big boy? Looks like we have the same day off. What are you doing today?"

"Er, nothing much. I was going to go into town but..."

"And you found you couldn't. Well, I'll tell you what. Since you're a real cute looker, I'll show you around today. Who knows, you might see some real interesting sights."

In a very short time Zack found himself back in her quarters. It soon became apparent that the interesting sights Shana was referring to were under her clothes. Zack was a virgin with a strict Baptist background offset by the surging hormones of a healthy seventeen-year-old. He barely made it into her before exploding.

Shana gave a slightly puzzled grunt as Zack rolled limply off her. There was a slight pause. "Not done much of this, have you?" said Shana, surprisingly gently.

"Umm—this was my first time."

"Oh my. If I'd known, I'd have done something special. Maybe not though, you'd never even have gotten into me if I had. Well, it looks like I'm going to have to educate you."

And she did.

Looking back on the next few months, Zack had the impression of being dragged, not too unwillingly, behind a runaway sexual train. Shana was lonely and childless. Her husband had taken up with a younger woman after she had failed to conceive in ten years, and more in pride than for any other reason she had elected to live on site at the plant where she worked. She was available to sort out production problems at any hour of the day or night (their lovemaking was more than once interrupted by Shana's pager) and she got a promotion and more money. But her life felt empty.

In the depths of her mind, Shana was never quite sure whether Zack was her lover or her child. Perhaps a bit of both. At all events, as they rutted on her sweaty bed she clutched him to her in a tight embrace, as if to try to fill the void she felt within. Zack learnt a great deal, but always had the feeling of being stifled.

Often, after they were spent, Shana would talk. She was curious about Zack's background, and he to a lesser extent about hers.

"What's a nice American boy like you doing in a dump like this? Sure, you can have a good time here," this with a suggestive wiggle, "but when all is said and done it's a dead end job."

In the beginning, Zack was unsure whether to confide in her his crusading zeal for the children. After a while, he approached the subject obliquely.

"Doesn't it worry you sometimes, having all those little kids slaving away under you?"

"Oh, they're no danger. The only reason for having you guys around is to keep them working."

"No, I didn't mean that. Don't you ever, well, feel sorry for them?"

"Who me? I suppose I did once, but you get used to it. They're not people, you know, just machines with hands. You keep 'em working as long as you can, then you get new ones when they're worn out."

"What happens to them when they're worn out?"

"Beats me. I just indent for some new ones, and the old ones disappear. None of my business."

And she would not be drawn further.

A few days later, one of the machines on Zack's floor jammed and a maintenance technician was called. It was necessary for Zack to stand near him while he worked and shoo the operators back to their posts. They had a tendency to gather around anything unusual, their mouths agape, occasionally holding hands with each other, silently watching but not quite comprehending with the remnants of their tattered minds.

The technician was a slim young Chinese with a pleasant manner. Besides the universal French, he was delighted to find that Zack could converse haltingly with him in his native language, and Zack was sufficiently bored to enjoy the challenge.

"Do these break down often?" said Zack.

"Not these ones. Some of the more complex ones on the other floors give us a lot more trouble. This one is fairly simple, but it tends to get clogged with cloth dust."

"I often wonder why they don't replace the operators with machines. Then they could work twenty-four hours a day instead of having to march new shifts in every twelve hours."

The technician grinned. "They use them because of a little thing called the human hand. Sure, we can make machines to be as versatile as humans, but they're expensive and need a lot of maintenance. These," he indicated the operators with a contemptuous jerk of his head, "are dirt cheap and don't need any maintenance."

"Why's that?"

The technician paused and looked at Zack as if seeing him for the first time.

"You're American, aren't you? Yet you must have been to China to speak the language. I guess you didn't really see what it was like in the poorer districts. Me, I grew up there and worked my butt off to get out.

"Listen, m'sieur. There are nearly two billion people in China. In the poorer areas that means standing room only. If the harvest is poor, people die—many of them. When the labor agents come round, the village elders practically beg them to take their ten-year-olds. The more the agents take, the more chance there is that the rest of them will survive until the next harvest. Sure, I don't like seeing them here—I could have been one of them—but their life here is a lot better than it would have been back home."

There was a fierceness about the way he said this that effectively ended the conversation. Zack stood around until he had finished, then went back to his normal work. It seemed that any interruption to the operators' routine upset them, and Zack had several disturbances to quell on that shift. As a result he carted off several limp bodies to the body shop. He was getting to be quite skillful with his nightstick. Even Abdul, who had hovered around initially like a broody hen now left him alone most of the time, which Zack took as a compliment.

The last time in that shift that Zack went into the body shop and laid a limp form on the trolley, the medic clucked her tongue. "She'll need to be replaced soon, by the looks of her."

"Why, how old is she?" asked Zack.

The medic picked up the limp wrist and scanned the barcode tattoo on it with a hand scanner. Crossing to her computer screen, she said, "We've had her eleven years, so that would make her twenty-one or so. That's about as long as they last."

Zack was amazed. "But she doesn't look twenty-one."

"No, of course not. They're treated to retard growth. Makes them easier to handle. For one thing, they're not allowed to reach puberty, otherwise you'd really have a tough job out there."

"What will happen to her now?"

"I shouldn't worry about that if I were you. There's a special unit deals with these things. Just puts them to sleep, quietly. Now be off with you, you've brought me quite enough to do this shift without standing around here gossiping."

The weeks and the months went by. Zack settled into a routine, mainly because there was little alternative. Twelve hours a day, six days a week. Most times he was in a production center, but occasionally he did a shift or two at a perimeter gate, albeit in a role where he couldn't access the gate opening controls. He still couldn't get his smart phone to work, but there was an internet café where he could send and receive e-mails. Strangely enough, when he tried to send descriptions of the child workers, the information didn't seem to get through, judging by the replies he got from his family.

Shana monopolized most of his off-duty time, but after a while Zack was surprised to find himself arranging his shifts so they didn't coincide with hers. He felt strangely guilty about this. After all, hadn't Shana told him how much she needed him, how she couldn't bear to see him even talking to another woman?

Perhaps Zack was maturing, or maybe Shana had given him confidence, but Zack was finding he liked talking to other women. Female operators didn't count, of course. Only the occasional one could command a few slurred words. But there were plenty of other women in the plant. A few like Shana lived on site, but most commuted in every day.

Whenever Shana caught him talking to another woman or even imagined he had, there was a blazing row.

"You lying, cheating, cunt-sniffing bastard, what do you take me for? You think I'm just another cheap whore you can pick up and put down again after all I've done for you? I wouldn't give you the drippings from my nose, you slimy streak of pig shit..."

Zack did not have Shana's facility with words, and in any case there was little point in him opening his mouth once she had started. She probably would not have noticed. She always calmed down after a while and then made love with added zest and abandonment. Of late, though, it seemed to Zack that her rages were becoming more frequent and more violent. Zack was by inclination a peaceful person and Shana worried him. Was this what being in love was all about? Maybe he should think seriously about being a monk.

The end came a few days after Zack's eighteenth birthday. They had had an even more blazing row than usual, or at least Shana had screamed at him louder and longer than usual, and then she threw a glass vase at him. She had thrown things before, but this time it hit him hard, cutting him on the side of the head. Zack stood there in shock for a moment, then lunged at her in rage. Shana stopped her tirade, looked at him in alarm then shrank back, frightened by what she had done. Zack grabbed her and shook her like a dog shaking a rat.

He paused, and realized in a moment of clarity that he was quite capable of killing her. In disgust at himself, at Shana and at the whole relationship between them, he released her and walked out.

As he strode away, Shana came running after him. "Come back, baby, I didn't mean it. I'll make it up to you..."

Zack turned on his heel. There were other people around, watching interestedly. "Get. Out. Of. My. Life. You. Bitch." He walked off, leaving Shana with her mouth hanging open.

He never spoke to her again. Shana blackened his name to the best of her ability, spreading stories of his impotence, cruelty and anything else she could think of. None of this did Zack any harm. Indeed, Abdul looked at him with new respect and grinned cheerfully at him the next few times he saw him. After a while, Shana found a new lover, and things calmed down.

Shortly after this, Zack was transferred to Operator Receiving. The security department had decided he was reliable enough, and needed someone with a gift for languages who could help with intakes of new operators. It was an iron-clad rule that operators came from a different part of the world. North African children might be, and frequently were, sold to labor agents, but always they went to plants in Asia or South America, or anywhere but North Africa. Zack's plant had a supply contract with a Chinese labor agency.

On his first day in Receiving, Zack reported to his new supervisor, a sharp-faced middle-aged woman with badly dyed hair (her grey roots were plainly visible). "There's a new batch coming in this afternoon. No billy clubs. They're not processed when we get them. The agency sends them in sedated, and we do the processing here. Any problems, you deal with them by talking to them. If things get out of hand, you'll have a hand-operated sedater needle, but don't use it unless you have to. That stuff's expensive. Any questions?"

Zack could think of plenty, but none that he thought Hatchet-face would think relevant, so he just shook his head and said nothing.

There were four other guards on duty with him, so he decided to follow their lead.

That afternoon, several closed trucks arrived, and disgorged a horde of children into the building. Zack was shocked. These were not the empty-eyed, indistinguishable automatons he was used to. These were children. Dirty, ragged, smelly, dazed from sedatives and weary with travel, but children, human children.

Luckily for Zack, there was no trouble that afternoon. He just helped herd them to where the receiving staff stripped, showered, injected, shaved their hair (crawling with lice in some cases, Zack noticed with a shudder), and put them to bed in a large room with a hospital like feel and smell to it. Whatever the injection was, they were asleep almost before they lay down. Zack saw the staff hooking up drip feeds and catheters before he left.

"What's next?" Zack asked his shift boss as they left.

"For that lot, nothing for the next week. They stay there while they're being processed. But tomorrow there's another bunch just coming out of primary processing. There's usually some action there. Bring your nightstick."

The next morning Zack was on duty when a batch that had been received the previous week was awakened. After the initial brain-burning they were confused, with just enough residual emotional capability to feel frightened. Most of them huddled in groups looking dejected and lost, but a few became violent. There was no point in trying to talk to them; they had lost the ability to understand. The guards' nightsticks were much in evidence.

It was a morning fraught with tension for Zack, and he felt exhausted at the end of it. "How long does this go on for?" he asked the squad leader.

"Not long. They'll go into primary training this afternoon for a couple of weeks, and that soon sorts them out. They use cattle prods there, same as on the production floors, but they can turn the power up on the training units. The ops soon get to know what's good for them.

"Meanwhile, there's the usual one or two who didn't make it through brain-burning. You can go escort the meat wagon round to disposal. They should be loading up at the rear dock about now."

An anonymous closed van was waiting. Zack got into the passenger seat beside the driver. In the back were some huddled shapes under a blanket. The driver, a small, thin, middle-aged man, did not seem to have any conversational powers beyond a disinterested grunt, so the trip was made in silence.

Operator Disposal was an anonymous building on the far side of the plant, well away from any of the production areas. It was in a wasteland of repair shops and storage yards, and was undistinguished except for its tall chimney. The driver made his way to the rear of the building and backed the van through a doorway into what was evidently an unloading dock. The outer door shut as the van came to a halt.

Zack followed the driver out and watched him open rear door of the van and pull the blanket away. Three small, naked corpses lay there. "Okay, you can do something for a change, don't see why an old man like me should have to do all the work," said the driver. He indicated a trolley on the dock, and Zack began lifting the corpses onto it. They were cold and stiff. He lifted them as tenderly as he could, as if his gentle handling could in some way compensate for all the indignities they had suffered.

"Come on, come on, no need to take all day," grumbled the driver. Zack wanted to shut him up, smash his teeth down his throat, but felt that violence would somehow be a further indignity to these children so he ignored him. The driver opened the inner doors of the dock and Zack followed through, pushing the loaded trolley in front of him. They moved down a short passageway and through a further set of doors. Near him was a conveyor belt, and beside it, stacked like cordwood, were several dozen small frozen corpses.

Several men in white overalls were loading corpses onto the conveyer. A supervisor was reading barcodes on the corpses' arms with a scanner. He turned round as Zack walked in. "You're just in time for the next firing. Just drop those on the conveyer with the rest." Zack did so, as gently and as reverently as he could. The other corpses were being thrown on the conveyer like sides of beef. The supervisor looked sharply at Zack. "First time here, is it?"

Zack nodded. "I shouldn't let it get to you too much if I were you," said the supervisor with a grin, running his scanner over the arms of the corpses Zack had brought in. "We do this all the time. And sooner or later someone's going to be doing it to you and me. When you finish your shift, get yourself a woman and screw her. That'll cheer you up," he said jovially, clapping Zack on the back.

Zack quickly walked out with his head bowed. He felt he had failed. He had come here to help these children, and here he was assisting at their funerals. No, you couldn't even call them funerals. More like garbage disposal. His eyes blinded by tears, he stumbled back

into the van. On the way back, the driver became talkative. "Allah be praised, but I'm glad I don't work there. Gives an old man like me the creeps. It's alright for youngsters like you, you've got your whole life in front of you, but for an old man like me..." and so on. Zack ignored him.

That evening, Zack got himself drunk. Being a Muslim country, alcohol was frowned upon, but it was easy enough to get hold of if you wanted it. Zack wanted it.

Soon, Zack's first year was up. Although his contract called for him to work a further four years with a hefty bonus at the end of that time, Zack had no intention of staying any longer. As soon as he was able, he made a trip into town, and never went back. He had his passport and enough money for a flight back to the US, and that was all he needed. He took the Gibraltar tunnel back to Spain and caught the first available flight.

Zack parent's were back in California by this time, and there Zack went. It was difficult to know what to say to them. "Hi, Mom, guess what, I've been helping to kill little children for the past year." No. If he were a Catholic, perhaps he could confess to a priest, but he was a Baptist, and a not very enthusiastic one at that. Yet he could not, must not, remain silent.

It was Sarah who solved his problem for him. She had seen her son leave, a rather serious but essentially likeable boy. Fifteen months later he had come back a tortured young man. When they were alone one day, she looked him full in the eye and asked, "What happened, son?"

Zack told her. Initially with dry eyes, then as the enormity of the past year bore down upon him, with tears, until at last he could barely speak. When he could go no further, Sarah held him for a while, barely able to believe him, knowing only that this was her son and he was in deep torment.

Finally, Sarah, the ever-practical mother, asked, "What are you going to do next, Zack?"

"I have to tell other people what's happening there. I have to tell the world."

Sarah thought awhile. Unlike Zack, she had been an adult when they were in China. She had a clear idea of the overcrowding and sheer competition for resources that was a part of life there. Although what her son had told her was new to her, it did not altogether surprise her. But if Zack felt that he had to tell people, if only to ease his soul, she would help him. He was her son.

"I know a journalist who works for one of the networks, Zack. This isn't quite her field, but she can introduce us to the right person. Why don't you start by writing it all down."

Mandy Steinhof was indeed a journalist, but her specialty was local politics. She had honed her skills of savaging elected representatives to the point where she could usually leave her audience with the impression that something fishy was in the works, no matter whom she was interviewing. She also played a good hand of bridge, which was how Sarah knew her. She approached Zack with the same cynical disbelief that she customarily employed with her other victims.

Zack surprised her. Most people she dealt with had a well-worn ease of manner on the surface, which usually concealed some murky depths underneath. There were always murky depths somewhere. Zack, however, was so totally unpracticed, open, and innocent that she simply could not conceive of him having any ulterior motives. Yet his story was interesting. Oh sure, one heard rumors about this kind of thing from time to time, but this was the first time she had heard it first-hand. She decided to investigate further.

"Leave it with me, kid. I think we're on to something here."

Mandy came back in a couple of week's time, apparently quite pleased with herself. "Okay, I've got the United Network interested in this. I think they're going to ask you for an interview shortly. Meanwhile, I'm going to give you a bit of coaching on interview techniques. There's a lot more to it than meets the eye. Don't fail me kid—I've got a lot riding on this."

The day of the interview came. Mandy drove him to the holovision studio, and expertly ushered him through the preliminaries. Finally Zack found himself facing his interviewer.

Magnus Wong was at the top of his profession. He could sense scandal like a retriever homing in on a decomposing rabbit. He could dissect an opponent with savagery, yet withal making himself appear a lofty guardian of the public interest. It was unfortunate that Mandy Steinhof's excited blunderings around the networks in the previous few weeks had attracted the attention of the global corporation that operated the Tangier plant, amongst others. They could buy the Magnus Wongs of this world with petty cash.

Zack, under Magnus Wong's expert probing, gave a brief version of his story. Strangely enough, it seemed to Zack, he never quite got round to talking in any detail about the child workers. Then:

"Are you aware, Mr. Gonzales, that there is a warrant for your arrest in Tangier, on charges of rape and child molestation?"

Zack was dumbfounded.

"Are you also aware that the minimum legal age for working in factories in Tangier is sixteen, and that the Tangier plant unions, where you worked for a few months, state categorically that there is no one under that age working in the plant?"

"But, but, that's all a lie..."

"While, of course, we can't dismiss your story out of hand, we do have a taped interview here with a Ms. Shana Boumedian, with whom I believe you worked at the plant."

And there was Shana, telling the world how she had worked in the same department as Zack, and how shocked she was when she found him one day molesting an innocent sixteen-year-old female apprentice, and so on and so on. Shana was enjoying her revenge. Finally. "...and you can't imagine how relieved I was when that monster was finally fired. I don't know what your laws say over in America, but I just hope and pray that you keep him there. I couldn't sleep easy in my bed at night if he ever came back."

Shana's English, though heavily accented, was intelligible to most viewers. Zack never got a chance to reply. The cameras zoomed in on Magnus, as he concluded, heavily and sorrowfully, "... and this I hope, will give us all pause to consider that the good name of Americans everywhere can be besmirched by the inconsiderate actions of a few undisciplined young people. Now, my next guest tonight..."

Zack was ushered out of the studio in a daze. Mandy was nowhere in sight. She knew a setup when she saw one, and one like this had to have big money behind it. She decided to fade into the background for a while. (She never played bridge again with Sarah.)

Zack never remembered how he made it home that evening. The enormity of what had happened did not really sink in until he was home. All his family had been watching—Sarah, Philippe and Martha— and they were waiting for him when he came back. Sarah said not a word, but hugged him tight.

He was never quite sure whether his father and sister believed his version of things or not. His mother made it quite plain that belief wasn't a consideration as far as she was concerned; he was her son, she stood by him, and that was that. But in spite of Sarah's support, he felt his life was destroyed. He knew what was happening out there, but nobody else seemed to care.

It was a few days later that he chanced to see the call for volunteers for Mayflower. Sick at heart, wanting only to put the whole world behind him, he applied. Six months later the news came that he was on the shortlist. He left for his initial screening with a feeling of relief that everything that had happened could now be put behind him.

CHAPTER 9

The requirements for the Mayflower were finally settled. Fifty voyagers, most of them in a deep coma at any one time, plus all their supplies pre-packed in landing craft, together with the landing craft for the voyagers themselves. All Sol Lansky now had to do was to complete the design of the ship that would take them there, and then build it.

"Very well, Sol," said Merriweather, "I guess you have your marching orders. Are there going to be any problems we need to know about at this stage?"

"Not really. There will be problems, you can count on there being problems, but then that's really what engineering is all about—solving problems as and when they arise. Engineers have been doing this ever since they started building the pyramids in Egypt.

"And we're heading into the unknown. Nobody's built a manned interstellar spaceship before. We're the first. We'll just have to make it up as we go along.

"I'll tell you one thing though, right now. Whatever we build has to work flawlessly for fifteen years or more in deep space and still be capable of maneuvering the ship into orbit around the destination planet at the end of it. There's only one sure way I know of doing that. Build it big, build it thick, build it heavy, and then triplicate everything. Sure, we'll probably be grossly overbuilding it, but I'd rather do that and be reasonably confident it's going to get to the other end than build it lightweight and stripped down, and not get there at all. As far as our technology is concerned today, you can either have a clunky monster that gets you there or a slim, elegant space yacht that might not."

"It's all very well to talk about big, thick and heavy, Sol, but this is a spaceship we're talking about, not an ocean-going freighter. How are you going to get this thing to fly?"

"No problem, because flying is the one thing it doesn't do. It will be built in space, it will move through space, and never land on any planet anywhere. It's a deep-space machine, nothing more, nothing less. When they get to wherever they're going, they'll need landers to bring them and their supplies down to the surface. There's no way this baby would survive a landing."

"Sounds as if it's going to be one monster of a machine."

"Oh, it will be. No doubt about it. And the bigger and heavier we build it, the more power it will take to move it, but then there's no real limit to fusion reactors, so we'll just build those bigger as well. That's why it's going to cost a lot of money. It won't be pretty, it won't be elegant, but it will work. That I guarantee. Just keep the money flowing."

And so the construction of the Mayflower began in orbit around the Moon. Lansky was in his element, riding herd on every detail. It went surprisingly quickly because in the latter part of the twenty-first century Lunar orbit had become a giant, sprawling shipyard, or more precisely a spaceshipyard. Huge orbital facilities, many of them owned by Astro-Mining Corporation, could fabricate sections of the ship which, on completion, just hung there in orbit until they could be integrated with the rest of the ship as it took shape. By the end of the twenty-first century spaceship design had become largely standardized, so sections of it could be adapted from standard modules. With this approach the ship could be built in less than three years, whereas a few decades earlier it would have taken ten years or more.

Some parts of the ship necessarily had to be manufactured on Earth, particularly some of the life support and hibernation support systems, but these were kept to a minimum because of the high cost of getting them into orbit.

The largest component of the Mayflower by mass, indeed the majority of its launch mass, was water for its reaction mass. This was readily available in the asteroid belt between Mars and Jupiter. It was mined as dirty ice, which was screened and distillation purified in the Lunar orbit yards using fusion reactors.

And as the ship took shape under Lansky's expert hands, so the party of colonists started to take shape under Lockmeyer's hands. Originally a short list of five hundred possibles had been identified from the millions of applications that the Mayflower Project had attracted. However, many of these had not been serious applicants— possibly they had just applied on a whim which they since regretted, and so failed to respond when told of their selection. About half of this number actually turned up for the preliminary screening.

Those that arrived had first to pass a physical screening. While genetic selection could tell what the applicants might possibly be like, it couldn't tell what they were actually like. Some of those that arrived were in poor physical shape or had significant health problems, to the extent that they were unlikely to survive the hibernation process of the voyage, not to mention the prolonged weightlessness, and so were rejected. More problematic was that several of the women, while otherwise in good physical shape, had had irreversible tubal ligations and so could never bear children. These too were rejected.

But the main screening was psychological. Julia Lockmeyer conducted all the interviews personally. Zilla Starr's was fairly typical.

"Do you realize you won't be coming back? When you get on board the Mayflower, you will never see the Earth again, never see your family and friends again. You will be gone forever, for the rest of your life."

"Yes, I do realize that."

"Does this worry you at all?"

"I suppose it does, to a certain extent. Don't get me wrong, I don't think I'm doing this because I'm running away from anything, I think I could have a reasonably fulfilling life here on Earth, but regret at leaving all of this is very much outweighed by the urge to do something special, do something with my life that will make a real difference, make a difference to the human race."

Which was precisely what Julia Lockmeyer wanted to hear. Several of the applicants seemed to think that they could come back whenever they wanted if things didn't work out for them, which was an immediate disqualifier as far as Julia was concerned, but the tall slim woman in front of her seemed to have a realistic view of the voyage. Julia continued on:

"When you get to your destination, do you realize that almost none of the benefits of civilization that you are used to will be

available. There will be no Net, no holovision, no theatres, no shops, no schools, no means of transport except your own two feet. You will be living much as your ancestors from several hundred years ago lived, where technology begins and ends with saws, axes, and ploughs."

Zilla grinned. "That's what makes it so interesting. I sometimes feel stifled by all the technology around me. I'm an artist, and I'm always trying to see what lies beneath the surface, what really makes things tick."

And the crucial question. "Do you realize that we are counting on you to propagate the human race on a new world? To put it bluntly, we hope you are going to have multiple births, and those births will be necessarily be under primitive conditions with little or no medical support?"

To which Zilla gave a happy grin. "Yes, and the more the merrier, without everyone around me giving me disapproving looks after my second one. I don't want to do what I see too often, women waiting until their late thirties or forties to have a single child. I want lots of fat little babies, and I want them now while I'm still young and springy."

And finally, "Do you have a boyfriend or girlfriend to whom you are attached? If so, and except for the unlikely event that they will also be part of the Mayflower team, do you realize you will never see them again?"

"No, I don't have one. If it's relevant, I have lots of friends of both sexes—and by the way I'm definitely heterosexual," Julia already knew this, "but I don't have a special attachment to any particular person."

She thought for a moment. "There are quite a few people I shall be sorry to say goodbye to, but I'm not afraid of that." Another slight pause, then, "I guess I shall be having children by one of the men on the Mayflower team. What happens if there's nobody on the team that I like or would want to have children by?"

"Don't let that worry you at this stage. There's still three years before the Mayflower sails, and you'll be training with the rest of the team in that time and getting to know them. If you decide for any reason during that period that you don't want to go you can leave at any time, no questions asked. But once the Mayflower sails and you're on it, that's it; there will be no possibility of leaving beyond that point. You will be committed for the rest of your life."

By such means the number was whittled down to seventy, of which fifty, twenty-five men and twenty-five women, were selected as the primary choices with the other twenty as backups.

When the names of the Mayflower voyagers were announced, there was a predictable flurry of media interest, and each one of them was subject to a battery of interviews and human interest stories. Zack's past was dragged up, and a couple of media stories appeared under the general heading of 'Sex predator included in Mayflower voyagers,' although the public enthusiasm for the whole Mayflower Project was sufficiently high by this time that the stories failed to gain any traction. Zack did however have an extra interview with Julia where they went over his experiences in the Tangier plant, followed by some discussions with Charles Lansdowne. The latter was not strictly interviewing him but was very interested professionally in whatever Zack could tell him about the personality suppression drugs in use there.

Maireed's case was a little different. As far as the Gaia Liberation Army was concerned, she had disappeared during an abortive operation in Los Angeles, missing presumed dead, and her sudden resurrection from the dead, so to speak, as a member of an expedition to which the GLA was opposed to the very depths of its being caused quite a stir at GLA HQ. (Her name also caused SoCal Security Section Chief Kaminsky, whom Maireed knew as Dogface, to laugh out loud and say, "Good for you, you bitch," but that was another matter.)

The rage at the hastily convened council of war at GLA HQ was palpable. That a Warrior Priestess of theirs should have betrayed them to this extent was insupportable. It was as if a Catholic archbishop had suddenly declared himself to be a practicing Satanist. Up to now the GLA had run campaigns to turn people against the Mayflower Project (with little success) and had tried various forms of industrial sabotage (with even less success), but this raised matters to a whole higher level. The decision was quickly taken to use all the resources of the GLA to terminate the Mayflower Project, and Maireed in particular, with extreme prejudice. The problem lay not in the GLA's resolution but in the execution of their decision. The Mayflower Project had by this time become uncomfortably aware of the depth of opposition to it in some quarters and had set up comprehensive security measures, in which SoCal Security as it happened played a large part.

The GLA looked at its options for terminating the Mayflower Project.

"We could step up our current anti-Mayflower PR campaigns, but the level of public enthusiasm for it is just too great for it to have much effect. We could try terminating the individual colonists, but there are too many of them and too many potential replacements, so we might end up with an all-out war on our hands, which won't do us any good no matter how it plays out. The backlash might do irreparable harm to us. Do we want to risk that?"

"No matter the risk, we have to do it. Gaia demands it." The GLA Senior Commander thumped her fist on the table in emphasis.

"How about sabotaging the ship?"

"The ship's being built in Lunar orbit, and we don't have any space operations capability worth speaking of. In any case if we simply destroy the ship while it's being built, it wouldn't be too difficult for it to be replaced. Ideally we should look for a means of destroying it when it's sufficiently far away from Earth that it won't be noticed, so there would be no incentive to send out a replacement."

"What about a time bomb on board the ship with a very long fuse so it goes off a year or more after launch?"

"It would have to be concealed somewhere that the crew on board the ship is unlikely to find it. After all, they'll have years and years to snoop around."

"How about a bomb in the supplies they intend to land with them on the new planet? I've heard these will be pre-packed into landing craft, and there would be no reason for them to unpack them while they're in space. A sufficiently powerful bomb would prevent them from completing their journey, even if it didn't kill them immediately. And just to make sure of things, we can booby-trap the bomb so even if they do find it, it will go off anyway."

"Do it," said the Senior Commander.

CHAPTER 10

There came a day when all fifty of the voyagers and colonists-to-be were gathered together in a secluded training camp in Oregon (not far, as it happened, from the Gaia Liberation Army's training camp). The launch date had its own ticking clock, which was the age of the voyagers. Anyone over twenty-five at launch would be unlikely to survive the enforced hibernation required by the journey, so the usual long drawn out, glacial pace of most government projects was given a sharp kick in the rear and told to hurry itself up.

Not that Sol Lansky would have any truck with anyone or anything who tried to slow his project down. Given the mandate to have everything ready by a fixed date, and with the enthusiastic support of Julia Lockmeyer, he happily steamrollered over everything in his path.

The ship, of course, had to remain in perfect functioning order for the fifteen subjective years that it would be in transit. "Build it big, build it thick, build it heavy, then triplicate everything," was Sol's dictum, and the expression BTH3 became the unofficial project motto.

Sol didn't normally pay much attention to the media, except for watching football when he had a moment to relax, which wasn't often. But even he began to be a little worried about the opposition to the project in the media, spearheaded by the GLA (and largely funded by it). To be sure, the bulk of the media were strongly in favor of the Mayflower Project, but a discordant note had begun to creep in. Headlines such as 'Should the human race impose itself on the galaxy' and 'Are we morally justified in going to another planet' began to appear, together with long articles querying whether a race that had indulged in wars, slavery, subjugation of women, persecution of gays and lesbians, maltreatment of indigenous peoples, factory farming and unsightly roadside billboards should have the right to spread its evil ways out into the galaxy.

The Mayflower Project already had a contract with a security company, but this was back in the days before spaceship construction had started. Something a lot more serious was called for now. After some prodding by Sol, a contract was signed with SoCal Security, since much of the work was being done in Southern California, and this was SoCal's home ground. A little while later, SoCal Section Chief Kaminsky found himself closeted with Sol. They hit it off almost immediately, recognizing each other as practical, results-oriented men who were prepared to kick ass whenever it was required to get the job done.

"You do realize that one of your voyagers, Maireed Shaughnessy, is a trained GLA saboteur? We picked her up a year or two ago trying to destroy the Astro-Mining plant in L.A."

"What!"

"The GLA have a large direct action cell in L.A. which we monitor as a matter of course, and we usually know when they're about to try some stunt or other. We picked her up as part of a team at Astro-Mining one night with a lot of incriminating equipment on her."

"What did you do with her?"

"Well, since we don't have formal powers of arrest, we can either quietly shoot undesirables and dump the bodies in a no-go area in L.A., which I really don't like doing if I can possibly avoid it, or scare them off. In her case we did a little blackmail by taking some photos of her and telling her we were going to make porn films with them—the GLA doesn't like that—then shipped her off to New York. Our affiliates there told us she seemed to have settled down as a school teacher so we didn't bother with her any further."

"I think I'd better get Dr. Lockmeyer in on this. It's her decision, at least until Ms, Shaughnessy starts throwing bombs around."

And Julia duly re-interviewed Maireed in a long, in-depth interview which covered, amongst other things, her time at the GLA training camp, details of which were subsequently checked out by SoCal Security. As part of Julia's many qualifications as a space medicine physician, she was a trained psychologist, which gave her a distinct advantage as an interrogator.

"Okay, Sol and Section Chief Kaminsky—"

"Fred."

"Okay, Sol and Fred. I think Maireed is clean. Yes, she did spend a year at the GLA Warrior Priestess training camp and was subsequently sent on a terrorist operation, but I don't think her heart was in it. The GLA picks up impressionable young people and feeds them a lot of BS without giving them much opportunity to think through what they're doing." Fred Kaminsky nodded his head in agreement. "In addition, unless she's a really good actress, and I don't think she is, her concern for her brother Sean, who I gather is a poet of sorts, just doesn't jibe with the mindset of a monomaniacal fanatic.

"Unless there is some overriding evidence that she's a danger to the project, I want to keep her, partly because of her DNA, but partly also because she seems to be the kind of capable self-starter that we need when they get to the new planet. The last thing we want is a bunch of wimps who will just sit around waiting to be told what to do."

And so Maireed remained on the Mayflower team. But Fred Kaminsky was paid to be suspicious.

"I'm prepared to accept that Ms. Shaughnessy is clean, because not even the GLA would be stupid enough to insert a saboteur who was recently picked up in a similar context, but I'm going to recommend that we do a quiet but intensive background check on each and every one of your colonists, including the backups. We're good at that; we do it all the time on new hires at high-tech companies. In addition, I think we should introduce a lot more physical security in the manufacturing end of things."

"Is this going to slow things down?" asked Sol.

"Not so's you'd notice. I recommend we introduce high-security ID badges, things like that, but I also want to have a very thorough systematic process for checking everything before it gets launched into Lunar orbit. Correct me if I'm wrong, but I suspect it will be a lot more difficult to check things thoroughly once they're in orbit.

"And while we're on the subject, I was looking at the ship's manifest, and it occurs to me that the ideal place for a bomb or something of the kind would be in the supplies the colonists will be taking with them. I understand that once they're delivered to the project they'll be stored on the ship as is without any further

processing, and furthermore they'll be packed into cargo landers and won't be disturbed until the journey's end, so if I was planning to plant a bomb, that's where I'd put it."

"Good point. If we temporarily store everything to be shipped on the Mayflower in a high-security warehouse before launching it— and we'll get your people to advise on the warehouse design and operation—your people can go over everything and check them out."

"We can save you time and effort there. We've already got quite a large high security warehouse and we'll just set aside a walled-off internal space for you. We'll guarantee very high security."

A few months later, Fred Kaminsky called Julia.

"There's two blacksmithing anvils in the cargo manifest. Correct?"

"Yes, that's correct."

"Although they look identical, one weighs about ten percent less than the other. Is there any reason for this?"

"Not that I know of."

"Okay then, we're taking both of them away and replacing them with identical ones, but this time our people will supervise their manufacture and delivery from start to finish."

And a few days later on a firing range a long way away, both anvils had small detonation charges exploded underneath them, and one of them destroyed itself in a massive blast that would have torn the Mayflower in half.

CHAPTER 11

While Sol had his problems with designing and manufacturing the Mayflower, Julia had hers with organizing and training the colonists. "Sol just has to ensure that his ship works for fifteen years, for most of which it will be in passive cruise mode anyway. I have to ensure that the colony survives and flourishes for two or three generations after they get there, until the colony is firmly established and thriving. Beyond that I can't foresee, but at least I can try to give them the best possible start."

"How are you going to do that?" asked Merriweather.

"We can give them a good physical start by dealing with any potential medical problems they may have. Each one of them is going to have the most minute and thorough medical examination that modern science can manage, and any potential problems such as appendicitis will be dealt with here and now. However, the real problem is that the ideal colonists and the technology to get them to the stars are a few hundred years out of sync. The ideal people to send would be farmers or trappers from the nineteenth century or earlier—people who are close to the soil, who can casually plough fields, chop down trees, build barns and houses, slaughter pigs, and so on. Of course we don't know if there will be trees or pigs on their new world, but what we need are down-to-earth generalists capable of adapting to any circumstances. I think we've selected a good bunch of young men and women, but very few of them have what I would call wilderness survival skills.

"And then of course there is the problem of their socio-political organization once they get there. There are so many variables that I really don't know what will be best for them. Do we set up a social structure now, with leaders and followers, or do we let them sort themselves out once they get there?"

"They probably will sort themselves out, regardless of anything we do now, so we may as well not burden them with a pre-arranged organization. After all, whatever we set up here on Earth, there's absolutely nothing we can do to enforce it once they get there. But if I were a betting man, I'd lay odds on them becoming a monarchy before too long."

"Isn't that rather a retrograde step? Surely they should be able to set up a functioning, grass roots democracy."

"Unfortunately, Julia, democracies either require that everyone is a completely rational being who will always follow the will of the majority, which in the real world is completely unrealistic, or they need an enforcement system to make sure that laws are obeyed. Don't forget that every—and I mean every—system of government relies ultimately on the use of force or a credible threat thereof. It may not often be used, but if it isn't there the whole system will rapidly collapse into chaos. Back in, say, Stalin's Russia in the twentieth century, the use of force was immediate, obvious, and brutal. But suppose you live in a very enlightened, tolerant democracy and you do something against the law—let's say, for the sake of argument, you make a habit of driving on the wrong side of the road. While you may be treated courteously to begin with and politely asked to stop, if you don't stop then eventually you will be asked less politely, and if you still won't stop you will be dragged off to jail kicking and screaming. The only real difference in this regard between Stalin's Russia and a tolerant democracy is the length of time between breaking a law and being forced to go to jail. Laws can't be optional, or there will be chaos.

"And of course to provide law enforcement you normally need a large infrastructure of police forces, lawyers, judges, jails, and so on. Our colonists simply won't have the resources for this, which means that they will be forced to adopt the simplest possible means of law enforcement—one strong man with a big stick, which is usually how monarchies arise in the first place."

"Ye-es, I guess you're right. But who chooses the monarch?"

"I suspect the monarch will chose himself—and when I say himself, I mean it will almost certainly be a man, not a woman. Brute physical strength and aggression are likely to be deciding factors. I also suspect that once our colonists get over the initial shock of landing on a new world, there will be some power struggles in which people are likely to be injured or even killed."

"I guess I'll have to live with that, or rather with the fact that I can't do anything to prevent it, as long as the killing is confined to the men. The women must be protected at all costs—they're the ones that have babies. But beyond the political side of things we ought to be doing something to prepare them for whatever physical conditions they're likely to meet."

"Er—what conditions are those? In spite of all the astronomers can tell us, the actual weather conditions and the native plants and animals and so on that they will have to deal with are completely beyond our ability to predict."

"But we can't just pile them onto the ship and tell them to get on with it when they reach the other end."

"Agreed. But what would be useful for them to know or to have practiced here on Earth?"

And so Julia was left to devise a training regime for the colonists. No doubt in the manner of all bureaucracies, various subcommittees could have been struck and would in the fullness of time have hired consultants and produced various weighty reports and training manuals, but Julia regarded this as simply a time-wasting means of passing the buck. After all, there weren't exactly a lot of people with experience in starting up colonies on new Earth-like worlds, so she decided she could do it just as well as anyone else. She therefore made up her own training plan, based on the desert island scenario.

"So you're washed up on a deserted island with not much in the way of resources other than your own muscles. (Can't send much in the way of machinery, it's too heavy, and besides, where would you get fuel?) What would you want to do?

"First of all you'd want to make some kind of a shelter, like a hut. Okay—what are you going to make it from? There may or may not be any trees, or anything like wood, so we'll have to teach them several techniques for making huts from all sorts of different materials— wood, plaited fibers, rocks, adobe, you name it.

"Let's assume they can eat the local wildlife. That may or may not be true, but let's assume it is for the sake of argument. They'll need hunting and fishing techniques—I doubt that many of them know much about it. Oh, yes, and how to gut, skin, and butcher animals. I'll bet that very few of our urban-dwelling colonists will ever have done that. Assuming of course that there are local animals, and that they are edible, and are built more or less like the ones on Earth…

"Then they will almost certainly want to plant crops, so they will need to learn how to plough a field. No machinery, probably no draft animals at first, so they'll have to do it themselves.

"In short, a wilderness survival course, augmented by some elementary farming techniques.

"With all of this we can count on accidents happening from time to time, so each and every colonist should have a good working knowledge of simple medical procedures such as stitching wounds and bone-setting.

"And then, let's not forget the most important thing of all, childbirth. There will be a lot of childbirths—if there isn't, the expedition will have failed. We should have several capable midwives."

And so a little while later an observer at the training camp would have seen a team of twelve men in harness pulling a plough while the thirteenth guided it. In light sandy soil it worked quite well. In heavy, clayey soil it was brutally hard labor.

However, it was hunting deer and subsequently butchering them that was hardest for most of them. If the closest you have ever come to meat is a neatly wrapped package from the supermarket, the raw physicality of converting a recently living creature into meat caused not a few of them to throw up the first time they tried it. Two of the colonists quit at this point and were replaced from the reserves. But after a few repetitions, most of them became sufficiently hardened that they could do it fairly well.

Jessica was the only one of the colonists who had any medical experience which didn't depend on a massive infrastructure of robotic equipment and advanced pharmaceuticals. Julia Lockmeyer may have had several medical degrees, but what she knew about childbirth under primitive conditions could be written on half a sheet of paper. The midwifery and general nursing course was largely devised around Jessica's experience.

Devising a training course and finding suitable instructors was one thing. Getting the colonists to concentrate on them was something else. One of the problems was that if you put twenty-five healthy young women and an equal number of healthy young men together, nature will take its course and romances will blossom, where the term romance encompasses everything from shy liaisons to uninhibited, carefree sex.

As far as Chuck Woodburn was concerned, he was in hog heaven. He had no inhibitions about tumbling any willing woman into the hay, and his air of tough confidence left him with no lack of partners.

In some cases there were genuine love affairs. Peter and Ingrid were both shy people who had always had difficulty meeting members of the opposite sex, and who tended to remain tongue-tied when they did. They chanced to be sitting next to each other during one of the introductory meetings and some kind of a spark flashed between them. Perhaps they recognized kindred spirits in each other, but they walked out of that meeting hand in hand and neither of them looked at another member of the opposite sex again. Both of them were virgins and they shyly shared a bed that night, gently exploring each other's body, confident that neither of them would be aggressive or hurtful to the other.

Jessica was a virgin and intended to stay one until the time came for having babies. Sex to her was akin to a sacrament, and she would not trivialize it by indulging in it prematurely.

Maireed carefully surveyed the group. A bed partner was going to be desirable during the training period before the ship sailed—presumably there wouldn't be much opportunity for sex on the ship because most of them would be in deep coma most of the time—but emotional entanglements were to be avoided, particularly at this stage. She found her ideal partner in Patricia Deutsch. Patty, as she was invariably known, came from a long line of what could best be described as good breeding stock. Many of her female ancestors had produced large broods of children, and Patty's softly rounded curves and gentle disposition, not to mention her detailed DNA analysis by the Mayflower selection team boded well for her future career as a mother. Quite why she had volunteered for the Mayflower was a bit of a mystery, even to herself; perhaps the thought of all those babies she would have was irresistible.

Maireed, being Maireed, once she had selected Patty lost no time in giving her a long, passionate kiss.

"Ooh, that was nice—but, um, should we be doing this, Maireed? I mean, aren't we supposed to be thinking about having babies?"

"Not for a long time, sweetheart. Not till we get there. Until then, you stick with me and I'll look after you."

"Yes, Maireed. Oh yes. Ooh yes, do that again…"

Unlike either Chuck or Maireed, Zack was shy and withdrawn. Not from lack of experience—Shana had seen to that—but from a feeling that he was a failure. He had tried to protect the slave children and had ended up being one of the slave drivers. He felt he was running away from the problem. Admittedly it seemed to be beyond his capability to do anything about it, but he was still running away. Zilla was drawn to him like a moth to a candle flame. An air of vulnerability can be a powerful aphrodisiac to those with a maternal instinct.

"Hi, you must be Zachary."

"Yep, but everyone calls me Zack."

"Okay, and I'm Zilla. So tell me about yourself. I guess we're going to spend the rest of our lives as neighbors, so we might as well start getting to know each other."

"There isn't a lot to tell really. I'm nineteen, my father's Mexican and my mother's from Kansas, and I've lived in several places around the world as I was growing up..."

"Lucky you. I've lived in the same suburb in Salt Lake since I was ten. I'd love to see other parts of the world—well, this world at any rate—but I guess I never will now."

"A lot of it isn't worth seeing, believe me. It's—oh, never mind, let's talk about something else."

"That bad? Wait a moment, weren't you involved in some kind of sex scandal somewhere or other?"

"No, that's a lie. I was framed to protect the organization I was about to blow the whistle on, and I don't want to talk about it." And got up to go.

"Hey, I'm not prying. I didn't mean to be—oh shit, I'm sorry, can we start again? I'm Zilla, and I gather you're Zack. We're going to be part of the same group for the rest of our lives. I haven't the least idea why they chose me, I don't know anything about my ancestors because I'm an adopted child, but I want to go to the stars and be a pioneer and have lots of babies, and by the way I'm an artist and I paint things. What about you?"

Zilla's rather breathless delivery mollified Zack, at least to the extent that he sat down again.

"I don't know why they chose me either. According to the media, we're all supposed to be exactly normal, but from a few hints I've heard we seem to be the exact opposite of it."

"Makes sense, come to think of it. If you're going to send a group to the stars it makes sense to send the very best you can find. I mean, I don't want to blow my own trumpet, but I don't think I'm average. I think I'm a lot more than average."

"I don't really know what I am or why I was chosen. I just applied because I was sickened by what I'd seen in another part of the world. I guess I just wanted out of everything, to try and do things better somewhere else."

Zilla had enough sense to say nothing at this point, but just took Zack's hand in hers and stroked it gently without looking at him. Gradually he started telling her his story.

"So I guess what you're saying, Zack, is that when there are too many people, human life gets cheap, and then nobody cares too much about what happens to other people as long as it happens a long way away?"

"I guess so. At least we won't have that problem where we're going."

"Not for many generations. It's never going to be our problem. But I guess it could happen eventually. I suppose by then we'll be able to do the same again, move on to the next solar system and start all over again."

CHAPTER 12

And so in the year 2101 the Mayflower sailed. She was neither pretty nor graceful, but when the mind grasped the scale of her there was a certain clumsy majesty about her, like an obese monarch. She was little more than a spacefaring tank-farm. Her mass at launch was over ninety percent reaction mass—water, in fact—while the voyagers and all their life-support systems and their cargo accounted for a mere two percent. Ploughs, anvils, and seeds figured high on the manifest, while the technological toys of the late twenty-first century figured not at all. For as Julia Lockmeyer had realized, and Sol Lansky too when he had considered the matter, if you cannot support and maintain your equipment it is better not to have it at all, because eventually it will break down and become useless. Better to learn how to do without it from the start than grow to rely on it and be crippled when it ceases to work.

All fifty of the voyagers together with Julia were ferried first to the Moon and then via a Lunar shuttle to the Mayflower. They gathered in the ship's gymnasium, which was the largest space available in the ship, where Julia addressed them one last time.

"In a few moments I shall return to the shuttle that is waiting outside. If any of you want to change your minds about going to the new world, you can make your way back to the shuttle with me and return to your former lives. This is your last chance to do so. There is no shame in this, because we are asking you to do something above and beyond normal human endeavor. Once the shuttle leaves, the Mayflower will start her main engines, and those of you that remain here will be committed to journeying to the new world and spending the rest of your lives there.

"For those of you who stay, this is my farewell to you. In the last few years I have come to know all of you, and every one of you has my love and my fervent wishes for your safe arrival and success on your new world. Be strong, be fruitful, be happy, above all be joyful.

"And now I am going to leave before I disgrace myself and burst into tears."

As she turned to go, many of the voyagers rushed to hug her one last time (this took some dexterity because they were in zero gravity, but then they were all young and fit), and Julia did indeed burst into tears. But she journeyed back to the Lunar base alone, for none of the voyagers changed their minds and accompanied her.

When the Mayflower had sailed, Julia returned to Earth, went home and quietly wept. Over the last three years the voyagers had become her children, the family of this childless woman. She had been instrumental in launching them towards a new world and a new life, and she would not see them again. There was an emptiness and a sense of loss, of desolation that she had never before experienced. It would be sixty years, more than Julia's life so far, before any news of their arrival reached Earth, and for the remainder of her life she would reach out to them with her prayers for their safe arrival.

Once the shuttle had left, an unfamiliar voice addressed the voyagers. "This is the ship's captain speaking. In case you're wondering, I'm not human; I'm an artificial intelligence, and it's my job to ensure that you all reach your destination safely. If anyone wants to ask me anything at any time, just say Mayflower and I will answer you. You can either do this out loud in public or via one of the various intercom phones you will see around the ship.

"The main engines are starting up now. Initially we will only be moving at a very low acceleration, about two percent of normal gravity, and we will build up to our full operating acceleration of one gravity in the course of about half an hour. I would like you all to float into a chair and fasten your safety belt until we have reached full acceleration, after which you will be free to go about your business."

And with that the voyagers felt a tiny tug of weight, just enough to keep them from floating out of their chairs.

Powered by her massive fusion engines the Mayflower accelerated at a constant 1g, and as a result the voyagers experienced the same weight that they would have on Earth. The ship would maintain this for ten and a half months, until it reached ninety percent of the speed of light, at which point the engines would shut off and the ship would cruise at this speed in a state of weightlessness until it started decelerating at the same rate in the final ten and a half months of its journey.

The first day or two after sailing there was constant radio traffic to and fro between the Mayflower and Earth, with media interviews taking up most of the bandwidth. However, interest faded fairly soon—there was little real news the voyagers could give, and with the ship accelerating at 1g it took less than four days before the round-trip radio time lag was an hour long, which made interviews with the voyagers more or less impossible. In a surprisingly short time, the media lost interest and the Mayflower and its voyagers soon faded from the public consciousness.

With all fifty voyagers awake, their quarters were quite cramped, but then it was not intended that the majority of them would be awake at any given time, except for the last three months of the voyage when all of them would be awake and exercising to build back their muscle strength before landing on their new world. Most of the voyagers went into hibernation within a few days of launch after radio ceased to be a viable means of two-way communication with Earth.

Each voyager had their own dedicated hibernation berth in which they would be fed intravenously and minutely monitored using robosurgeon technology. All any of them had to do was strip naked, lie in their berth, and then say "Ready for hibernation, Mayflower" to start the sequence. (If anyone got into the wrong berth by mistake the ship would recognize them and gently tell them to go to their own berth.) Some of them modestly wore a bathrobe as they got into their berth then threw it out just before starting the sequence, whence it would be picked up by one of the maintenance robots that crawled around the ship, but most of them had become so used to each other that they had no qualms about walking naked to their berth. In any case everyone was young, fit, and healthy with good-looking bodies.

Some, like Peter and Ingrid, went to hibernation hand in hand. After one last embrace, one last kiss, Peter picked Ingrid up and lifted her into her berth, who then smiled up at Peter and said "I love you," after which she initiated hibernation and consciousness fled. There was no guarantee that they would be awake again at the same time during the voyage. Individual wake periods were staggered to prevent overcrowding in the living areas, so that no more than three or four would normally be awake at any one time. The ship had its own schedule and kept to it.

Once the hibernation sequence had been initiated, the berth sealed itself and its occupant felt a slight prick with a needle. The next thing he or she would be aware of was being gently massaged by the robosurgeon and feeling very weak after being in a coma for up to four years. Although most of the voyage would be in zero gravity, each of them would be wrapped in a protective exo-skeleton for the first few days out of their hibernation berth while their enfeebled muscles regained some of their strength.

Because of the need for a three-month period between each hibernation session, each person's hibernation berth would be locked for that three months. There was no compulsion to go back into hibernation at the end of the wake period, but most people did anyway, from boredom if for no other reason. There was usually a changeover once a month—at least one person coming out of hibernation or going back into it—which helped if two people in the awake group took a dislike to each other. Apart from this it was necessary to keep them occupied, a fact of which Julia Lockmeyer had been well aware during the ship's design phase. The ship provided an enormous library of music, books, videos and computer games, although there was little for them to do physically apart from exercising in the gymnasium.

Much of each person's wake periods were spent exercising to rebuild muscles that had lapsed into feebleness as the combined result of coma inertness and zero gravity. Indeed, for most of them the periods between hibernation seemed in retrospect to consist of little else than exercising, eating and sleeping. But once they had regained some muscle strength, aided by muscle-stimulating drugs in their food, there were compensations. Sex in zero gravity was definitely interesting, and the Mayflower's designers had foreseen this and provided padded cubicles, with optional music and videos, in which this could safely take place. Bouncing around with a partner in a weightless state in the unconfined shipboard spaces could be dangerous otherwise.

Chuck Woodburn, amongst others, took the opportunity to explore the possibilities of zero gravity sex. When there was no up or down, remaining locked with one's partner could be a problem. "Oops, come back here honey" and "Come and catch me" were familiar sounds when he was in a sex cubicle.

Some of the voyagers never came out of hibernation. Each person would be woken if the monitoring system detected any problems, but sometimes they could not be woken and passed into death. Five men and two women were lost in this way and never completed the journey. The ship had its own fusion-powered crematorium, and the bodies of the dead were automatically conveyed to it at night when the awake group was sleeping (the ship maintained a twenty-four hour light/dark cycle to mimic day and night on Earth).

Their bodily remains were blasted into space as incandescent gas clouds, becoming part of the fabric of the universe for all eternity.

Three months before the end of the journey, all the remaining voyagers were woken and spent their time exercising to build up their muscles again. The Mayflower was well into its deceleration phase by this time so this was done at normal Earth gravity, and most of the voyagers were exhausted by it and spent their time sleeping when not exercising or eating. But without this build-up they would have landed as puny weaklings incapable of even standing upright in normal gravity. As it was, their muscles would not have fully regained their strength again when they landed. It was just hoped that they wouldn't meet any conditions on landing that required them to run fast or lift heavy weights, but this the Mayflower designers could not foresee. Some things just have to be taken on trust.

In the year 2133, thirty-two years after leaving Earth, although less than fifteen years in shipboard time owing to relativistic time dilation, the Mayflower entered the solar system of its destination planet and maneuvered into orbit around the New World (no one had thought of a name for it yet), her tanks almost empty of reaction mass.

For several days the ship's planetary observation sensors were busy building up a detailed picture of the surface, mapping it, analyzing the atmosphere and searching for any indication that human life might not be sustainable on it. About three quarters of the New World was ocean, with two major land masses and several smaller island chains. While no signs of intelligent life were found, this didn't mean there wasn't any, or that the local wildlife wouldn't look upon the colonists as convenient dietary supplements. And there was only one way to find out...

The ship's artificial intelligence captain finally gave permission to launch the scout ship with its crew of three. While the ostensible reason for scouting was to check out the main landing site that had been identified during the mapping phase, everyone knew that the real reason was to see if the scouts could stay alive on the surface. This could turn out to be a suicide mission, because while the scout ship had enough fuel to get down to the surface and then fly around for a while, it most emphatically did not have enough fuel to get back into orbit if conditions proved hostile. Once they were down, they would stay down. If they couldn't survive on the New World there was no point in going back to the Mayflower since she wouldn't be going anywhere else, so those left on board wouldn't survive in the long run either.

Chuck Woodburn had mixed feelings as he climbed into the scout ship with his crew partners. On the one hand he felt excited and relieved that he was finally going to reach the destination they had all been working towards for so many years. On the other hand he was nervous to the point that he had had to dash back to relieve himself at the last moment. They would be the first of the human race to set foot on a planet outside their home solar system, and since Chuck as scout commander would be the first to get out of the scout ship when it reached the surface he would be the first of the first. He had no idea what to expect. But as his militia training had taught him, when in doubt, make light of it...

"Okay, guys and gals, in case we get eaten by bug-eyed monsters the moment we land, it's been nice knowing you!"

Then the scout ship was on its way. None of its crew said much on the way down; they were all too nervous and apprehensive. Finally, they landed on what appeared to be a grassy plain near a river. The crew sat in their craft for a short time, debating what to do next. The scout ship's sensors indicated a breathable atmosphere very similar to that of Earth, but the acid test had yet to come—actually breathing the atmosphere.

"Okay, guys, this is going to be a bit like pulling off a sticky bandage. Do we do it all at once, zip, or do we do it gradually, a bit at a time?"

"You mean, do we crack the hatch all at once and start breathing the air, or do we let the air in bit by bit?"

"So what's the worst that could happen to us if we do it quickly?"

"The worst? Er—we die a long, slow, painful death, or maybe get turned into zombies?"

"Gee, thanks. But on the other hand, if we can't safely breathe the air, then the whole expedition will have failed because the rest of them won't be able to breathe it either, so why don't we just give it a try and see what happens?"

And with that, Chuck cracked open the main hatch and let the New World's air flood in.

Chuck took a deep breath. The air certainly seemed to be breathable, no pains in his chest, constrictions of the throat, spots before his eyes, or weird psychotic effects. They all sat just breathing the air for a few moments, then Chuck unfolded his legs from the cramped quarters of the scout ship and climbed down onto the ground. So far, so good. He wasn't being attacked by strange monsters; the grass, or whatever it was, wasn't dissolving his boots or reaching up to strangle him. In fact everything seemed calm and benign. He walked a few steps away from the ship as the other two got out.

Gradually the scene began to resolve itself. He was standing on a green, grassy plain sloping gently down to a river a mile or so away. Perhaps a botanist would have objected to the term grass, but it was good enough to be going on with. Near the river were some shapes that through his binoculars looked like trees or large bushes. Off to one side near the horizon was a range of hills. The sky was blue with fleecy white clouds, and the sun, which looked much like the sun on Earth, was pleasantly warm and a gentle breeze was blowing. It wasn't quite Earth-like, yet there was nothing he could immediately single out as alien—no nightmarish plants or animals, no glittering rock formations or unearthly cities. It was all a little disappointing, one might even say boring.

Boring is good, thought Chuck. Interesting would probably mean being attacked by weird monsters, and right now I'll settle for boring.

First things first. He clicked on his wrist microphone (very much like the one he had been used to as a militiaman) which put him in touch with the Mayflower via the scout ship radio. After receiving the beep, beep which announced that the Mayflower was within line of sight in her orbit, he said, "Scout commander to Mayflower. The Eagle has landed. We're outside breathing the air, and we're alive and well. Stand by for further signals." He could hear the sighs of relief from the Mayflower in his earphone.

The other two joined up with him. "Everyone okay? Alright then, let's take some photos and upload them right away just in case anything happens, then we check out the main landing site. After that I think we should spend a full day and night here before giving the okay to the rest of them."

One of the photos which showed Chuck with the scout ship to one side and a panorama of the New World behind him made its way back to Earth and became as famous in its way as the Mona Lisa, except that Chuck had an unequivocally broad grin on his face.

During the rest of that day, they explored down to the river and back and identified a landing site well back from the river. They wanted no possibility of landers putting down in the river by accident. When night fell, two of them climbed back into the scout ship and shut the main hatch, while the third stood on guard outside, changing over every few hours. While the planet seemed benign enough, they were not yet prepared for all of them to spend their first night outside. Who knew what strange life forms might prowl around after dark?

Since they were still alive and well the next day, they signaled as much to the Mayflower and set up a radio beacon on the landing site they had selected. With scant ceremony, great relief, and much trepidation the main body of the colonists began transporting themselves to the ground. The more robust parts of the cargo were landed hard, the more delicate parts, themselves included, landed rather more softly. Both types of lander used atmospheric friction at high altitude to bleed off their orbital velocity, then used giant parachutes and air bags for the actual landing. The only difference in this respect between the cargo landers and the personnel landers was the size of their parachutes and air bags; the cargo landers could save space and weight by using smaller ones.

One of the last tasks in orbit was to send a lengthy message back to Earth confirming that they had arrived safely and found conditions capable of sustaining life, together with summaries of the planetary data gathered by the Mayflower and photos of the landing site taken by the scout ship crew. It would be twenty-eight years before Earth received their message, transmitted via the great parabolic antenna the Mayflower carried for this purpose. They would not hear from the voyagers again; the antenna was too bulky to be shipped to the ground delicately, and it would not survive a hard landing.

When the landing had been completed, the Mayflower used the very last of its reaction mass to break free from the New World's gravity and plunge itself into the New World's sun, lest there should be intelligent life on the planet and the massive bulk of the Mayflower hurtling down in a fiery descent should cause harm to them. There would be no homecoming for this Mayflower.

CHAPTER 13

Zilla backed slowly down the short ladder and stood upright. She felt dizzy for a moment, but the uncompromising solidity of the ground beneath her feet helped it pass. She shut her eyes, clung on to the ladder for a moment more, then drew a deep breath and turned around.

In front of her was a jumble of scenery which made no sense to her for the moment. She drew another deep breath. This time, away from the familiar ambience of the landing craft, the smell of her new world made itself known. Not offensive, not threatening, just... different. Outside of her experience. She stood in an almost trance-like state, just absorbing the look and smell of the new world.

Zilla was awoken from her reverie by the next person backing down the ladder and bumping into her. "Sorry," she said reflexively, moving a couple of paces to one side. She turned to help him. He too stood uncertainly for a moment, looking around in a half-comprehending fashion, until Zilla gently propelled him to one side to make way for the next person.

Soon, all ten of them were standing on the ground. For a few moments, no one said anything. They stood near each other, for comfort and protection, looking around them with eyes of innocence and wonder. Every now and then a voice would say something like, "We're here—we're finally here," as if to prove that its owner was awake and not dreaming. Zilla felt suddenly afraid and reached out with her arm to the nearest person. It was Karl, who had bumped into her coming down the ladder. They stood for a long moment with their arms around each other's waists.

Predictably, it was Maireed who broke the spell. Practical, energetic, forceful Maireed. "Okay, you lot, sightseeing can come later. Let's get everything unloaded and the camp set up."

Under Maireed's direction some of them went back into the landing craft and started unstowing their cargo and pitching it out of the hatch. The others dragged it a quarter mile or so to the spot where the crew of the first lander (they were the second) had begun setting up camp.

There wasn't a lot of cargo. The bulk of it had come down in unmanned landing craft which hit the ground harder than humans could withstand. All the colonists had with them were supplies for the first few days, while they gathered themselves together and set up a permanent camp. They had descended to the planet in four separate landers. "Bloody silly to go all that way then lose everyone in a single hard landing," as Sol Lansky had said so many years ago, so there had been four separate landing craft for the colonists, plus four cargo landers and the advance party's scout ship. In the event, everything reached the surface safely. However, they were a little more spread out than they would have liked.

The landing site was on a broad plain, with hills to the west (or at least in the direction of the setting sun, which by definition was west) and limitless horizons to the south, east, and north. A river flowed a mile or two to the south. It was a logical choice. When putting down clumsy landers in unknown terrain, you tried to avoid any surprises such as ravines or marshes. The river was a concession to the frail needs of the humans, as opposed to the even frailer needs of the landing craft.

Chuck's scouting party had set up a beacon, and everything was supposed to land within a mile of it. The four colonist landers had come down within a few hundred yards of each other, but some of the unmanned supply landers had come down up to five miles away. There was a big collection task ahead of them.

Zilla dropped her load on the ground and collapsed beside it, panting heavily. Although everyone who had survived the journey had been awake and exercising for the last three months, they were still puny weaklings when they landed. The ship's deceleration-induced gravity during those months was the same as that of Earth, and their new planet was not much different, but nearly fifteen years of weightlessness in a drug-induced coma does no good to human muscles. Their food for those last three months had been heavily laced with muscle-stimulating drugs, but even so...

"Come on, we can't stop now, got to get everything organized," said Maireed's voice behind her.

Zilla squinted at Maireed's angular figure. "Piss off, Maireed, let me get my breath for a bit." She was beginning to get a little annoyed with Maireed. Sure, somebody had to organize things, and no doubt

Maireed was doing a fine job of it, but surely she could carry a few things once in a while? With a groan, Zilla got to her feet and tottered back for another load.

Maireed had a loud, strident voice, and worked on the principle that if you jumped straight in and issued orders in an authoritative voice, people would naturally accept you as the leader. It worked, because most of them were in a mild state of shock at finally being on their new world. But it was difficult to keep slogging away without taking time off to examine their new home. A few people started drifting off in the direction of the river and the bushes or trees that grew nearby, but were quickly pulled back by Maireed's strident shout. "You can look at those later, you guys, but right now there's work to be done. Besides, it might be dangerous out there."

Zilla was attempting to shoulder a load at the landing craft when Chuck Woodburn put his hand on her shoulder. "Take five, kid," he grinned at her. Chuck, being one of the scout crew, had been here a day or more longer than everyone else. He was evidently fitter than most of the others, for with a rifle slung over his shoulder he easily picked up the load she had been about to carry and started off with it. An instinctive thought rose to her mind: Patronizing bastard, I suppose he'll be wanting to open doors for me next, then the absurdity of the situation hit her and she grinned to herself. "Thanks, Chuck," she called to his receding back.

The heap of supplies grew untidily at the campsite, and a few tents began to spring up. Several of the colonists were slumped on the ground exhaustedly, and there was a sluggish air about the site. It reminded Zilla of the morning after a party. Suddenly she realized she was actually sitting on the ground, with her bare hands in contact with its alien soil, and had been breathing its alien air for the past few hours. For a moment, panic threatened to engulf her. Visions arose of monstrous bacteria eating at her flesh, rotting her lungs, swarming in alien fury in her bloodstream. Then with a sigh, she shrugged inwardly. She was just too tired to care.

Nearby, Maireed was similarly slumped, her angular frame leaning against Patty's more softly rounded body. Although she had not done much of the heavy work that day, she had been everywhere, exhorting, commanding, and generally making sure that things were done as her sense of fitness demanded. She was quite hoarse, and resolved to find a couple of lieutenants through whom she could pass her orders. A leader's voice was a precious asset, and should not be wasted by having to give every command personally.

They had slept their first night wrapped in sleeping bags. Most were in tents, but a few hardy souls, overcome by awe at their new surroundings, or just plain curiosity, slept outside and viewed the stars. Peter and Ingrid, for whom general physical exhaustion had damped their ardor during the final three months of the voyage, happily shared a tent and resumed their love affair. Whatever transpired on this new world, they had each other, and that was enough.

The landing site had been chosen in a mid-temperate zone in the northern hemisphere, and it appeared to be early summer. The night was mild, which was just as well, for they had no fuel for a fire. Perhaps we should have made the effort and gathered some wood, thought Zack. What happens if some of the local wildlife comes visiting? He clutched his rifle a little closer, and realized that so far they hadn't seen any signs of life except for some apparently harmless insect-like creatures and one or two things in the sky a long way off which could have been birds. I guess we must have frightened all the local wildlife away, assuming there is any. I suppose we'll find out all about them sooner or later, but meanwhile we'd better keep our eyes open.

The instincts of civilization die hard and very few of the colonists had thought to keep watch that first night. Most of them had an 'it'll be okay, nothing's going to happen' attitude, and in any case were too exhausted to stay awake. In the end only Chuck and Zack had agreed to keep watch, with Zack taking the first watch, Chuck the second. Zack kept himself awake by strolling slowly around the camp with his rifle slung on his back.

The rifles were not supposed to be there at all, since it was very much against civilized principles, or more precisely the principles of people who live in well-ordered, well-protected societies, to bring instruments of death and destruction with them. It was Sol Lansky, more than three decades ago, who had remarked "Bloody silly to go all that way and get eaten by tigers as soon as you get there." Whereupon a dozen hunting rifles and several large boxes of ammunition had appeared as if by magic. A few, like Chuck, had fallen happily on them and had spent a couple of afternoons test firing them on a range. Others had refused to have anything to do with them, while yet others, including Zack and Jessica, had reluctantly accepted that they might be necessary and had almost furtively spent time learning to use them.

Zack's large feet bore him with surprising softness around the sleeping camp. Near one of the sleepers who had elected starlight rather than the confines of a tent, he stopped as the figure moved its head, then thrust an arm outside the bag. "Is that you, Zack?" said

Zilla's voice. "I might have guessed you'd be on patrol. I'm too excited to sleep—can I join you?"

"Uh-huh. I could do with some company to keep me awake."

They walked slowly around the camp a couple of times, and then stood at a point where they could view all of it, insofar as the dark of the night would let them. While the new world had two tiny moonlets, they were barely visible so the nights would always be dark. Their eyes had adapted to see each other's outlines but little more.

"Why are we here, Zack?"

"That's a strange question. And in case you hadn't noticed, it's a bit too late to change your mind."

"I know that, silly. But it struck me this evening as I was trying to sleep. Ever since I was first told I had been accepted, god only knows how many years ago now, I've either been frantically rushing round training and generally getting ready, or just being a vegetable in transit. I've never stopped to ask myself, why?"

Zack chewed this over for a bit. He was not afraid of thinking in philosophical terms, but was unaccustomed to putting such thoughts into words. "I suppose that just saying onward and upward is a bit trite, but it's as near the truth as I can get. I think I had the feeling when I volunteered that Earth was overcrowded and worn out. There was no place for us any longer. It was almost as if we were being thrown out of the nest because we'd grown too big for it."

"And now we're here. Do you think we'll survive?"

"Don't see why not, barring some nasty surprises. But have you thought about our descendants?"

"You mean, do we have enough of a gene pool so we don't inbreed? They said back on Earth we'd be okay."

"That's not what worries me. How are we going to educate our children?"

"You mean setting up schools, and all that?"

"Yes and no. Back on Earth, we had a huge infrastructure to pass on the present generation's knowledge. Schools and universities, book publishing, not to mention pretty well all of human knowledge available via the Net, but here—nada. Zip, zero and zilch. This generation—us—is going to be far too busy just trying to survive to spend much time schooling the next generation. Our children will be hayseeds and theirs savages."

Zilla was silent for a moment. "I think that's probably what will happen," she said softly. "And maybe that's what is meant to happen. It will be a rebirth of the human race, leaving all the bad things behind us."

"And maybe some of the good things too," said Zack. "This might be a second Garden of Eden. I've always wondered what the fruit of the tree of knowledge tasted like."

The next morning Maireed awoke in a thoroughly bad mood. She had insisted on her own tent so she and Patty could share a sleeping bag in reasonable privacy, but it was the first time she had ever slept anywhere but a proper bed. She had managed to avoid all those ridiculous camping trips back on Earth while they were in training, and was rather depressed at the thought of having to sleep on the ground for the foreseeable future. She resolved to get someone to put a comfortable bed together for her as one of the first priorities for the colonists, and that made her feel a lot better.

But her agile mind had spent part of the night considering how she was to be leader of the new colony. This, after all, was her whole reason for volunteering for the Mayflower. Maireed wanted to be the leader (the queen in fact, but she hardly dared say it even to herself) so badly she could taste it. She had tried canvassing for support while on the voyage, particularly during the final three months when everyone was awake, but most people were intent on rebuilding their muscles and seemed to have little interest in thinking about how things were going to be organized when they landed. Now that they were here and the time for preparation was ended, perhaps things would be different.

There were sounds of activity outside as Maireed emerged bleary-eyed from her tent. "Where's the coffee, then," were her first words, and magically a cup of hot, steaming coffee was thrust into her hand. A few contemplative sips, then her ever-ready voice started up again.

"Right then, let's get this show on the road. First things first. I want a meeting of everyone as soon as possible to set up operating committees and proper structure, so we know who's doing what, and so forth."

"Er, we thought we'd better start by going after the supplies that came down before us," said a voice, rather timidly.

The response came with great vehemence. "We can't have people wandering all over the landscape, getting into Christ knows what sort of trouble. This has got to be properly organized, or we'll all be in trouble. Now, everybody over here, and let's get things organized." The last few words were in a strident bellow that demonstrated the full force of Maireed's lungs.

In a few minutes, most people had gathered around Maireed, who by that time was standing on a pile of stores, looking down at them. "Who the hell's that, still in the sack," she said. That, as it happened, was Zack, who had finally gone to sleep a few hours previously after handing over the watch to Chuck. "Somebody get him over here, whoever it is."

Zack arrived, not in the best of moods, in time for the last half of Maireed's speech. "...welcoming everyone to our new world. We're all lucky to be here, and I want you all to know that I'm going to do my very best to ensure that this world is run on sound democratic principles from the start. What we're going to do today is set up an executive committee which will in turn delegate its responsibilities as it sees fit to make sure that everything that's necessary for your comfort and survival is done."

Jake Johnson, a dark-skinned, intense young man, had been listening with impatience and when Maireed stopped momentarily for breath, jumped in. "We can't just acclaim a committee. We must have an election so that the committee is truly representative of the people."

"Thank you, Jake," said Maireed, smoothly, "I was coming to that. We'll take nominations from the floor—Patty, would you be our recorder—and we'll vote on them by a show of hands. The sooner we get this business out of the way, the sooner we can all have breakfast."

Perhaps it was the urging of their empty stomachs, or perhaps most of them were still dazed at being on a new world, but the election of the executive committee was over in twenty minutes, with Maireed as chairperson, Jake as vice-chairperson, three slightly dazed and hitherto silent colonists as members and Patty, at Maireed's request, as secretary. "She's so good at this sort of thing, you know." Jake had sought to question Maireed's assumption that she would be chairperson, but made the mistake of referring to the position as chairman. Maireed promptly demanded of the colonists whether they thought it right that the committee be headed by someone of such obviously sexist tendencies, indeed, she had misgivings as to whether he should be on the committee at all. However, she sensed that the colonists were becoming just a little tired of the whole business, herself included, and would be in a positively rebellious mood very soon. She therefore smiled graciously at them, caroled, "Breakfast, everyone," and jumped down from her platform, thereby signaling the end of the meeting.

Zack had lounged on the edge of the group the whole time, regarding the proceedings with a slightly incredulous air. When it was over, he looked toward Zilla who was standing nearby, with a slightly puzzled expression on his face. She grinned back. "Come on, we can always vote the loud-mouthed bitch out of office later on if we don't like her."

"It's not that. I came here to get away from goddam committees. I suppose she'll want us all to address her as Madam Chairperson from now on."

"Don't be a grouch, Zack. Come and get some breakfast, then you can catch some more sleep later on."

CHAPTER 14

Maireed wasted no time in getting her newly-minted committee to work. She was now, at least in her own eyes, the leader of the colonists. Use it or lose it, she thought.

"Right," said Maireed, "this is the first meeting of the Executive Committee, and the first thing we have to do is set an agenda, which should include ratification of our Constitution, which was set out for us on Earth, copies of which are in the binders which we have here."

And indeed, among the supplies sent down with the personnel landers were some lightweight binders containing what the expedition organizers back on Earth so many years ago had thought would be useful instructions and information. They even contained the helpful information at the front that they were copyright of the US Government, 2099.

While the committee droned on in the background, the more practically-minded of the colonists—for so they had begun to think of themselves—got on with the humdrum tasks of gathering the supplies from the cargo landers. "Come on, Chuck, let's do something useful," said Zack.

Chuck and Zack had long recognized each other as being practical people who got on with the job in front of them and let others do the talking. Only about half the colonists seemed to be physically capable of any kind of prolonged labor, and of these perhaps half were willing, this first full day on their new planet, to make any kind of effort after the initial excitement of landing. Many of them seemed to be unwilling to leave the landing site, as if the realization that they were finally and absolutely cut off from Earth was just sinking in and the landing site was their last tenuous link with their home world. In the end Zack managed to get eight others besides Chuck to set out for the nearest cargo lander, about a mile away from the camp.

As they set out, Maireed came running over.

"Where the hell do you think you're going?"

"We're off to get the supplies unloaded from the cargo landers. Where do you think we're going?" said Zack in a rather annoyed tone.

"Not until the Executive Committee authorizes it, you don't. We can't have people wandering off without letting us know where you've gone. What if there were an accident and we had to come and rescue you?"

"Oh, piss off, Maireed. Go play with your committee; some of us have got real work to do."

And with that Zack walked off in the direction of the nearest cargo lander. Chuck and a couple of others followed, but Maireed immediately started haranguing the remaining half dozen who stood around sheepishly in the face of this assault. In the end the working party was reduced to only six individuals including Chuck and Zack.

The first item to be unloaded in each of the four cargo landers was a light cart with large wheels. Each lander held a cross-section of the colonists' supplies so that if any one of them did not survive the descent the colonists would not be totally bereft of something vital.

Unloading and moving the supplies a mile or two would have been easy enough for a crew of healthy young people, but their muscles were atrophied from years of hibernation and weightlessness and it would be some time before they regained their full strength. We're a bunch of tottering old grannies, Zack thought, but he pushed himself as far as he could. He felt he owed it to the others to set an example. After all, he was the one who had organized this trip to the lander.

The next items to be unloaded were sections of a prefabricated hut. Back on Earth the planners had assumed that the colonists would need it to store the other supplies as they were unloaded, but it meant that some of the first items the crew had to unload were the largest. Not so good for their feeble muscles.

"Okay, one more time—heave," gasped Zack, sweat running down his face. Getting this section down to the ground was supposed to be easy with the winch mounted in the lander, and indeed they had practiced it on Earth, but somehow it missed the cart waiting below and slipped to the ground.

Finally they managed to get a couple of sections of the hut onto the cart. It was supposed to be capable of holding all four sections, but looking at his crew and realizing the limits of his own muscles Zack decided it would be best to start with a part load.

"Take five, guys."

"Screw that, let's take half an hour. I'm pooped."

And with that most of the crew flopped onto the ground.

"Did anyone bring any water?" asked Boris.

Oh shit, I forgot, thought Zack, but he didn't say it out loud for fear of sounding foolish in front of the crew. In fact he had thought of it, but the altercation with Maireed had driven it out of his mind.

"No, but there's a stream over there. I'm going there for a drink."

"Jesus, Zack, you can't do that. You don't know what's in the water. It might poison you."

"Well, we're going to have to drink the water sooner or later, so we may as well do it now."

And with that, Zack strolled over to the stream about two hundred yards away.

Walking to a stream to get a drink of water seemed like the most natural thing in the world, but the closer he got the more he realized that this wasn't the same world. The thought of alien microorganisms floating in the water almost made him turn back, but he forced himself on. He was determined not to show weakness in front of the crew. Besides, somebody had to try the water, so it might as well be him.

Feeling rather like a condemned prisoner going to the gallows, Zack knelt cautiously on the narrow pebbly beach by the stream, looking for alien monsters in the water. Seeing none he cautiously dipped one hand in the stream, half expecting it to be taken off by some piranha-like creature, but nothing happened, so he cautiously licked the moisture off his hand. It didn't taste of anything in particular, so he cupped his hands and took a small mouthful. Much like spring water back on Earth, he thought, and drank some more.

Turning around, he saw the others had followed him.

"Tastes okay, but wait half an hour to see if anything funny happens to me. If I'm okay in half an hour, I guess we can say it's fit to drink."

"Yeah, but what if there's something in the water that doesn't show up for a day or so?"

"That's a risk we're going to have to take. If we can't drink the water we're screwed anyway."

Zack lay on his back and gazed at the clouds in the sky, which looked much like clouds on Earth. Water vapor is still water vapor no matter which planet you're on, he thought. And with that his lack of sleep the night before caught up with him, and he closed his eyes and fell asleep.

While Chuck had few qualms about seeing Zack asleep (he'd spent too many nights on patrol as a militiaman not to know that you took your sleep as and when you could, and in any case Chuck had also been on watch the previous night so he knew why Zack was sleeping), some of the other retrieval crew members fretted nervously.

"Do you think he's still alive?"

"Sure he is; you can see him breathing. Let the guy have his sleep. We'll wake him in an hour. Why don't the rest of you take a break."

And with that, Chuck lay on his back and feigned ease and calm while trying to hide the fact that he too was nervous in case the water turned out to be poisonous. One thing militiamen knew was that nervousness was infectious and had to be stamped out. If one man in a unit started fretting it could quickly destroy morale and turn the unit into a panicked mob. Even when you had to retreat you never turned and ran blindly.

After an hour during which their thirst grew, Chuck gently shook Zack's shoulder. Zack woke up smoothly enough.

"Feeling okay, are you?"

"Sure, why not?"

"Well, you drank some of the water."

With that Zack stood up and stretched his arms.

"Never felt better. In fact I'll have another drink. Why don't you guys come too."

And he led them over to the stream where they all drank their fill.

The trip back was uneventful but tiring. As they pushed their cart back into the campsite, Maireed greeted them with a sneer.

"Well if it isn't our little heroes. So what have you brought back for us?"

"Half a hut, if you must know."

"Half a hut? Half a motherfucking hut?" Her voice rose so that everyone within earshot could hear. "Is that all you could do? Next time the committee will get this properly organized so we can bring back something useful.

"And while you've been gone, your committee has been doing something useful, like making plans to test the water. Didn't think of that while you were swanning off, did you?"

"No need to bother about that, we've already tried it and it's drinkable."

"You did what, you stupid bastards? You mean you drank the water without testing it first?" Maireed's voice rose to a scream "These guys are in quarantine; they're probably swarming with alien viruses."

"And if the water isn't drinkable, what are you going to do about it? Order some more from Earth?"

At that moment Jessica arrived on the scene. Her calm demeanor and sheer physical presence meant she was one of the few colonists that Maireed instinctively knew she could not browbeat. "I gather you've been the guinea pigs for us, then."

"Yep, doesn't seem to be a problem so far."

"Well, I guess that means it's not chemically harmful, but we don't know about any bacteria or viruses it might contain, so I'll keep an eye on you guys for the next few days. Meanwhile, the rest of us can boil the water before we drink it—we've probably got enough fuel for that, and if not those things over there look like trees so they'll probably burn."

And with that, Jessica turned back to organize things.

Maireed and Zack maintained an armed truce for the next few days. Maireed knew instinctively that she had to maintain the appearance of being in charge if she was in fact to remain in charge, so she busily gave orders, in the name of the executive committee of course. Bossy she might be, but stupid she was not.

One of the first orders she gave was that Zack was in charge of the workforce delegated to retrieving the stores from the cargo landers. Zack would have continued doing this anyway, but it looked to the rest of the colonists, at least to those who weren't paying much attention, that Zack was now working as a loyal servant of the committee. Not that Zack cared much, one way or the other; as far as he was concerned the work had to be done, and he might as well get on with it. At least Maireed wasn't getting in his way anymore.

Zack managed to organize two teams of ten apiece. He would have liked a third but that would mean he was in charge of almost three quarters of the colonists, and Maireed had definite views about that. Lieutenants were useful, but they should never have too much power.

"We need to balance the cargo collection with other base creation activities, Zack, so twenty people is the max we can afford for this task. Anyway, I'm sure you'll organize it so the job gets done as soon as possible."

And with that, Zack realized he would get no more without a major battle, so he decided he might as well save his breath and get on with the job.

The next two or three weeks were exhausting. Over fifty tons of supplies had to be collected from the four cargo landers and wheeled back on the transport carts to the main campsite. Zack had the carts from all four landers unloaded and assembled, and had each team of ten working on a separate lander for the first two, both of which were within a mile of the campsite. Each team filled a cart, then half the team wheeled it back to the camp site while the other half filled the next cart. However, the last two landers were four or five miles away— somehow the landing system devised by Sol Lansky's engineers was not as accurate as it might have been—so Zack had both teams working on the same lander, since there would usually be two or three carts in transit at any one time.

Maireed had organized separate teams at the campsite to unload the carts and store the supplies. At least she's managed to do that, thought Chuck, who by now was beginning to take a dim view of Maireed's usefulness, since the latter seemed to spend most of her time debating governance matters with her committee. Chuck had definite views on this; in his opinion committees were something you did in your spare time after the real work had been done. In any case, as far

as Chuck could make out they seemed to spend most of the time arguing with each other.

Each night Zack's cargo teams collapsed into their sleeping bags; each morning they woke up with aching muscles, but gradually their bodies started to get back into shape again after their long hibernation. Day by day the piles of supplies grew at the campsite, until finally the last lander was stripped of the last useful item.

CHAPTER 15

The original campsite was abandoned for one nearer the river. They had to have water, and there was no point in being further from it than they had to. The new site was a broad meadow around which a loop of the river slowly swirled. To one side was a spur of higher ground while on the other side was a marshy area through which flowed into the main river the stream from which Zack's team had drunk on their first cargo retrieval trip. It was a lush, comfortable-feeling place, even though some of them had misgivings about it.

"What if the river floods?"

"No problem, we'll put everything back from the river a little, and we can always move everything onto the higher ground at the side, where the grass, or whatever it is, looks drier."

So it started, but the lure of that green freshness was too much, and some of their tents and storage huts were perhaps a little nearer the river than prudence dictated.

"Don't worry, we can shift everything in a couple of hours if it looks as if the water's going to rise."

Even so, Zack and a few others were never comfortable with the new site. It wasn't the water; he just didn't like the site, but was voted down, or more precisely was told by Zilla not to be so grumpy.

As the initial flurry of activity of setting up a base camp—gathering supplies from the landers, digging latrines, gathering firewood, exploring their immediate surroundings—subsided, a curious lassitude settled over the camp, an air of 'okay, what's next?'

Zack and Chuck usually hung around together in the evenings when the day's work was over, and frequently Zilla joined them. They often made their evening meal together. While the food supplies sent from Earth consisted of vacuum-packed nutrition bars of various kinds, in gourmet terms they were little more than chewing exercises. However, among the supplies were packets of various spices and flavorings, and with some water and a little ingenuity different combinations could be boiled up together to make more interesting meals. Many of the colonists experimented in this way, with more or less palatable results. There was even a hard dough mix which could be eaten on its own (just), but when crumbled and mixed with water would make a reasonably bread-like substance, provided that an oven was built to bake it. Chuck and Zack by dint of experimentation managed to build a small oven out of stones which worked quite well.

Between supper and sleep, a remarkably short time since they were usually exhausted at the end of each day, was a time for conversation.

"Shouldn't we be plowing fields or something?" said Zilla one evening.

"Yeah, but I don't think this is the right place for it."

"You've said that before, Zack. Okay, tell us why."

Zack thought for a while. He had never had to put this into words before, and marshaling his thoughts into a coherent argument had never come easily to him. Eventually:

"I guess if I had to put it into one word—shelter. This place is too wide, too open. If we were a nomadic tribe of a thousand or more with herds and flocks it would be ideal, but there's only a few dozen of us, no herds, no flocks, and no means of defense if anything does attack us. And I'll bet it gets pretty windy and chilly in the winter."

"I think you're right, Zack," said Chuck, "but you're not going to get anything happening without the Exec on your side, so you'll need to convince them. In any case, I don't think most people would be too enthusiastic about moving right now."

"Why not?"

"Because they're frightened," chimed in Zilla. "I know I am. It's only just hit me in the last day or so when I've had time to think, but back on Earth we were cocooned in civilization. Okay, it may not be so bad for you, Chuck; you've been used to working out in the boonies, but me—I've never been anywhere where I couldn't access the Net, never been anywhere where there weren't shops and theatres and transport to get to them. Even while we were at the training camp we knew instinctively there were civilized facilities within reach if we needed them. And yes, I know, we knew all of this would happen when we signed up, but the stark realization of it all is only just coming home to me. I'm scared. I just want to huddle in one spot and pull a blanket over myself."

She looked as if she was going to burst into tears, but prevented herself. Doing it in private with just one man for company was one thing, doing in front of two men with dozens of other people within earshot was something else.

Zack thought about it for a moment. "I guess I'll have to try and convince the Exec Committee, but I don't know that I'm going to have much success. I'm not Maireed's favorite person right now."

The next day Zack did indeed try. Maireed's response was predictable.

"What the hell are you talking about, Zack? For chrissake, take a look around you—see any little green men with ray guns out there? There may be a time for swanning off and exploring, but this isn't it. Right now we need to work as a group to get things organized here!" Zack forbore to mention that the camp was pretty well organized anyway, but decided not to argue.

That evening he related this to Chuck and Zilla again.

"I think Maireed is as frightened as the rest of us; she's just better at hiding it. Droning on with her committee is really just doing something she feels comfortable with because she can't think of anything else to do."

"Well, we can't just sit around here eating up our food supplies; we have to start doing something."

Zilla seemed to have a better sense of what they should be doing than Chuck, who, for all his outdoorsy, tough guy self-confidence was beginning to look up to Zack as the leader of their little group. "If this was three hundred years ago, we wouldn't have any problem in getting on with farming or hunting or whatever," she said. "That's what folks did in those days, at least that's what the peasants did."

"Yeah, but three hundred years ago they wouldn't have been able to get here. Seems that once you develop the capability of getting here you lose the capability of doing anything useful once you do get here. I agree with Zack. Sooner or later we're going to have to move, it's just that now is not a good time to tell everyone, just after they've busted a gut getting this lot organized."

"Good time or no, sooner or later it has to be done."

"Yeah, but be practical, Zack ol' buddy," said Chuck, "getting everything moved into place here took enough effort. Telling everyone they have to do it all over again ain't gonna make you Mr. Popular."

"I don't think I'm here to be popular. I'm here to help start a viable colony of us humans. If that means we have to move somewhere else, then so be it."

"What sort of a somewhere else did you have in mind?"

"That's just it, I don't know. All I know is that I feel in my bones that this isn't the right place. We need to find a better place."

Zack was a self-sufficient loner by nature. It simply didn't occur to him to organize an expedition with several people. Once he had decided to do something, he just went ahead and did it. While he was more than capable of organizing working parties to do something needing many hands such as unloading the cargo landers, if it could be done by one person he automatically went and did it himself. That evening he loaded food, ammunition and a few other items into a backpack, took an axe and one of their rifles, and quietly left before dawn.

As he turned in to his sleeping bag that night for a few hours rest before setting off, Zack had the feeling that he at any rate was about to do something useful instead of just sitting around wondering what to do next.

CHAPTER 16

Zack started off in the pre-dawn half-light before anyone else was stirring. His plan was to follow the river upstream, towards the hills in the west from which it appeared to issue. Much of the riverbank was marshy, so he followed parallel to the river about half a mile away. It was easy to follow, because there was a dark green line of trees along the riverbank on both sides.

He walked perhaps fifteen miles that first day, over gently undulating grassland. Although he had had nearly three weeks of good food and exercise, his muscles still had a long way to go before he could be described as fit, and he was weary by day's end. He camped near a stand of trees and lit a fire, more for company than for the heat it provided, for it promised to be a mild night.

In truth, he was more than a little frightened. Like most dwellers on Earth of his time, real solitude was foreign to him. Several times that night he nearly started running back to the main camp in panic. But he steeled himself to stay; he had to do this on his own, although he knew not why. Something was wrong with their new colony. He could not put it into words, yet he could taste it, smell it, feel it. He had to be by himself to think. His intention to explore was just an excuse to be by himself, and he knew it.

He slept finally, a couple of hours before dawn, and woke up when a large bird flew screeching overhead. It could have been a crow except for its leaf-like tail. After his heart stopped pounding, Zack decided it was harmless, and got on with the business of breakfast, which consisted of a couple of vacuum-packed nutrition bars. But he did wish he had a large plate of eggs and bacon and fried potatoes. Somehow, chewing concentrates just wasn't the same.

The second day was easier. His legs were stiff for the first few miles, but his heart was lighter. He knew he would be frightened that night, and the next, and the next, but now he also knew he could face his fears. He felt he was in control, and walked with a firmer stride.

By the end of that day the ground was undulating in a series of shallow ridges. At the top of each ridge he could see hills beyond. He finally reached them on the afternoon of the third day, a slowly rising slope in front of him. Since the end of the previous day, the trees had grown more numerous. Strange looking trees, some with long triangular leaves growing in pairs and metallic-looking bark, others rather like silver birches with fern-like leaves, but all undoubtedly trees. But their wood burnt well, and at the end of the day that was all he cared about.

About noon on the third day, Zack was walking through a meadow of grass-like plants, knee-high in places and waist-high in others. On the far side of a clump of trees he came across a group of animals grazing;

they looked so obviously part of their environment that at first he barely registered them. Then he stopped and gazed in wonder.

Like animals on Earth, these had four legs each, and heads, and possibly tails as well, but beyond that he could not easily describe them. They were neither deer, nor horse, nor sheep, nor any other animal in his lexicon. Yet they were undoubtedly cropping the grass, or whatever one called the ground cover, and since he was downwind of them he could also smell them—sweetish, with an acrid aftertone.

Zack slowly sank down onto his haunches and observed them for a while, and thought about what he was seeing. I guess Mother Nature must be an engineer, he thought. Four jointed legs is simply the best design for moving over rough ground at speed. Anything else, such as wheels or slithery stuff doesn't work as well, at least not in most cases. And if you have four legs, you need some sort of a connecting spine, then all the life-support equipment, like the digestive system and so on, gets slung in between. You then put an orifice at one end to ingest food, another one at the other end to excrete waste, and the rest is just detail.

Suddenly, one of them must have sensed his presence and flicked its head, presumably as a warning to the others. The whole herd of a dozen or so immediately galloped away with a delicate, flowing gait which seemed rather out of place with their stumpy bodies. Zack stood watching them go. After some time the thought occurred to him: They were afraid of me. That means they're afraid of other things, and those other things probably have big teeth. Go carefully. He gripped his rifle tighter and looked around him before walking on.

The river valley here had narrowed, with steep, tree-covered slopes on either slide. Zack did not relish the thought of walking through thick forest, so he kept to the higher ground away from the river, where the trees thinned out. A couple of times he crossed small streams which appeared to run into the main stream lower down, and once or twice he saw fish-like shapes in the water. He was tempted to try catching one but decided that such experiments could wait. He had plenty of food, and if his catch turned out to be poisonous there was no possibility of help.

That third night he camped among the trees, since he had no other choice. While it was still daylight he gathered a large pile of firewood and resolved to keep his fire burning all night. When night fell he could hear things moving through the brush nearby, and wished he had some companions to keep watch while he slept. Eventually, he fell asleep, his head pillowed on his backpack, rifle clutched in hand. He was awoken sometime in the night by something sniffing near his ear and scratching at the backpack. He sat up and in blind panic fired his rifle (and as it happened, missed his foot by a few inches). In the brief illumination of the flash he thought he saw a fox-sized creature fleeing. With great effort he prevented himself from blindly fleeing in the opposite direction, and set himself, with shaking hands, to build up the fire again. He slept no more that night.

On the fourth day, the hills rose steeply on either side of the river valley, and Zack followed their line on the northern side. The tree cover thinned out on the crest of the hills. Looking south, down into the valley, he saw the trees near the river were large and luxuriant-looking, while the river itself, when he could see it through the trees, sparkled in the sunlight. With sudden resolve he made his way down the slope into the thicker forest, and after an hour or so of pushing his way through thick undergrowth reached the river. He was sweating heavily by this time and there were insects buzzing around his head, although none of them landed on him or bit him. Perhaps he smelt too alien to them. Give the little critters a few days to acclimatize to me, and they'll soon get over their inhibitions, he thought. He wondered, not for the first time, how compatible their biochemistries were, and whether any of this world's flora or fauna would be edible by humans.

The river at this point was clear and fast flowing over a rocky bottom. There was an island with a few trees in the middle of the stream, which looked like a good site for a camp, and the river did not look too deep, so he started wading across. The water reached to his crotch, but no higher, although halfway across he nearly lost his footing when a fish-like creature about a foot long leapt out of the water near him. After reaching the island without further mishap and scouting around briefly, weariness compounded of lost sleep and aching muscles overcame him, and he lay down to sleep in the shade of a large tree.

The sun was in the west when he awoke. According to the observations they had made before landing, the day here was about twenty-six hours long, and they all had had problems adjusting their circadian rhythms to this cycle. Zack felt refreshed but disoriented when he awoke, and imagined briefly he was back on the ship. In a half-awake state he wondered what an otter-like creature with reddish-brown fur was doing in the ship, sitting on its haunches, solemnly regarding him. Realization flooded back in, and he lay very still, looking back at the creature. He slowly moved to sit up, but it fled at his movement, although he could still see it at the water's edge, evidently torn between curiosity and safety.

Using very slow, and what he hoped were non-threatening movements, Zack opened his pack and pulled out a protein concentrate bar. Breaking off a sizable chunk, he gently tossed it down the slope towards the creature. You can be my guinea pig, he thought. If you eat this, then I guess I can eat you, or your relations. He sat back against the tree and waited. Soon, the creature twitched its nose several times as if sniffing the air, then crept very slowly and very cautiously towards the food. It reached it, sniffed it several times with great concentration, then nibbled a bit, and finally attacked it with gusto, all the time keeping one eye on Zack. When it had finished, it looked quizzically towards Zack, who reached into his pack again and dropped another chunk, but this time only six feet away.

Charlie (Zack didn't know if it was a he or a she, and didn't particularly care, but Charlie seemed to fit) sat on its haunches and stared back at Zack. "What, me, come that close to you? Do you think I'm stupid or something?" it seemed to be saying. But hunger, or possibly gluttony, got the better of it and it gradually crept closer. With every line of its body poised for instant retreat, Charlie reached out a front paw, which Zack noted had three heavy-looking blunt claws, seized the food in its mouth, then scuttled off to a safe distance to eat it.

We should put a marker plaque down here, thought Zack. On this spot, the first off-planet food was eaten by Charlie—do you have a last name? Probably not, so I guess we'll have to give you one. Charlie Brown. Well, Charlie, you've had your feast, now it's time for mine. As soon as Zack moved to stand up, Charlie fled back to the river and dived in with fluid grace. If that protein bar doesn't kill you, I have a feeling you're going to be back. I'd better look out for my pack from now on.

Zack had fished a few times back on Earth—eons ago it seemed—and had brought a hand line with him. On the far side of the island there was a rocky beach, and beyond this the river seemed to be deeper and slower moving. Several times he saw fish jumping out of the water, possibly for insects. Taking this as a good sign, he baited his hook with some more protein bar and cast the line in the water. Almost immediately, he was rewarded by a tremendous jerk on the line which would have torn it out of his hands hand he not been gripping the plastic reel firmly. Deciding that there was no need for finesse, he simply locked the reel and walked backwards, having to exert considerable force as he did so, and eventually dragged a writhing, struggling fish about eighteen inches long onto dry land.

The fish had been delicious. Grilled on a green twig over a bed of hot coals, its taste had been like a cross between chicken and eel rather than what Zack considered to be fish, but lying back against his tree in the dusk, he felt comfortably replete and at peace with this new world. His pack was now suspended eight feet in the air from a branch of the tree in case Charlie decided to come visiting. With his rifle and axe close at hand, Zack was content to watch the stars come out. He thought about what he would do the next day, how the colony would consolidate its foothold and expand, how pleasant it would be to have a companion—Zilla, perhaps—with him right now...

He awoke with a jerk as thunder crashed around him, was temporarily blinded as another lightning bolt tore into the ground nearby, and his eardrums were pummeled with thunder again. Rain hissed down, soaking him. He tried to stand, but his foot skidded off a wet tree root and he fell heavily. Disoriented in the dark and the rain, he no longer knew where the tree was, nor his rifle and axe. A lightning flash lit up the scene, but he was facing away from his campsite and could see nothing familiar. Rising panic gripped him and he felt the hunted animal's urge to run blindly. With an effort he mastered himself, but remained crouching until the storm was no longer directly overhead and the rain had slackened a little. Finally, he stood cautiously upright and looked for his tree. It took him several lightning flashes to do so, but eventually he felt confident enough to crawl towards it and search with his hands for rifle and axe.

His hands closed upon this rifle, but at that moment another lightning flash seemed to be reflected oddly back at him. The next flash showed more clearly; the river was rising, and much of the island was now underwater. He slung the rifle on his shoulder and redoubled his search for the axe. When he found it, he hefted it in both hands and buried its head in the tree about eight feet above the ground. It was too dark to find the footholds he had used to climb the trunk earlier when he had suspended his pack out of reach of Charlie, so he stood with his back against the tree and strained his eyes to see the water which he could hear rushing past through the sound of the falling rain. The lightning had nearly stopped, no stars were showing, and the darkness was complete except for an occasional distant flash.

Zack tried to gauge the river by its sound, but this became superfluous when his feet were lapped by the rising water. The river slowly rose to his knees, and the current threatened to pull him over. He cautiously edged round to the upstream side of the trunk, put both arms around it and prayed to the Gods, whoever and wherever they might be on this world, that it would rise no further.

Dawn found him in the same spot, a wretched, bedraggled, shivering castaway standing thigh deep in the middle of a river which was two or three times the width of yesterday. The rain had stopped, although the sky was still overcast. The shallow section of the river through which he had waded to the island was now over his head, and the current was fast. He felt trapped.

Zack stood for perhaps half an hour after it became light enough to see his surroundings, first in thankfulness for the light and the cessation of rain, then in increasing misery. He was trapped. Eventually, he supposed, the water would go down, but when? Finally, it became light enough, and the trunk dry enough, for him to attempt to climb it.

He was cold, his muscles were stiff, and in any case had not yet regained their full strength. More than once he nearly fell, but the knowledge that if he did he would probably be swept downstream by the current spurred him on, and finally he reached the first fork of the trunk, from which he could reach the branch on which he had hung his pack the previous day. His axe he could see buried in the tree trunk below him. He decided to leave it there for the time being.

His wet clothes clung to him, but at least there was no wind. Hunger gripped him, and he began to haul his pack towards him. A sudden thought struck him. As far as he could make out, there had been no ill effects from eating the fish the previous evening, unless of course it had made him hallucinate the storm and the flood. Somehow, Zack did not think so; his cold wet clothes were altogether too soggily uncomfortable to be a hallucination.

Zack stayed in the tree for a day and a night, until the river had subsided somewhat. The tree was large enough for him to climb up and down for exercise to warm himself, and he had food. He stripped and cleaned his rifle, taking great care not to drop any of the parts into the water below, and took off his clothing to dry it when the sun finally shone that afternoon, but apart from that, boredom was his enemy. At night, he tied himself to the trunk to guard against falling out, but sleep was impossible except for a few catnaps.

As he sat in his tree and felt the helplessness and futility of his position, it gradually dawned on him that this was what had worried him earlier about the colony. Helplessness and futility. They had come to this planet in their pride and self-assurance, yet when they arrived, somehow the purpose seemed to have drained out of them. They had no true leadership, no one to point them in a direction and say, "There! That's where we're going to go, that's what we're going to do, so follow me." Like him, they seemed to be sitting in a mental tree, helplessly gazing around them, waiting for something to happen. They had gathered all their supplies, had set up some huts and tents, and now sat around eating those supplies and discussing politics. Politics indeed! There might be time for that when they had established themselves as a viable tribe, ensured their survival, and built a village. But now was not the time. Now was the time for doing, not talking.

CHAPTER 17

Zack's absence wasn't immediately noticed at the main campsite. After the exertions of setting up the camp and recovering all the supplies from the cargo landers, there was not a lot of activity, so if anyone thought about Zack at all they assumed he was sleeping. Chuck and Zilla realized he had gone, but by unspoken agreement they said nothing about it to anyone else.

It was that afternoon when Maireed's committee, discussing some point about distribution and control of supplies, wanted some details about the amount and storage of the supplies and needed Zack's input.

"Where's Zack got to, Chuck?" asked Jake Johnson who had been sent to find him. (Maireed took every opportunity to use Jake as a gofer just to remind him who was boss.)

"Gone."

"What do you mean gone?"

"Taken off exploring. He went early this morning. He must be miles away by now."

When Jake reported this back to the committee, Maireed predictably went ballistic. She came storming over to Chuck.

"What the hell do you think you're doing, letting Zack go off without reporting it to the committee? We're the elected representatives of everyone. We have executive responsibility for everything that goes on here. How the hell can you expect us to keep everyone safe if you let idiots like Zack go wandering off on their own getting into God only knows what sort of trouble? Don't you realize it could be dangerous out there? He's putting other people's lives at risk, having to go and rescue him if he gets into trouble, which he almost certainly will."

Chuck had a grin on his face during Maireed's tirade, which did nothing to calm her down. Eventually she stopped to draw breath.

"Zack's doing something useful, like finding us a better place to live, unlike your goddamn committee which is just wasting time. And for the record, I don't know where Zack's gone, so we couldn't rescue him even if we wanted to. So why don't you just go back and play with your committee?"

And with that, Chuck turned his back and walked off.

Maireed wasn't satisfied with this, although running after Chuck was too undignified for her. She stood her ground and used the full force of her lungs.

"Does anyone know where that idiot Zack has gone? Zilla, you're thick with him, what do you know about this?"

Zilla had guessed he was going and had guessed he was probably heading towards the hills on the horizon—it was, after all, the only reasonable direction to take, considering that any other direction would only lead to much the same scenery as they were in now—but decided to play dumb. She just shrugged and said nothing, and hoped the dim, stupid look she had adopted would protect her from further hectoring by Maireed.

Baffled and frustrated, Maireed returned to her committee meeting and immediately set to work drafting a series of rules and regulations about people reporting their movements to the committee. While it wouldn't do anything to make Zack come back, it at least gave her a club with which to beat anyone else over the head who decided to go off exploring on their own.

The herd moved ponderously on its well-established migration path. Large black shaggy quadrupeds, they had very little intelligence but well-honed instincts which generally caused the herd to move as a single body. It had been a long trek since their last watering place; they were thirsty, and they could smell the river not far ahead. But there were other, alien smells which made the herd skittish. In the end thirst won and the herd quickened their pace as they drew near the river.

Chuck's instincts for danger had been well developed during his time as a militiaman. Those that didn't have well-developed instincts in city areas where snipers often regarded militiamen as target practice tended not to live too long. Two days after Zack had left, Chuck's instincts probably saved the colonists from being wiped out. It was perhaps the faintest discernible vibration through the soles of his feet that caused him to look up to the ridge of the gentle slope leading away from the river and see a black tide rolling down towards him.

He stood gazing at the sight for a couple of seconds, not quite comprehending what he saw, then shouted an alarm.

"Everyone, get up top, away from the campsite. There's a stampede coming."

Some of the colonists saw where he was pointing and immediately took off, but many of them just stood uncomprehendingly, not understanding what was happening or what to do. Chuck ran around trying to get then to move.

"Move it, you stupid bastards! You'll be trampled to death if you don't."

By this time the rumbling noise of the herd galloping towards them was quite audible, as well as the vibration felt through the soles of their feet, and almost everyone made it out of the way as about five hundred creatures, vaguely like black buffalos, thundered past on their way to the river.

All except Peter and Ingrid who were sleeping in their tent after gentle but passionate love-making. The animals were densely packed together, and the ones headed directly for their tent could not have moved to the side even if they had tried. In any case they had tough, wiry coats and were used to smashing their way through undergrowth, and the tent to them was just another form of undergrowth. Peter and Ingrid died in each other's arms as wave after wave of half-ton creatures thundered over them, crushing their bodies to pulp.

The colonists stood on the high ground adjacent to their campsite, aghast at the sight below them. It was only when Chuck started a roll-call that it was realized that Peter and Ingrid were missing. One or two of them remembered more or less where their tent had been, but since it now seemed to be in the middle of a herd of large black shaggy creatures milling around, no one volunteered to go down and look for them. They slept that night in the open on the high ground above the herd, which seemed to have no desire to follow the colonists, but kept to the meadow near the river.

The herd remained in the meadow for a day and a night, cropping the abundant ground cover and slaking their thirst. Finally, in the middle of the next day the entire herd, moving as if a single mind controlled them, waded and swam across the river, shook themselves dry on the other side, and carried on their way. An hour later it was as if they had never been there—except for the trampled meadow, the crushed supplies and tents of the colonists liberally covered in dung, and the remains of Peter and Ingrid's tent.

Predictably, it was Jessica who went to them first. She had had plenty of experience with blood and death in Zimbabwe, but even her stomach was turned by what she found. She could see she needed some help, and decided that of all the remaining colonists, Chuck would be one of the ones least likely to throw up when he got there.

"Chuck—get over here and bring two sleeping bags with you."

Between the two of them they managed to put the bodily remains of Peter and Ingrid into sleeping bags. They felt instinctively that they should not be buried where they lay, in case the herd came back and defiled their burial place, so Chuck fetched one of the transport carts and between the two of them they wheeled the bodies onto higher ground.

They were buried side by side in a joint grave later that day. While they had died tragically and unnecessarily, the colonists felt by unspoken agreement that their gentle love for each other should be honored by burying them together.

Meanwhile, what remained of their supplies had to be rescued. The storage huts seem to have been used as scratching posts by the herd, and one had collapsed completely while two more were bent out of shape. While the huts were marvels of lightweight engineering, they were never designed for this level of mistreatment, and the three damaged ones had burst open and their contents strewn over the ground to a greater or lesser extent and subsequently trampled by the herd. By the time they had buried Peter and Ingrid and assessed the damage to their supplies (Maireed insisted that the Executive prepare a recovery plan before any work was done), the sun was setting, and work was necessarily stopped until the following morning. Nobody wanted to sleep among the wreckage of the campsite so they spent the second night sleeping in the open on the high ground. At least they had food; the previous day they had fled in such a hurry that all their supplies had been left behind.

Later that night, it rained heavily, the first real rain the colonists had experienced on the New World. Many miles upstream, Zack was up to mid-thigh in water as the swollen river surged past him. When the colonists woke the next day, the river had risen several feet and the campsite, with food, seeds and equipment strewn over it, was now a shallow lake.

CHAPTER 18

When the flood had subsided somewhat, Zack strapped the rifle and axe to his pack and, holding the pack above his head, waded from the island back to the riverbank. The water came nearly to his shoulders, but moving carefully he managed the crossing without mishap. While sitting in the tree, he had seen a tributary stream coming into the main river a little way upstream and decided to explore it.

A gentle upward slope along the tributary took him beyond the flood zone, and about a mile further on the ground leveled out into a broad meadow full of flowers—at least they were plants with brightly colored heads which he assumed were flowers. There were a few trees here and there, with a denser forest further upstream. Gentle hills rose on either side of the south-facing valley. It was sheltered with a stream flowing through it and access to the main river lower down, and the ground had a fertile look to it. Here, thought Zack, is an ideal spot for a village. And somehow I have to convince the others to move here.

Making his way back through the lower slopes of the hills towards the main camp on the plain it rained a lot of the time, but by then he had grown accustomed to it. Sleeping in the forest at night no longer troubled him. It was not so much that there were no large predators; Zack had seen evidence of their kills more than once to convince him that they existed, although he had not yet seen one. But he had grown in stature during the last few days. No longer was he a timid creature, jumping at his own shadow. He walked with the confidence that, until something showed him otherwise, he was the lord and master of this forest and these hills.

We probably won't take this land for our own without a fight, and the big predators probably won't just slink away. But take it we will.

He hoped that they would be more humane and understanding than his race had been in the past, and kill only to drive predators off, not to exterminate them. But kill them they would, if necessary, because Zack intended that the valley upstream would be the first home of human beings on this world, and he would lead them there. For a brief moment he felt sorrow for invading their territory, and upsetting their established order. Then he dismissed the feeling as a half-remembered snatch of poetry came into his mind: "The old order changeth, yielding place to new."

We have a duty to be decent stewards of this world, he thought, and not screw it up any more than we have to. But more importantly, we have a duty to the human race—that's us—to take this world for our own. And we shall do that, come what may. And with that he set his footsteps firmly back towards the plains below.

Zack slogged his way back across the plain. The grasses, or whatever one called them, were taller and thicker than they had been at the start of his journey, and it was hard going in places.

But he was stronger and fitter than he had been then, and made light of the journey.

He had been gone eight days when he came within sight of the main campsite. Standing on a slight rise of ground he could see that the river was in flood as it had been upstream. It was evident that this was a seasonal occurrence; the trees and bushes on either side of the river grew at the margins of the flooded area.

It was also evident that the camp had not fared well. The original site where they had erected the huts was flooded, and some of the huts looked distinctly bent out of shape. A new camp had been thrown up on the higher ground to one side, but it looked ragged, as if tents had been pitched hurriedly, with piles of stores dumped at random. Zack hurried forward.

He saw Zilla at about the same time as she saw him. She dropped what she was carrying and ran to meet him.

"Zack, thank god you're back. This place is a mess." She wanted to run into his arms and burst into tears, to lay down her burdens for a while, but she was too proud, too independent to do so. So she stood there looking at him for a while, then did so anyway. Zack had never been in this situation before, never had a woman throw herself at him for comfort/protection/succor—whatever it was, Zack gave up trying to work it out, put his arms around her, and decided it made him feel good. Very good.

"What happened?" said Zack gently, after Zilla had more or less stopped making snuffling noises against his shoulder.

"We got run over by a herd of buffalo, that's what. Well, they weren't actually buffalo, but they were huge, black shaggy things with four legs, and there were hundreds of them. We were camped right in their path, and they just charged through us on their way to the river. They seemed to stop and drink, then hung around grazing for a day or so before moving off. The first we knew about it, a couple of days after you left, was a noise like distant thunder, which you could feel through the ground rather than hear, then they were on us. We scattered onto the high ground, but Peter and Ingrid were in a tent by themselves and didn't make it out in time. They're buried over there, what's left of them."

"And after that, I suppose, the river started rising?"

Zilla nodded her head, remembering trying to pull themselves together after the herd had left, then waking up the next day and seeing with horror the water drowning the campsite. Zack began to see a pattern in it; the river flooding every year at this time, and the herd on its seasonal migration somehow timing it so they arrived just before the river became too deep to cross. The beautiful meadow on which they had camped was fertilized with dung every year, then flooded. Small wonder it grew lushly.

"What about the supplies?"

"Not good. I think we've lost about half of what we originally started with. Anything breakable which wasn't in the huts got trampled into mush, and is underwater mush by now. The storage huts were damaged, and a lot of their contents were trampled into the mud as well. We've dragged out more or less everything we can find to the new camp, but it's chaos over there. Everyone is depressed, and a lot of the time they just sit around moping. Zack, you've got to do something."

"Don't worry, I will."

Together they walked to the new camp. Zilla was right; there was an almost tangible air of depression about the place, more like a refugee camp after a war than the home of colonists on a brave new world. Perhaps the colonists and those that sent them had underestimated the sheer cultural shock of landing on an alien world with no possibility of return. Previous explorers on Earth had always known at the back of their minds that, no matter how far they went, no matter what perils they encountered, sooner or later if they survived they could return home. It had taken a few weeks for the realization that there would be no homecoming here to sink into them at a gut level. This, and now their first unkind blow from their new world. It was too much for them.

The colonists reacted in different ways. Many of them became lethargic, with an air of 'why bother, everything's gone wrong,' but some rushed around, accusing, blaming, and generally letting off steam. Maireed was one such. She saw Zack, with Zilla close beside him, walk into the camp.

"Well, look who's finally deigned to grace us with his presence," she shrieked to the camp at large. "About goddamn time you fucking showed up. Where the hell were you when we needed you, you goddamn creep?"

Zack gave her no answer, but started to walk around the camp, greeting everyone he met. "I've got something to say to you all," he said to each one, "so let's everyone gather on that flat space over there."

Maireed followed him around for a while, then stomped off to gather her committee together. Finally, they were all standing together. Zack, still wearing his pack, his rifle slung over his shoulder, casually holding his axe in one hand (he was so used to them by now he was barely conscious of them) looked more purposeful and aware than any of the rest of them. "Seems to me," he said, "this is a lousy place to live. You'll be dodging buffalo and floods every year, and I shouldn't be surprised if it gets a bit cold and windy in the winter. I've found a sheltered valley where we can have a decent life, grow crops, catch fish—they're good to eat—and bring our kids up in safety. I'm going to lead you all there."

"Not so fast, mister," said Maireed, arms folded over her chest, standing at the front of the crowd with her committee members. Jake, for once, was prepared to support her; feuding could wait when the committee closed its ranks against an outsider. "We're the Executive Committee here; we were democratically elected by everyone"—this with a sweep of her arm to indicate the colonists behind her—"and no goddamn coward who sneaks off when there's danger has the right to speak unless we say so. Right now we need everyone we've got to clear up this mess, so take that ridiculous stuff off your back and start doing some work. Right now—like cleaning out the latrine. Later on, the committee *may* consider what you have to say, but we're in charge here, and don't you forget it."

To Maireed's dismay, Zack burst out laughing. "Listen, all of you," he said. "Committees and chairpersons and all that crap belong back on Earth, but not here. We came here to get away from all that. Tomorrow, I'm going back to where we can make ourselves a decent life, and no goddamn committee is going to stop me. Those of you who want to come, then come. Those who want to sit around in this godforsaken spot and play games with Maireed, then do so. But I'm going tomorrow."

"Don't listen to that motherfucking creep," shrieked Maireed. "You'll never go anywhere as long as I'm in charge here. I'll see you dead first. I'll wipe that fucking smile off your face for a start."

So saying, Maireed advanced on him, her face red, spittle flying from her thin lips. As she advanced the few paces towards him, Zack thought that her angular person seemed to encapsulate all the problems that were infecting their small group. Maireed wanted to be the boss—no harm in that, of itself—but to be the boss without having the capability to be a true leader. A leader, above all, had to be able to inspire others to follow them, and that Maireed was patently unable to do. Without leadership, the colony was doomed—they would sit around here until all their supplies were gone, or another disaster wiped them out.

As she reached him, he lifted his axe above his head and brought it down like a god of the ancient world, cleaving her skull in two. Blood sprayed out and her lifeless body sagged to the ground, pulling his axe down with it. He put his foot on her chest to steady himself as he wrenched it out, and the thought came unbidden to him: I have slain the dragon.

Zack faced the colonists, standing frozen in their places. He hefted his axe, dripping blood and gore, into the air.

"I am the King," he roared.

CHAPTER 19

The colonists stood frozen in shock for a few moments. Meanwhile Zack, still holding aloft his gory axe thought to himself, Did I really just do that? I guess I did. I'd better do something about it then.

"Right, you, you, you and you, get shovels and dig a grave over there," he said in what he hoped was a commanding voice, pointing to a flat empty space away from the area occupied by stores and other paraphernalia. "Well, what are you waiting for—get moving. And you Patty—fetch me her sleeping bag."

The roar of Zack's not inconsiderable voice broke the spell, and Patty fluttered off to do his bidding. He felt as Maireed's executioner he at least ought to place her in her sleeping bag, which would become her funeral winding sheet. More than that, there was a half-formed feeling at the back of his mind that as well as king he was now the priest, and dealing with the dead was a priestly function.

When Patty brought Maireed's sleeping bag to him—carefully avoiding her body and the area around her soaked in her blood, as indeed did everyone else, he noticed—he picked up Maireed's body and laid it upside-down in the bag, trying not to notice the two halves of her head gaping open as he did so. He zipped up the bag and pulled the flap at the top over her feet which were sticking out. As he stood up he thought, Keep them busy. Don't let them mope.

"Right, let's get the supplies organized. I want all the huts up on the top here. Chuck, Karl, Boris, see what you can do to repair the damaged huts. I can see a lot of stuff still down there in the meadow, and some of it seems to be in plastic wraps, so get down there and start pulling it out..." and so on for several crisp commands.

Much to his surprise, Zack found the process of giving orders a lot easier than ever he would have imagined. There appeared to be no doubt in everyone's minds, his own included, that he was the boss, and there was no need or inclination for diffidence, no need to say please, just give crisp, confident orders and they would be obeyed. But he did notice that people were physically avoiding him, making detours so as not to come near him as if he was an unexploded bomb that could go off at any time. Okay, he thought, if that's what they want, that's what they can have, as long as they do what I say.

And with that he started picking up some of the heavier loads and moving them to the high ground, to show them that kings weren't above manual labor.

Shortly before sunset they buried Maireed. Zack simply picked her body up in its sleeping bag, walked with it to the newly-dug grave, and gently dropped it in, then signaled to the grave diggers that they could fill it in. No ceremony, Zack felt that the colonists would rather forget the whole affair and pretend it had never happened. The next day Zack had a marker made giving her date and place of birth, and the date of death. There was some discussion—not argument, Zack noticed that no one was prepared to argue with him—about the date of death, since no one was certain of the current date back on Earth. In the end, Zack settled it by naming it the twenty-eighth day A.L. (After Landing).

After burying Maireed, they made fires and sat around them. Zack knew instinctively that he would be by himself—no problem there, he was a loner by nature—so he just pointed to someone carrying firewood and said, "Make my fire there," and it was done. One of the advantages of being a king, he thought, is that you don't have to ask, you just tell people what to do and it gets done.

Jessica had joined Zilla and Chuck and a few others beside their fire.

"What kind of a bloodthirsty monster have we let ourselves in for?" she said quietly but bitterly. "I saw plenty of violence in Zimbabwe, but never anything to match this. I thought we came here to be rid of this, not to see it happen all over again. Is this the way we're going to settle disputes from now on, with unrestrained violence? Because with Zack in charge I can't see things being done in any other way."

"You can disapprove of him all you like, but you can't fault him for style," said Chuck. "Ain't no doubt in anyone's mind right now as to who's boss, and that's the way it should be. Screw democracy and little Hitlers like Maireed, right now we need a real leader, and we've got ourselves one. I'm not going to challenge him, and I can't see anyone else doing it. We're a tribe, not a bunch of uprooted voters from Earth, and a tribe needs to be told what to do, not sit around talking about it."

"I've never seen blood before," said Zilla in a rather tremulous voice. "Yes, of course I've seen cuts and nosebleeds, but never blood resulting from violence to this extent. I don't know what to think. I think I'm still in shock. I shall probably have nightmares about it. Where I grew up there was always safety, always patrolmen and women, violent death was something you read about but never saw. And suddenly someone you like and think you know does something like this. What makes it so terrifying is that there's no comeback, no consequences. He won't be arrested and go to jail, because there isn't anyone to arrest him and in any case there's no jail. I'm frightened."

Chuck patted her hand. "Don't worry, kid, this was just a one-off, lancing a boil poisoning the tribe. Things are going to be okay, you'll see."

"How the hell can you say that," rejoined Jessica. "What's to stop him swinging his axe at anybody else he doesn't like. We ought to restrain him by force, treat him as the criminal he is."

"All you'd get if you tried that, assuming you could get the others to go along with you, would be a general melee in which a lot of people would get hurt, possibly killed. And for what? We're a tribe, and a tribe needs a leader. It was the same in the militia. A bad leader is better than no leader at all, and I don't think Zack is going to be a bad leader. I'll not back you up if you want to challenge Zack for the leadership, because that's what you'll be doing if you try to restrain him. This is leadership in the raw—put up or shut up."

Jessica fell silent for a while. She was outraged by Zack's violence, her soul revolted against it, yet some tiny voice within her seemed to say that perhaps the tribe was in a better state now that Zack was in charge. At any rate there seemed to be a more positive air about the

place, an expectation that something useful was about to happen, that nobody was sitting around moping any more. She was confused, and so decided to keep her peace, at least for the time being.

Zack had intended to begin the march to their new home the very next day, but he found that organizing the move took longer than he had thought. While one of the storage huts had been completely destroyed by the herd, it proved possible to repair the two damaged ones by taking them to pieces and rebuilding them with a little mechanical ingenuity. Under his direction, the three remaining huts were moved to higher ground about a mile from the river, where he hoped they would be safe from any other migrating herds of animals, and all the stores they could not take were stowed in them. The carts, when they had finished using them, were tied to stakes pounded into the ground next to the huts. It was lengthy and sometimes backbreaking work, particularly when shifting things such as anvils, and the weather was becoming hotter as the season approached high summer. But it kept them busy, and their morale improved noticeably when they saw that Zack was both willing and able to lead by example.

Finally on the third day after Maireed's death, they were ready to move, nineteen men and twenty-one women in all out of the forty-three who had survived the journey from Earth. Zack had debated with himself whether to leave a party to guard the huts, but decided it would be futile. If another invasion of animals arrived like the last one, there would be little they could do about it, and barring intelligent beings, nothing was likely to break into the huts. Besides, he felt it was best they move as a single group. We're a tribe now, and I am its king, he thought. Tribes should stick together.

CHAPTER 20

The line of colonists spread out across the plain beside the river. Each of them was laden with as much as they could carry. Zack had considered using the carts, but the ground was unsuitable for them, particularly in the treed areas. Perhaps later on they would use them when transporting heavy items like the anvils, but right now they were better off with individual packs.

Zack had one of the largest loads, partly because he was one of the strongest and fittest, and partly because in his newfound role as king he felt he should set an example. He could either impress them with his status by carrying nothing at all, or carry a large load and make light of it. He chose the latter. His axe he carried over his shoulder with his rifle; it seemed now to be his symbol of kingship. While many of the others had axes, Zack noticed they carried them inconspicuously strapped to their packs. It was as if none of them wanted to give the appearance of challenging him.

He was rapidly learning the essential loneliness of command. He understood instinctively that as king he had to command, not discuss.

Later, perhaps, it would be expedient to set up a King's Council to advise him, but his word must always be law. Democracy was a luxury for settled, established cultures. Here, there was no state, no church, no history, and no law. He could not be all of these, but at least he could make a start by being the law.

The tribe moved as fast as its slowest member, and that was a lot slower than Zack had moved on his first trip. The first night out many of the colonists were uneasy, as indeed Zack had been. Until this moment they had always spent their nights in sight of the landing craft, or huts, or something solid which reminded them of Earth. Now they, the children of Earth's largely urban society, felt totally divorced from Earth and its comforting ambience. They had camped near trees and before dark had lit campfires, huddling around them for comfort as their remote ancestors had done in pre-history back on Earth. But without their tribal chief, some of them, if not most, would be starting to panic. Zack spent his time that first evening going from fire to fire, telling them of the sheltered valley awaiting them and generally doing his best to allay their fears.

By the end of the second day's trek, after spending a lot of the first night as sentry, Zack had realized that he couldn't do everything himself, and needed some lieutenants. Chuck was an obvious choice. From his background as a militiaman he was accustomed to giving and taking orders, and in addition he was one of the few colonists with an easy familiarity with firearms and the outdoors. But who to choose for the other lieutenant?

Zack's gut instinct said Jessica was the best choice, but was it wise to have her in a leadership role? He was vaguely aware of her animus towards him, although this didn't worry him too much, but was it advisable to have a woman in a leadership role in the new social order that would no doubt emerge? Back on Earth any difference between the sexes in this regard had long been discarded, but then back on Earth a woman's lot was not confined to bearing and rearing children, nor the man's lot to hard physical labor and protecting his family from predators, both of which were likely to be the case here. In the end, Zack decided to go with his gut feeling. That evening, he asked Chuck and Jessica to join him at his fire.

"I need some lieutenants. I want you two to be them. I'm going to divide everybody else into two groups and I want each of you to lead a group." Somehow, the word lieutenant with its military connotation seemed more fitting than mere deputies. Perhaps in due course they would become dukes?

Chuck had no problem with being one of Zack's lieutenants. He was happy that there was a real boss now, rather than a squabbling committee, and if Zack had promoted himself, he had done it in a way that left no doubt in anyone's mind. Besides, Maireed had been getting to be a pain in the butt as far as he was concerned.

"Chuck, sentries are now your responsibility."

Zack knew enough about the local wildlife to know that there were large carnivores around. While he hadn't seen one, he had seen enough of their kills to know that whatever they were, they were quite large, so setting sentries at night was only sensible. He was about to tell Chuck how he wanted them set, but stopped himself. Chuck probably knows better than I do how to set sentries, he thought. Kings don't need to deal with details, they just pick the right person and let them get on with it. All he said was, "Include me on the roster at the beginning of the night. I want everyone to know I'm on watch."

As Zack expected, Chuck knew how to set sentries and make sure they did their job. On the first night he got very little sleep, being awake at every changeover, but then as a former militiaman he was used to going without sleep. One of the sentries objected to getting out of his sleeping bag in the middle of the night (he was cuddling his girlfriend at the time), so Chuck pulled him out and thumped him hard two or three times, then made him do his two hour shift. When word of this got round, and Chuck made sure it did, there was no further reluctance to doing one's shift. Chuck was an efficient enforcer.

Unlike Chuck, who had a hardnosed approach to leadership and tribal welfare—is the leader doing a good job, never mind how he got to be leader—Jessica was conflicted. She was still horrified by Zack's killing of Maireed. How can you possibly act as his lieutenant, how can you have anything to do with this murdering, bloodthirsty monster? said the voice of indignation within her. But then a quiet little voice in her said something about she who was without sin casting the first stone. You killed a man back at the mission, and you would have killed more if they hadn't run away.

Yes, but that was to protect the people at the mission.

But isn't Zack doing much the same here—leading us into a safer place? And Jessica thought of how Zack had spent the previous evening going from group to group, calming their fears and giving them reassurance.

In the end, Jessica rationalized to herself that being one of Zack's lieutenants would be for the good of the tribe, telling herself that she could thereby hope to curb Zack's worst excesses if he should turn out to be a real monster.

Zack for his part was a little worried at first about giving a command role to Jessica, since he was not sure how the colonists would react to a woman in charge. Certainly, back on Earth, merely to query the ability of a woman to take on the highest leadership roles would have invited a deluge of opprobrium, but this was not Earth; this was nature in the raw. In the end, what mattered was not gender but personality. Jessica was calm, quietly confident, and most of all, showed no indecisiveness. She led her group with ease.

It was the middle of the third day of the march, with still some way to go before they reached the hills, when Zack had a chance to talk to Zilla. He fell into place with her as she was walking. She looked at him briefly then cast her eyes down and said nothing.

"What's the matter, Zilla? Are you angry with me?"

"No—what do I call you now? Sire? My Lord? I'm not angry, just confused."

"Zack will do nicely when we're alone, although I think in public you're going to have to do what the rest do and call me Sir. But what are you confused about?"

"I don't know. If I did, I could tell you. Oh, I suppose Maireed's death, and you now being king, and, and, I don't know, just about everything."

"Well, why don't you come and talk to me about it tonight, after supper, by my fire." The practice had grown up, quite naturally it seemed, that in the evenings they sat around fires in groups of half-a-dozen or so, but Zack had a fire to himself. Whether this was out of respect or whether they were shunning his company, Zack neither knew nor cared. He was used by now to spending evenings and nights with just his campfire for company. If he invited one or more of them to discuss matters with him, they would come, but it seemed natural for them to return to their own fires afterwards.

By the third night the colonists had begun to settle into a routine and were getting more practiced at setting up camp. They carried tents with them, but the nights were warm and most preferred to sleep out in the open in sleeping bags. Zilla came to his fire after she had eaten, and stood there rather uncertainly. Zack smiled up at her until she sat down near, but not close to him.

"What's up, Zilla?"

Zilla stared into the fire for a time, hugging her legs with her chin on her knees. "I don't know. No, that's silly. Besides, I've already said that.

"I think perhaps it's the loneliness. I know, I've never actually been on my own since we left Earth, all those years ago. But I feel this aching silence inside me. I think I'm in mourning for all the things of Earth we've lost for ever—all the family, the friends, the close, familiar things..."

What Zilla really wanted to say, but had neither the words nor the confidence to say them to Zack even if she could articulate her thoughts, was that his killing of Maireed had shown brutally and starkly that they had indeed left Earth with all its customs and societal norms, and were heading out into the unknown. Maybe some day there would be a new established order in which she could feel at ease, but right now she seemed to be on a cliff top with an unknown future in front of her. It was not so much loneliness as uncertainty that was troubling her.

She broke off and sobbed gently. Zack wanted to hold her in his arms, the natural instinct for a man to comfort a woman in distress, but something in her pose held him back. She wanted comforting as much as she had ever wanted anything, but this was not the right time for him to go to her.

It was useless to say they had known from the beginning it was going to be like this. They had known in their heads, but not their hearts. It was like the death of a mother. The full realization of loss does not come until you walk away from the graveside.

Zack wondered to himself why he did not feel the loss so strongly as the others. Perhaps because he was by nature a loner. Not for him were troops of friends; he would not have known how to deal with them if he had them. But listening to Zilla, the thought came to him that, like it or not, these people were his responsibility. He had taken on the task of kingship and it seemed that his people (*his* people!) had willingly accepted him. More than that, they had thrust their burdens on him. So be it, he thought. But I don't want to do it on my own.

When Zilla's sobs had stopped, he gently spoke her name. She looked at him, her head tilted sideways on her arms, her eyes still blurry with tears.

"Zilla, like it or not, I'm king. I think the rest of them want me to be king. I don't think they'd let me give it up, not unless I screwed up badly or just walked off and left them, and I'm not going to do either. But I want someone with me. Will you be my queen?"

Zilla jerked upright with a hand to her mouth as if she was suppressing a scream. For a space of perhaps five seconds she sat frozen, staring at him. Then, staring down at her knees, she spoke haltingly, as if choosing her words with great care.

"If you wish, my lord, I shall do as you say. But if I have any choice in the matter, I beg you, don't choose me. I can bear you children, I think, but I don't think I can be a companion to you."

It was Zack's turn to stare open-mouthed at her.

"But, but, I thought we, well, you know, liked each other?"

Zilla smiled sadly at him. "I did. I think I still do, and I admire you tremendously. But you have blood on your hands."

Zack spent the next day in a daze. He gave orders where necessary, although he was learning that the fewer he gave, the better. A king commands, he does not nag. But apart from this, he spent the day in rather vague introspection. At times he was gloomy, at others angry. At times he had an urge to punish Zilla in some way, but realized that this was foolish and would achieve nothing. He looked back at his killing of Maireed and pondered it.

If I could go back to that point, would I do the same as I did then? I think I would. I think what I did was necessary for our survival. But it doesn't mean I have to like what I did, or like myself for doing it. And it seems the others don't have to like me either. Respect me, yes. But like me, no.

By the end of the day, he was a little closer to coming to terms with himself.

I chose to be king, and it turns out it's a lonely job. All right, I accept it. So be it. But I will be a strong king, and a good king—in that order.

And finally, just as he was falling asleep that night, beneath the stars: I think I tasted the fruit of the tree of knowledge today. Perhaps that's what kings have to do. But it's a bitter fruit.

CHAPTER 21

The carnivore lay in a hollow in the ground surrounded by long grass, near where Zack had seen the grazing herd on his first trip. It had brought down one of the herd and was tearing chunks from its still warm carcass, when it caught a strange, acrid scent on the breeze. It lifted its head, still holding a mouthful of bloody meat, and carefully sniffed the air. It was a large animal, nearly two hundred pounds of teeth, claws, and brindled fur, but not quite large enough to be disdainful of any competition.

There was no doubt about it. Some creatures with an unknown smell were approaching. They didn't smell like grass-eaters, nor any other creature he knew. He could feel their footsteps now, a faint but quite detectable trembling in the ground under his belly. They were large, but the rhythm of them was strange also. Fight or flee? But it had been a long time since his last kill and he was hungry. Fear and hunger warred briefly in his fuzzy brain, then hunger won.

They were coming directly towards him. Couldn't they sense him? Why were they still plodding in that maddeningly deliberate way towards him? Whatever they were, hunger and an instinctive feeling that he was superior to them made him decide to stay his ground.

The colonists were strung out in a long line, without any particular order. Zack was usually at the front, but he often walked back down the line to make sure there were no problems. So it happened that he was halfway down the line as they were walking through knee-high 'grass' when Zack heard a grating, animal snarl followed by human shouts and screams, and looked up to see a tawny blur leap out of the grass at the front of the line. He immediately started running the hundred yards or more to the spot, but stopped after twenty yards to shuck his pack onto the ground and unsling his rifle. He continued on at a run, rifle in one hand, axe in the other.

The carnivore had leapt at the nearest colonist, Tanya, a short, dark woman who had been walking directly towards it. It had finally made up its mind that it was the king around here, it had superior weapons to anything else that moved, and it certainly was not going to allow anything to disturb its meals. Their plodding approach had convinced it that they were competitors, not prey, and it intended to show that its rule was absolute, and there was only one penalty for transgression—death. It landed on Tanya with claws and jaws extended, smashed her to the ground, sank its fangs into her throat and its claws into her body and started tearing at her.

When Zack reached the scene, two other men were there with rifles, neither of them being Chuck who was down at the rear of the column when it happened. One seemed to be trying to fire with the safety catch still on, while the other was dancing around trying to get a clear shot without hitting Tanya. Zack ignored them. He was suddenly angry, blindly angry. These were his people this creature was attacking, and nothing and nobody was going to harm them while he was king. He approached the animal at a dead run, making an incoherent roaring noise in his throat. It was still tearing at Tanya's body as he cast his rifle aside and raised his axe in both hands. The creature leapt off her body as it sensed his approach and the threat he represented, and twisted around with lightning speed to attack him. But it was too late. As it leapt, Zack's axe landed, taking it in the shoulder, nearly severing its front leg, and continuing on deep into its chest.

Zack staggered back at the impact, his axe nearly torn out of his hands. The creature, although mortally wounded, clawed its way along the ground towards Zack in a paroxysm of pain and rage. Zack lifted his axe once more, leapt backwards to avoid having his leg shredded by the creature's remaining front claws, then aimed hastily but carefully and buried his axe in its skull. The creature gave one or two violent twitches, then collapsed into the limpness of death.

Still running on automatic, Zack pulled the axe head out of the creature's skull (a brief thought flashed through his mind: I seem to be doing this a lot lately); then he stood above the carcass, leaning on his axe and breathing heavily. Suddenly the reaction hit him and he started trembling. You stupid idiot, he thought, you could have been killed doing that. Why didn't you use the rifle?

Because these are my people, came the unbidden thought, and I will avenge them.

He controlled his trembling with an effort and walked the short distance to Tanya's body. She was very evidently dead. Her corpse would have been an obscenity in a slaughterhouse, and his first instinct was to throw up. He nearly did, but the newfound knowledge of his kingship helped him to control himself. He untied her pack straps, rolled her body over, all the time trying not to see the gaping wounds, then took off her pack. Detaching her sleeping bag, he unrolled it and spread it out, then lifted her still warm body into it and zipped it up. The top of her head showed, but that was unharmed and looked almost as if she was sleeping, at least until the blood started soaking through. I should have waited, he thought, but it was important to get her out of sight.

He stood up and looked around. All the remaining colonists were gathered around in a loose semi-circle, watching him with awed expressions on their faces. Some of them who had been at the back of the line thought he had killed Tanya himself until they saw the animal's carcass. Enough of this, he thought, keep them busy. They can think about it later.

"Right, I want guards with rifles posted. There may be more like our friend here out there. Every person with a rifle—and you, Jake, take mine—spread out in a defensive perimeter. Chuck, see to it. I want a party to dig a grave for Tanya. You, you, you, and you. Dig it six feet deep on that flat space over there. Make sure you stay inside the guard perimeter. Jessica, do whatever you can to prepare her for burial. I want another party—you and you—to drag this carcass away from here. Get it out of sight and smell. You and you, accompany them with rifles. The rest of you, stay inside the guarded perimeter and get a fire going. We could all do with some coffee after this." Personally, I could do with a good slug of brandy, he thought, but that'll have to wait until we start growing crops and build a still. Two, three years, maybe?

He looked down at himself and realized for the first time that he was drenched in blood, both the animal's and Tanya's. He hoped none of it was his, but it revolted him and he couldn't go any further without washing it off.

"I'm going down to the river to wash this mess off. I want a rifleman—you, Boris—as a guard with me. Chuck, cover the gap left by Boris." So saying, he marched off towards the river holding his axe without looking back.

Jessica had been near the front of the column and had seen and heard Zack go roaring past making a noise in his throat rather like AAAARRRGH and then hurl himself and his axe at the creature. The battle between the two of them and Zack's swift victory left her startled, but with a new view of the world as it now was. Perhaps this is why we need someone like Zack as the leader, she said to herself. I guess there's a need for violence when you can't just call the cops. Her remaining horror and anger at Zack for Maireed's killing drained away as she saw him in a new light. Besides, a man who protects the tribe like that is rather attractive, she thought, with an inward blush at her temerity.

The river was about a mile away, and he was gone nearly an hour. He returned with clean clothes, clean body, and clean axe. He strode back into the camp in his underpants with his guard trailing behind him, the rest of his damp clothes under his arm, his axe on his shoulder, and a nauseous fluttering in his stomach from delayed reaction. He accepted a cup of coffee and stood sipping it slowly, hoping it would stay down. Meanwhile Jessica quietly took his damp clothing from him and spread it out to dry. She had retrieved his pack and had readied some dry clothing for him. Zack was touched. It was the first time any of them had done anything for him unasked.

By the time Zack had finished his coffee, the grave was ready. We can't just drop her in there like Maireed, and quickly cover her up. I'll have to have some kind of ceremony. Oh lord, what do I do?

Jessica hadn't been able to do much to make Tanya's body any more ready for burial than it already was, but she had placed some long branches under her sleeping bag and two ropes underneath the branches, so the body could be picked up and lowered into the grave rather than just being dropped in. It seemed more dignified, more respectful, somehow. With two people on either side of her, Jessica being one of them, they slowly carried her to the open grave. At Zack's signal, they lowered her in. Standing on one side of the grave, he looked at the colonists gathered on the other side.

"Tanya wasn't the first of us to die an early death, and she probably won't be the last. We came here knowing that not all of us might survive. But we, the colonists, are going to survive. We came here to claim this world for our own, and by this gravesite and Tanya's body, I swear to you, this world shall be ours. We shall have children, and they shall have children, and we shall fill this fair world with our people."

Almost unconsciously he picked up a handful of soil excavated from the grave and trickled it on top of Tanya's body.

"Tanya, we must leave you here. But we shall not leave you in our thoughts. We shall not forget you."

And the colonists murmured, as if in benediction, "We shall not forget you."

Jessica looked at him as he spoke and thought back to Sister Mary's death. This is what a leader does, she thought. Whatever I might think about him, he's doing what has to be done to the best of his ability. He's taking the burden upon himself as I did back then, taking all our hopes and fears on his shoulders. I wonder if he feels as uncertain and confused as I did?

And with that her last reservations about Zack as leader, and indeed about him as a man, melted away.

They filled in the grave and hammered some branches into the ground to mark the site. Later, they would make a more permanent marker. For the time being, Zack thought it best to press on while it was still light, to put some miles between themselves and Tanya's death place. But now and henceforth, they would travel as an army, with scouts and flank guards. No more long straggling line. Zack did not intend to lose any more of them if he could help it.

That evening, Jessica came to his campfire and quietly prepared his evening meal for him. After they had eaten she fetched her sleeping bag and silently zipped hers and Zack's together while Zack watched in a rather bemused fashion, realizing that after Zilla's refusal the problem of who his mate and companion was going to be had been taken out of his hands. Finally, Jessica said, "I've told Chuck you won't be doing sentry duty tonight."

By then night had fallen. Jessica wondered briefly whether she should modestly get into the joint sleeping bag and undress there, but decided she might as well start as she intended to continue, so standing near the fire—they were a little way away from the rest of the tribe—she slowly undressed in front of Zack. When she was naked, Zack did the same. They stood looking at each other for a short while, and then, pleased by what they both saw, they got into the sleeping bag together.

Jessica was a little hesitant at first—she was, after all, a virgin, and gave a slight grunt of pain as Zack entered her—but thereafter clung firmly to him. She was determined that Zack should be in no doubt that he had a willing partner.

King Zack now had a queen.

The next day the tribe continued their march towards their new home. Zilla's mind was a little easier, after seeing Jessica spend the night with Zack. She had to admit to some jealousy, but, *After all, I did turn him down—well sort of—I just reacted with blind panic when he asked me. I don't really know why I did that, 'cause he's not an unattractive man, and he is the king. Maybe I just don't want to be the queen.*

And indeed the more she thought about it, the more she realized that being a colonist and a mother was quite as much responsibility as she wanted. Being responsible for anyone else besides her future children was not something she looked forward to.

During their time on this world, several of them had paired up with one another, and while the march seemed to have accelerated the process, Zilla hadn't yet made up her mind about a partner. She'd had sex with one or two of the men (the birth control drugs they were automatically given on board the Mayflower weren't due to wear off until a month or two after landing), but none of them really appealed to her as lifelong companions, and while having multiple sex partners might be attractive, she had enough sense to realize that this was very likely to lead to trouble in a primitive society, which theirs was undoubtedly going to be.

Later that day Zilla stumbled on an uneven patch of ground. Chuck, in whose division she was, happened to be beside her and caught her arm as she fell, keeping her upright. "Okay then?" he said as she regained her balance.

Her mind went back to that first day after landing when he told her to take a break. She looked at him this time and thought, I'm not going to get upset about him helping me this time—he can open all the doors for me he wants. Mad, passionate love would be nice to have, but a strong, competent man as my partner is more important. Besides, if I don't grab him soon, somebody else will.

She let her body soften and lean against him for a moment. No words were exchanged, but Chuck knew he was being given an invitation. "See you tonight, then," was all he said, and all that needed to be said.

They reached the valley late on the fifth day of their march, gathered firewood, lit fires, and sat around them with a feeling of relief. They had a sheltered place to live; they had a king (and a queen) to make order out of chaos. Life would be good. The next day they would start their new life, but for tonight they could relax with a sense that they had finally made a real beginning.

By the time they reached the valley there were twenty women and nineteen men. There was a sense of purpose among them now, as if the knowledge that they had made a new and more auspicious beginning had sunk in, and more pairs began to form between men and women (with intervention by King Zack a couple of times, quietly aided in the background by Queen Jessica, to sort out disagreements and problems), until eventually there was only one woman left without a mate. Poor Patty, she whose womb was a cradle of fertility, had

had a woebegone, helpless air about her ever since Maireed's death. Her support and prop had been taken away, and she was adrift without a compass.

It was Jessica who decided her fate.

"You do realize we've got one woman left over, Zack," she said one night a couple of weeks after reaching the valley.

"Yeah, I know. What the hell do we do about her?"

"We can't let her womb go to waste. There's too few of us to allow that happen."

"So what do you suggest?"

"She can't just float, that would cause all sorts of problems. Someone will have to have two wives. And since you're the king..."

"Okay, I see what you're getting at. I think Patty would say yes. I can't see her wanting to live on her own for the rest of her life. But what about you? How do you feel about it?"

"Not too good, but I guess I can live with it. But let's have one thing clear right from the get go. I'm your queen, your number one wife. Within this household I'm the boss woman, and don't you forget it."

Zack looked at Jessica's sturdy, self-confident figure and decided that she would probably be the boss woman no matter how many other wives he had. And truth to tell, he was happy to have it so. Growing up back on Earth, his mother had been a similar tower of strength, running her household with unquestioned authority and protecting her children like a lioness. He might be the head of the tribe, but he was more than happy to have Jessica as the head of his household. He took her hand in his.

"Deal," he said. "And besides, I don't think you're ever going to have any babysitting problems with this arrangement."

And it came to pass in the generations to come on the New World that while lesser men might have only one wife, the King, by law and custom, was permitted to have two.

EPILOGUE

Zilla stood at the door of her hut, looking with bleary eyes into the pre-dawn sky. Marc, her newborn son, suckled hungrily at her breast, while Victor, now fourteen months and only recently displaced from her breast (so much for the theory that a woman wouldn't get pregnant while breast feeding), tugged at her skirt and whined. Part of her wanted to push him away and concentrate on Marc, but instinct told her that he needed reassurance and affection, so she drew him closer and cuddled him against her leg.

Her right arm grew weary with Marc, and soon she would need to change to her other breast, but she felt too tired to make the move and disturb both children at once. As she stood there half asleep, the sky rapidly lightened, the rim of the sun peeked over the horizon at the end of the valley and a blaze of light transformed the landscape, as if awakening from somber dream to bright reality. Her posture became more erect, and clasping her children closer the thought flooded into her: This is my world. Not just another faceless unit in a teeming sea of humanity, but a proud pioneer, a landowner, a citizen of this new world. Smiling, she shifted Marc and clasped Victor with her other arm without being aware of her actions, and stood reveling in the sunlight and the gentle dawn breeze.

The village (no one seemed to need to call it by any other name) stood in a wooded valley through which flowed a stream fed from the hills above. Soon, the men would be going out into the fields, or felling trees and pulling stumps to enlarge the fields. It was backbreaking work from dawn to sunset, and already Zilla could hear Chuck stirring in the hut behind her, making the grumbling, mumbling noises he usually made at that hour. She wondered sometimes how the tough militiaman she had paired with a couple of years ago had turned into this peasant clodhopper, but to be fair to him, he was probably wondering how she had turned into the bedraggled earth mother that she undoubtedly was at this hour. One thing was certain: They both had a great deal more muscle than they did two years ago.

Victor brought her back to the present by peeing down her bare leg (he wasn't wearing a diaper). Incredibly, to herself at any rate, she smiled fondly at him and said, "I guess it's breakfast time then." As she turned to go back into the hut holding Victor's rather grubby hand, she wondered briefly at her good humor, and then thought that perhaps they were all of them just getting closer to the everyday realities of life. Most of it had gone outside the hut anyway.

Breakfast was porridge that had been simmering all night on the embers of the fire. Chuck was on his knees blowing the embers into flame, and filling the hut and the porridge pot with ash in the process. He never seemed to have the knack of concentrating his effort in one spot. "Here," she said, "hold Marc for a moment while I do that."

Mumbling something to the effect that he could manage, Chuck gave a couple more puffs just to demonstrate that he really could do it if he put his mind to it, then gratefully exchanged places with Zilla. He had some difficulty initially in standing upright, since sleeping after a long day of heavy labor on a bed consisting of a bag sewn from part of a lander parachute and stuffed with dried leaves and grasses gave him a stiff back in the morning, but he was so used to it by now that he barely noticed.

Breakfast took Chuck no longer than was required to gulp down his bowl of porridge, and then he was off. The King had said he wanted every man at first light in the area beyond the northern end of the big field, to drag out the newly-felled trees and start pulling the stumps. When the King gave a direct order like that, it was wise to obey.

When Chuck reached the clearing, the King was already there, directing operations. Chuck was one of the last to arrive. "Funny, isn't it, how the men with the best-looking wives always arrive last in the morning," bellowed the King. He had a loud cheerful voice at this hour of the morning, and an elephantine sense of humor. But Chuck didn't mind, nor the chuckles of the other men. In fact he felt rather smug about it.

All the work would have to be done by muscle power alone, and it was going to be brutal. Chuck thought briefly how it would be if they had draft animals. There were some animals that seemed to have the right physique, but so far no one had managed to capture any, let alone tame them. They would probably have to start by capturing some foals (calves? pups?), and that would almost certainly involve killing the adults, a thought which still made Chuck feel a bit queasy in spite of the hunting and subsequent butchering they had recently begun doing. He dismissed the thought, spat on his hands, and picked up his axe. They needed to expand their cultivated area so the trees had to be cleared, or at least the King said so, and nowadays that was good enough for everyone.

Back at the village, Zilla suddenly heard the outraged cry of a newborn baby. The Queen (funny how nobody called her Jessica any more) had been up all night with another of their tribe giving birth, even though she herself was heavily pregnant. Zilla reckoned she would probably act as midwife when the Queen gave birth, and although she was still a little nervous at the thought of that responsibility she looked forward to it.

Birth, children, crops, hunting, fishing. Life had become very simple, and Zilla was very happy to have it so.

Twenty-six years later, back on Earth a very old woman named Julia Lockmeyer was visited in her nursing home by the President of the United States with the news of the Mayflower's arrival on the New World. After seeing the data sent back by the Mayflower, and in particular the photos of the landing site with members of the scout ship crew standing in the open next to their ship, she smiled gently. "Why, that's Chuck Woodburn standing there. I remember him, a nice young man. He's probably a grandfather by now." With a few tears rolling down her withered cheeks, she closed her eyes and quietly murmured, "Nunc dimittis."

That night towards dawn she quietly passed away, with a smile on her face.